CHASING CLAIRE

HELLS SAINTS MOTORCYCLE CLUB

ALSO BY PAULA MARINARO

Raine Falling

CHASING CLAIRE

HELLS SAINTS MOTORCYCLE CLUB

PAULA MARINARO

Montlake
Romance

Text copyright © 2015 Paula Marinaro

Published by Montlake Romance, Seattle

www.apub.com

Amazon, the Amazon logo, and Montlake Romance are trademarks of Amazon.com, Inc., or its affiliates.

ISBN-13: 9781477827826
ISBN-10: 147782782X

Cover design by Jason Blackburn

Library of Congress Control Number: 2014955024

Printed in the United States of America

This book is dedicated to my very own Harley Man . . . my husband and the absolute love of my life, Pasquale Marinaro.

CHAPTER 1

I had been on my feet for hours. And hours. And hours.

And I was feeling that pain everywhere.

The small muscles in my upper arms ached from lifting the heavy trays. The larger muscles in my lower back screamed from being bent and stretched. My left ankle hurt where I had twisted it. And despite the pain relievers that I was downing like candy, my headache just kept getting worse.

One more time.

Just one more time.

If the fat guy sitting in the second booth near the door called me over *just one more time* to stare at my tits, wink at me, and order "one more with lots of head, darling," I was going to pull open that dirty mouth of his and pour an entire pitcher of beer down his throat.

Usually I didn't mind helping out at Ruby Reds, but enough was enough.

I looked around at the sea of fools who occupied the red and black leather booths, and wondered where the hell they all came from. Crownsmount wasn't exactly a booming metropolis. It was a small town, nestled among some other small towns, with the major city about fifty miles east. But the area did support two private colleges, so I guess the tequila bar had become a draw.

Ruby Reds was owned by the Hells Saints Motorcycle Club, which had been founded and was now run by my surrogate father,

Prosper. Though we lived in the Southeast, there were chapters all over the United States. Just recently, the Saints had also expanded into Europe. In an effort toward more legitimate business practices, my sister's husband, Diego, had recently been named vice president.

I emphasize the word *effort*. This not-so-merry band of outlaw men still had a long way to go before *legitimate* could apply to them, however loosely the term was used. But Prosper Worthington was a smart guy with a somewhat ironic sense for business, and under his rule the Hells Saints MC had made some strong alliances with like-minded criminals. Financially speaking, at least, they had come out the better for it. So I had to give them props. I didn't know much, but from what I had seen from the corporate side of it, my adopted family of badasses were doing okay.

What seemed like a lifetime ago, my sister and I had found ourselves in a dangerous place and had gone to the MC for help. After things had been made right, we decided to stay on. It might not have been perfect, but it was safe, and it had been just what we needed. As it turned out, staying on had come with its own set of complications. A set of complications that I tried hard not to think about, because when I did, it made my head swim and my heart ache.

A stint in rehab, a few dead folks, a couple of kidnappings, one really scary car chase, and the dramatic, premature birth of my first niece were just some of the highlights that had taken center stage during our time with the club.

Yeah, my life had never been what one might call quiet, or even close to anything that could even remotely resemble normal. But in the past couple of years, I had found myself in situations that trumped even my low expectations for a shot at an average life.

And it wasn't just me.

I could also add my best friend and roommate, Glory, to the pot of hot mess. Glory had the unlikely distinction of being a former all-nude dancer, turned recluse, turned fisherman. And I had the strong feeling that the evolution of Glory had just begun. The thought exhausted me.

My life.

My headache.

And then there was Reno. He was where the heartache came in.

Reno and I had been . . . hell, I had no idea what Reno and I had been. But for a while it had been good. Really, really good. And then it wasn't anymore. The thought of him made my eyes mist and my heart hurt. I was pretty sure that it was my fault that things had gone the way they had, but I just didn't know how to make them right. And, really, I didn't even know if he wanted things to work out between us. I only knew that whatever it was that Reno and I had been working toward, we weren't doing that any more. Sometimes I missed him so much that it was hard to breathe.

And then there was *that other thing*. And *that other thing* was the stuff of nightmares. *That other thing* was the kind of thing that even if you never talked about it or willingly thought about it, it was still right there with you.

The other thing invaded my dreams.

Try as I might to avoid it, in the past year or so, my life had taken on all the elements of a Greek tragedy. The determination that it took for me to rise above the doom and damnation wore me out and sapped all of my strength.

But I wasn't beat, yet. I was a Winston woman, and if nothing else, that was enough to get me through.

Most days anyway.

I took a look at the clock. I had fifteen minutes left to my shift, then I was free for the weekend.

CHAPTER 2

I pulled off my apron and made my way toward Raine's office in back of the bar. Attached to it was a large, well-lit bathroom. Inside of that bathroom was a shower that supplied enough hot water to keep me happy.

A shudder of pure pleasure shot right through me as I felt those stinging jets of full-on heat hit my sore, tired muscles. I laid my palms flat against the tiles, bent my neck under the spray, and let that steaming water run straight over me. Sighing, I felt a gradual release of the tension that had permanently taken up residence in my overused, tired, bunched-up muscles.

Reluctantly, I stepped out of the hot shower and into a cloud of fragrant steam. I took the thick cotton towel and rubbed my skin hard, feeling the blood flow back into my tired body. Starting with my legs and working my way up, I massaged in some lightly scented body lotion until I began to feel somewhat human again. The fragrance was called "In the Midnight Garden." It had been a favorite of mine for years and it was the one luxury that I consistently treated myself to. I didn't always take the extra time to use it, but when I did, it enveloped me in the soft scents of yesterday. The smooth, creamy mix made me think of the past. Both the good and the bad.

In the Midnight Garden reminded me that no matter how bad things seemed, they could always be worse.

Making a strong effort to hide the dark blue, telltale smudges of lost sleep, I grabbed every girl's best friend, otherwise known as concealer, and dabbed a little under each eye. Then I brushed on some mascara and covered my lids with a light coppery shadow. I rimmed my baby blues with twenty-five dollar eyeliner, and tinted my lips with gloss.

Tipping my head forward, I flipped my hair upside down and dried it for maximum volume.

Satisfied that the strong effort would bring strong results, I stood back and looked at myself in the mirror.

Expectantly.

Hopefully.

And then . . .

With a heaping helping of disappointment.

The artfully made-up eyes that stared back at me still looked troubled. Turning away from the mirror, I let out a heavy sigh, wrapped the towel tighter around my too-thin body and rifled through the duffle bag. I pulled out my underwear, jeans, and the T-shirt that I had packed before I left for work. I always changed and showered after every shift, even if I was just going home. The greasy oil from the fryers, the spilled beer, and the piles of cash I handled all day long made me feel like a breeding ground for micro-organisms. Even if that wasn't the case, today was special and I did not want to take a chance of passing on any germs to my niece.

Today was Willow's first birthday, and I was number one on the celebration committee.

After slipping on my bra and panties, I pulled the T-shirt over my head and tugged on the loosely fitting Levis. All my jeans hung a little too low on my hips now. But there were worse things than dark circles and baggy pants. So, pushing those worse things aside, I zipped and belted. Then I combed my long hair into a loose side braid. After stopping at the bar to grab a cold one, I headed out.

It was only a short drive before the busy, two-lane highway turned into an easy single stretch of road. From there, the asphalt eventually made its way to a long, smooth, graveled private lane leading to Diego's property. I thought about my adorable niece. She was still so precious and new to this world. With her little Buddha belly and big blue eyes, she was love wrapped up in a soft pink blanket.

Despite a rocky start, Willow would have a good life. My sister would make sure of it, no question. Of that, I was absolutely certain. And that certainty brought me back to a place I rarely visited, the dark alleyway of my own childhood.

Funny thing, that trip down memory lane. For some, it was a leisurely Sunday morning drive coasting down a pretty, tree-lined avenue.

For others, it was a high-speed midnight chase along a dry, cracked highway.

For me, it was the highway.

Definitely the highway.

Growing up in a house with a dead mother and a perpetually grieving father hadn't exactly been a recipe for happiness. Add to that pot of sorrow one cupful of loaded guns and a sprinkle of getaway cash, and there you had it. A heaping helping of danger—my childhood.

By the time my sister was twelve years old, she ran our household. Raine had cooked, cleaned, done the laundry, and set the alarm for school each morning.

Raine Winston had taken care of business.

Everything had fallen on my older sister, because in all the ways that mattered to two little girls, our father had been a useless drunk.

I blamed my mother. She should have known better.

Jesus, even at four and a half years old, I had seen that one coming. But, out of some sort of misguided bullshit, Maggie, Magaskawee, my mother, had condemned us to that life.

At eighteen years old, my mother had found herself in the unenviable position of choosing between the two outlaw men who loved her.

She chose the wrong one.

Our father, Jack, had been a weak man, made weaker by his dependency on the love of a woman who would not live to see her thirtieth birthday. Our mother had been the love of Prosper's life. Prosper was Jack's best friend. When my mother died, he had been our only hope. Prosper had whisked us away one warm summer night, and had given us the outlaw-biker version of normal. Because that version had come with a sunny house by the lake, a funny, loving woman named Pinky, clean sheets, and plenty to eat; I had loved that normal. I had thrived on that normal. And when I heard my eight-year-old sister laugh, for what seemed to be the first time, I knew that we were where we belonged.

Then Jack had come for us.

First just for a visit. Then for longer visits.

Our father came back to us with his clear blue eyes filled with uncertainty and something that looked like love. My child's heart had opened wide to let that in. But it had turned out to be a big mistake to trust Jackie-boy. Because he didn't have it in him. He just couldn't do it. He could not be what two little girls needed.

The thing that I remembered most about the subsequent years of my childhood was the deep sense of underlying fear. Because my father spent most of his days in an alcohol- or drug-induced stupor, nothing ever felt solid or safe in our world. Even though Raine was no more than a child herself, she had tried hard to give me the sense of security that I craved. In the chill of the night, my big sister would snuggle tight with me under the blankets, and whisper soft words about a magical safe place where we could go if things ever got too bad.

I knew that Raine had meant for those words to comfort me. But, there were times when I would lie in bed and wonder just how bad things would have to get before we could Houdini our way out of this world and into that one. I learned, frustratingly early on, that big sister's ideas of "when things got too bad" and mine were worlds apart.

But, I also knew that things could have been a lot worse for us. Thanks to Raine's diligence, we were never the dirty kids or the stupid kids.

Thanks to Jack's apathy, we were also never the kids whose parent showed up drunk at school events.

Those kids had been Clay and Della Jenkins.

To this day, I can still remember their horrified little faces every time they watched their mother arrive shit-faced at all the important elementary school events. Even now, almost twenty years later, I can still recall the mean-spirited laughter that had echoed through the hallways.

No, we were not those kids.

We were the kids who had stood with Clay and Della, solemnly slipping our small hands into theirs, in solidarity and understanding.

We were the kids who signed our father's name on permission slips and report cards.

We were the kids with the perfect attendance, because school was the only place we felt safe.

We were the invisible kids.

CHAPTER 3

A gray storm cloud gathered up ahead. I felt a rush of cool air dance through the open car window and tug at my hair. The intermittent rays cast by the sun peeked through the lush, green foliage. The shadows splayed against my windshield like black confetti.

A sign of trouble yet to come.

I pushed the thought away and pressed down on the accelerator. Speeding up quickly to get past the darkening shadows and into the light of the lowering sun, I saw my sister's happy little home come into view.

I smiled at the sight.

Raine and Diego currently lived in an eyesore of a double-wide on the edge of a grassy knoll. The ugly trailer sat at odds with every bit of natural beauty that the property had to offer. However, the unit was a temporary and necessary measure while Diego worked with Crow, one of the brothers in the Hells Saints MC, to build Raine's dream home.

As my car crested the hill, I could see the smooth gray cement of the foundation and the sturdy straight angles and outlines of wall joists, studs, and beams. The shell of the house had begun to take shape. To my unending surprise, the Hells Saints brothers rocked the whole craftsman thing. They had descended upon the property with an impressive amount of trade skill. In the rare instance that one of them couldn't plumb it, wire it, or frame it, they knew someone who could. With their do-or-die approach to things, I honestly had no doubt that the house would be perfect. It wouldn't dare to be anything less.

Rattling in protest, my small, rusty, tin can of a car sputtered, heaved, and spit out a few billows of exhaust before it finally came to rest at the top of the hill. Tired old girl, and I knew exactly how she felt.

Gathering up an armload of presents, I headed toward the sound of celebration. I walked through the door to find Prosper holding the gurgling baby in his big, strong arms. Willow and her grandpa were engaged in a tug of war, the prize being a favorite blanket. Willow pulled and waited in gleeful anticipation for Prosper to pull it back. This seemed to be the funniest thing in the world to the baby girl, and she laughed out loud. Every time she let out that giggle, the rough, hardened outlaw smiled at the baby with such devotion that I could feel his love fill the room. Her eyes were the color of rich, round blueberries, her tiny mouth was cotton-candy pink, and she had a small smattering of dark hair that Raine insisted on gathering on the top of the baby's head in funny little bows. Despite all of the girly trappings, Willow grinned up at her grandfather with that same intensity as Prosper.

She squirmed and wiggled in her grandfather's arms. With every move, there came the soft, swooshing sound of a little bum covered in padding. Pulling and tugging and determined to triumph, Willow's chubby baby hands gathered up the soft cotton blanket. There was absolutely no doubt in my mind who the winner was going to be. Prosper was putty in Willow's hands. All the little sweetheart had to do was to gurgle and point to have her every wish granted.

We all knew that the relentless spoiling had to stop at some point, but for now it was all good. We were good.

Prosper's wife, Pinky, stood close by his side. Dolly, Pinky's sister-in-law and best friend, sat at the kitchen table and smiled at the scene before her. Diego leaned back into the deep cushions of the couch with his arm casually draped around his pretty wife. The proud papa looked relaxed and content.

I thought for the millionth time that my sister had never looked more beautiful. Motherhood had turned my sister's thin frame into something lush and womanly. Raine's naturally slender hips had grown slightly wider and her breasts were still round and full. An air of peace and contentment radiated from her these days. I was eternally thankful the burden that my sister had carried for so long had been replaced with the comfort and ease that comes from being well loved.

And so it begins, I thought to myself. *The next chapter.*

Hearing the screen door slam behind me, I felt a whoosh of air and saw flashes of white-blond hair and elegant long limbs enter the circle of admirers. As Glory rushed past me, I stepped back and exchanged a look with my sister. Raine smiled—we all loved Glory—but I saw the familiar lines of worry crease Raine's brow as my sister looked down at my belted jeans. The slight straightening of her spine told me that Raine had missed nothing. I knew it was just a matter of time before she would demand the conversation that I was unwilling to have.

Sighing, I turned my gaze once again to the precious baby girl and gave silent thanks that it had all worked out the way it had.

It had seemed like forever that Raine and I had been hanging on to the tail end of a very long shit storm. But, thank you Jesus, we had finally gotten through the other side of it. And, if being on the other side of it brought this happy place of grinning fools and gurgling babies, then I was good with the events that led us here.

Almost.

I was almost good with it.

I just wished the nightmares would stop.

Because that not-sleeping-well thing was really beginning to take its toll.

The minute my head hit the pillow, *it* was there.

It was still there.

I could see *it*.

Hear *it*.

Smell *it*.

The sick thud of metal meeting tree. The ping of bullets shot too close to my head. The smell of burning oil, burning leather, burning flesh. The sights, smells, and sounds of death and destruction permeating right through to my soul.

And it hadn't even been my first trip down the fright-fest highway.

Not by a long shot.

But, this time I was stuck.

And unlike ever, *ever* before, I was trapped in that place all alone.

CHAPTER 4

Raine watched as Claire moved toward the door of the crowded little trailer. Apparently, Glory had found a new online store, and together the two roommates had bought everything in pink that the shop had to offer. Claire was going out to Glory's car to bring in the rest of the gifts.

As she heard the door slam behind her younger sister, Raine let out a worried sigh.

Raine was happier than she had ever thought possible. Her life with Diego and their child was more than she had ever dared to hope for. Life was damn near perfect for her.

But she knew that it wasn't that way for Claire. Life was far from perfect for Claire.

Raine was worried about her.

And not just a little.

In the past months, that worry had moved from a general concern for her sister's well-being, to a deep and growing suspicion that something was very wrong.

Ever vigilant, Raine had watched Claire, and what she saw scared the hell right out of her.

She knew that something dark was sitting heavy in her sister's heart. And she knew that whatever it was, it was pushing her into a state of isolating despair.

Whatever it was that was lurking deep in the dark recesses of Claire's mind, she wasn't talking about it.

Whatever *it* was, Raine was watching it eat her little sister alive.

Sighing deeply, she stood and stared at the doorway. Glory's eyes met Dolly's from across the room. Diego immediately got up and wrapped his arms around his wife. The scowl on Prosper's face gave way to the worry that he felt in his heart.

"She'll be okay, Babe," Diego said softly to her.

Raine wasn't so sure.

"Does Claire ever sleep?" She turned to Glory. Glory hesitated, then looked at the sea of faces now staring back at her. "Some. She's sleeping some."

"Bullshit," snarled Prosper.

Sensing the shift in tension, Willow began to fuss and reach for her mother. After he placed a soft kiss on her forehead, Prosper relinquished Willow to Raine's arms. The walls of the small trailer seemed to shake as the big man's voice hit every corner of the room.

"The girl looks like the fucking walking dead. She's back to skinny, and those circles under her eyes . . . goddammit."

He paused, then asked, "Christ, she ain't using, is she?"

Raine felt herself wince.

"No!" A chorus of women's voices let out a loud protest.

"Jesus, Prosper," Pinky hissed at her big husband. "Don't you dare go there."

"Woman, you know better than to talk to me about how to handle my girls." He arched an eyebrow at her and glared.

Pinky, undeterred, glared right back at her husband. She put her hand on his arm and shook her head slightly in warning.

Prosper ignored that warning.

"Goddammit. Somebody's got to go there. I am sick of pussy-footing around this bullshit. She needs to talk it out. Whatever it is. This shit needs to come out before it swallows her whole."

Raine felt a sudden shiver move right through her.

Someone has just walked over my grave, her mother used to say.

She felt Diego's muscled arms move tighter around her, warming her. Frowning deeply, she leaned in against her husband. Then Raine turned to Prosper. Her worried eyes met his determined ones. Prosper was not asking for anyone's permission, but with a slight nod she gave it to him anyway.

He was not wrong.

And if anyone could get to the bottom of whatever was causing the change in her funny, caring, loving little sister, Prosper was the man for the job. No doubt about it.

CHAPTER 5

W hat did I miss?"

I had heard them through the screen door—those badass women protesting. Prosper made his way toward me. His big body cast a shadow against the wall.

"Claire, honey, you don't look so good. I know you ain't been sleeping. Can't help but wonder if you've been putting powder anywhere but on that pretty face of yours?"

And there it was.

"Christ," I heard Diego mutter under his breath.

My sister stood beside Diego, suddenly very busy with a drowsy Willow.

"Damn it, Prosper." Dolly pushed him out of the way and started to walk toward me. I guess what she saw on my face made her stop.

I stared hard at my family. One by one. "You think I'm doing blow, Prosper?" I pushed those words out and sent them to swarm around their heads like angry wasps. "Is that what all of you think?"

At least they had the grace to look embarrassed.

Well. Not all of them.

Prosper was coming right at me. Fast.

When he linked his tattooed arm around mine, I stiffened in protest. But he just held on tighter, pulled me right out the door and dragged me across the wide expanse of grassy field. Then he sat my ass down hard on a big boulder.

Damn him.

Not only had he just humiliated me in front of our entire family, but now the big man made me wait. He slowly pulled out a fresh pack of smokes, tapped them lightly against his palm, unwound the thin cellophane strip, dragged one out, and lit up.

Then Prosper drew deep.

Twice.

"Jesus, Claire, you look like shit," he said, one eye squinting as he slowly exhaled a thin streak of white smoke.

"Yeah, heard that the first time." My voice shook with anger and my eyes burned bright. I thought about the concealer, the mascara, and the In the Midnight Garden effort that I had put forth just a short time ago in hopes of avoiding a scene exactly like this.

Game. Over.

I brought a hand up to smooth my hair.

Prosper took it and covered it with his own.

"What the fuck is it?" Prosper's words were harsh, but his tone was gentle. The touch of his big, callused hand on mine warmed me.

"It's not coke," I whispered raggedly. The accusation sat heavy on my heart.

Prosper was the hero in my story. In my eyes, he was everything a man should be: a provider, a protector, and a teacher. Prosper was everything that my birth father, Jack Winston, had not been. Long before my father's death he had become nothing more than a sad shadow to me. Prosper was my dad by choice. Having his love and respect didn't mean just a little something to me. It meant everything.

Despite everything I had fought my way through. I could not believe that it had come down to this.

Was I that girl to him now? The ex-junkie daughter living on borrowed time?

Great. Just fucking great.

"So tell me, Prosper, is relapse the family go-to now? Is this where it lands every time I lose a few pounds or spend a couple of restless nights?" I looked at him hard and felt the sting of unshed tears.

I didn't deserve this.

Not even a little bit.

Prosper took a full minute before he answered me.

"No, Claire. It's not. If you tell me it's fucking not, then it's not." He looked at me, assessing.

"It's not." I met his gaze straight on.

When my father moved to pull me into his big strong arms, I let him.

Sighing against his chest, I inhaled the clean, soapy scent of his skin. I settled into him like a child, taking strength from the raw power that radiated from deep within this man.

He was my safe place. I wanted to blow out a wish that would find me small enough to be tucked into his pocket, nestled tightly and close to his heart.

"Is it that bad, honey?"

"Yeah, it's that bad." I breathed it out. Finally, finally releasing it.

"Give it to me, honey. Give it to your ol' Prosper. You need to talk this shit out. It's eating you up. I can see it. We all can see it. Open up and let it out. There's nothing you can't tell me. Nothing I can't fix."

I sighed, knowing that Prosper was right.

There was nothing he couldn't fix.

I knew that he would take whatever I gave to him. Then, he would twist it, turn it, and stomp all over it, just to make sure it all came out for the good.

I knew that Prosper would do whatever he had to do, or needed to do, to protect me.

I knew that Prosper was the *lay down your life for the ones you love*, kind of guy.

I knew that he was the kind of guy, definitely the kind of guy, who would lie to protect the ones he loved.

And I knew that he had lied to me.

CHAPTER 6

The man I considered my father pushed me away from him then. But he kept a tight hold on me with both his hands, and he looked straight into my eyes.

"You not letting it out to Raine or Glory, I get. Maybe you don't want to lay whatever this is at their door. But shit, Claire, it's me you're talking to now. Yeah?" He spoke from his heart.

"Yeah," I said. My heart answering his.

"So talk to me, honey. Let's get rid of this shit today and move the fuck on."

He sighed deeply, his eyes dark with worry.

Prosper was throwing me a lifeline. But I couldn't find the words that would lift me up out of those dark waters. I didn't know how to describe the fear I felt. I didn't have a name for what happened when I closed my eyes.

I sat for a minute, my mind searching for those words. Then, having found them, it took some time before I gathered the courage to reach down and pull them out.

Prosper gave me that time.

"They're dead because of me." I fought the urge to clap my hands over my ears at the sound of my own voice.

Prosper's gaze grew hard.

"Who is dead, Claire?" Prosper asked.

"You know who's dead, Prosper." My gaze grew hard in return.

"That's what it is? You're burning daylight worrying about that piece of shit and his murderous she-bitch?" Prosper growled.

Yep, that was it. That sure as hell was it.

How could that *not* be it?

I nodded while images of eternal damnation played out in my mind.

"I killed Manny, didn't I?" I forced my voice into steadiness.

And there it was.

The sum of all my fears.

When Raine and I had left Manny Rieldo, he was lying on the ground with his balls pinned to the top of his thigh by a nail gun and his head dented in from a claw hammer. In a desperate attempt at escape, my sister and I had attacked him the minute he had opened the van door.

My plan had been to save our lives. And it had worked. We were alive. But in the process of saving our own lives, had I cost Manny his?

I hadn't known for certain. Not until the night after the big meet. Prosper had come to tell me and Raine that all was well. He had assured us that Manny had been taken care of.

He had assured *us* without looking at *me.*

Prosper had delivered his *all is well* message without a glance in my direction.

And that's when I knew.

In my heart, I knew.

Manny had been taken care of all right.

By me.

CHAPTER 7

Prosper looked at me for a long time.

"I need to know," I whispered. Even as the words came out of my mouth, I felt that cold black shadow move over me again.

He sighed deeply and put his hand up to smooth my hair.

"It's done, Claire. What does it matter who did it? It needed doing, and it's done."

"It matters," I said, desperate to make him understand. "I can't stay in this dark place of not knowing, Prosper. It follows me, like a monster that I can't get away from. I need to face it to move on. I need to face it to somehow move past it and into whatever light there is left for me."

Then simply:

"If I killed him, Prosper, if Manny was dead when you found him, then I have a right to know."

Prosper's eyes met mine with such searching intensity that I had to force myself not to look away. After what seemed like forever, he nodded once, then lit up another smoke. He drew deep three, maybe four times before he spoke.

"Yeah, honey. That claw hammer cracked the sonofabitch's skull open. And so fucking what? He was going to kill you, your sister, and the baby she was carrying. Manny Rieldo was a piece of shit who had a death wish," Prosper growled.

"No one wishes for that, Prosper." I could feel the beat of my own guilt-ridden heart.

"That's bullshit. *Bullshit*, Claire. Men like Manny Rieldo make a decision to die every day. He marked his fate the minute he got involved with that psycho snatch, Ellie," Prosper said.

"He had a life, Prosper," I countered. "He had people that he mattered to. He had a mother."

Prosper glared at me.

"*Everyone* has a mother, Claire. Adolf Hitler, Joseph Stalin, Saddam Hussein, they all had mothers. This cocksucker, Manny? His mother's name is Luisa Sievas. Bitch is meaner than a junkyard dog. That whole family is crazier than a bunch of shit house rats."

"But still, Prosper." A tear escaped down my cheek.

"But still nothing," Prosper growled and he wiped that tear away. "Jesus, Claire. You have got to stop doing this to yourself."

A pause from Prosper, and then:

"Did you mean to kill him?" Prosper drew deep from the cigarette, his eyes squinting over the curl of smoke.

"What? No! God no! We had to get away. From him and that crazy woman." I took a deep, ragged breath. The pounding of my heart would not let me speak.

I tried again.

"Raine and the baby . . ." my voice grew weak and trailed off.

Thinking back to that night, I honestly had never been so scared in my life, and I had a long list of scared to choose from.

Prosper's eyes crashed and burned into mine. Then he nodded and inhaled deeply. He crushed the cigarette between his fingers, threw down the butt, and stomped it out. Hard.

"Goddammit, Claire. Look at you. You're still so freaked, you can't even say the words. Manny Rieldo and his bitch were going to kill you and Raine. Then that she-wolf, Ellie, was going to straight-up carve that baby right out of your sister's belly. Make no mistake about that."

He paused to let that awful truth sink in.

"Why are you making yourself sick over that piece of shit? Do you ever lie awake nights thinking about what would have happened if you had *not* had the balls to lay that sonofabitch out?" he asked me. "That's the kind of shit that should keep you up nights. Not putting that piece of crap to ground. Believe me when I tell you, you did him a fucking favor, Claire."

"A favor?" I stumbled over the words.

"Yeah. A big one. Rieldo's name was high on everyone's shit list. Among the other desperate acts of random violence that the stupid fuck let himself repeatedly get talked into committing, he was a goddamn canary. He had just cut his time short by three years, and that was not for good behavior," Prosper continued. "The Italians are all over shit like that. It was just a matter of time before Manny Rieldo's wagging tongue flushed this whole uneasy alliance down the shitter. If that had happened, the body count would have been a lot higher than two. Claire, this was not Manny's first time at the crazy snatch rodeo. Fucker was a magnet for desperate and disturbed. And everyone, including that mother of his who you are so concerned with, knew it. From what I hear, Manny Rieldo's dick has been leading him on a merry chase of bad decisions since puberty. Because of that tendency and a whole lot of stupid, he has been living on borrowed time."

Prosper paused, reached into his cut and pulled out a silver flask. When he offered it to me, I didn't hesitate. I took a deep swallow and felt the burn hit my belly.

As my eyes began to water, I handed the tequila back over to Prosper and watched him take a long pull. His eyes didn't water, and my guess was that not much burned in Prosper's belly. He took one more hit, and he put it aside.

Then he continued on.

"Claire, I love who I love, and that shit goes deep with me. You, Raine, Pinky, and that baby in there, I'd take a bullet for any of you. No question. That makes me a good man in your eyes. I get that, and I'm glad for it. But, honey, I'm a mean, tough, murderous sonofabitch who shows absolutely no mercy when dealing with garbage like Rieldo."

He looked at me long and hard.

"You and Raine were taken from a goddamn doctor's office. You were thrown into a van and driven out of town by two crazy, felonious fucks who had murder on their minds. There was no way, no possible, conceivable way, that you were going to survive what the two of them had planned. Not once Ellie got down to business. And you know that, Claire. Deep down inside, under all the guilt and fear and fucking remorse for something you should feel no regret over, you know it. Manny Rieldo gave you no choice but to take that hammer to his head."

Prosper took my hand in his and put it over my left breast.

"You feel that, honey? You're alive. Raine and Willow are alive. Because of you. Because you are one brave, quick-thinking motherfucker yourself, you saved the damn day."

Then my father finished with *this*.

And *this* scared the crap right out of me.

"Claire, you listen to me now, and you listen hard. As far as anyone outside this club knows, it was me. I took that sonofabitch out. *It was me.* From this day forward, *it's still me.* You understand that? This thing ever, *ever* blows back, I handle it. *We* handle it. Me and my boys."

He inhaled deeply and blew out the words sharply, punctuating every point. "You don't talk about this to anybody. *Nobody.* You ever feel the need to share with big sister, or Glory, or anybody else, you think again. You get what I am telling you?"

If I hadn't gotten it before, I sure as hell was getting it now. Blow back.

"I got this, Claire. I put a lid on it and I am handling it. But I cannot do that if every jerk-off on the corner gets wind that somethin' don't add up. You understand me?"

Jesus.

"Do you get what I am saying to you, Claire?" Prosper ground it out, slower and louder. His eyes held mine, making sure that I got it.

"Yeah, I get it." I nodded hard.

I worked to swallow the lump in my throat, because I absolutely did get it. And its name was retaliation. And retaliation could make the scary town of my nightmares look like a trip to the circus.

Prosper and I sat together for a while after that, taking in the light of the setting sun. After a time, he pulled out his mouth harp, and treated me to a medley of ragtime rock 'n' roll. I leaned back onto the heat-soaked rock and closed my eyes. For the first time in months, I let myself rest.

Despite the very scary finish, that cloud was lifting.

My father's words had cracked the door of the prison of my own conflicted and guilt-ridden mind. I hadn't been trapped alone in scary town after all. A posse had been right behind me the whole time.

And everything my father said was true. I had never intended to harm Manny or Ellie. I had not set out to take a life. I had set out to save one.

And I had. I *had* saved a life. Three to be exact.

Good for me.

I began to feel vindicated in a way I had not felt in a long time. Vindication is a heady thing. I decided to go with that high. The crippling sense of despair, and guilt, and the fear of eternal damnation was beginning to lift.

CHAPTER 8

A few weeks after my showdown with Prosper, the relief that I felt that night began to grow into a restorative sense of peace. My nights were now spent in a deep and dreamless sleep. My days were filled with a sense of purpose that I had not felt in a very long time.

I was ready for a night out.

Glory and I drove up the private road that led to the Hells Saints compound. It wasn't long before the strains of music, the rumble of exhaust pipes, and the sound of loud, raucous laughter assailed us.

No doubt about it, Prosper's boys knew how to throw a party.

It seemed that every weekend there was something to celebrate; the patching in of a new member, the time-served release of a brother, marriages, divorces, births, and depending on the circumstances, sometimes even deaths were all causes for wild revelry.

Glory, Raine, and I didn't always join in. As a matter of fact, more times than not, we avoided the gatherings at all costs. Glory called the parties "the dining, drinking, drilling, and debt festivals." The boys ate, drank, and sexed up their fill, that was for sure. And just to make it interesting, there were always a few high-stakes games of cards, billiards, or darts thrown in. But tonight the celebration centered on Pinky's birthday, and none of us wanted to miss that.

The party was fully under way by the time Glory and I got there. Spits were turning, kegs were tapped, and the tables groaned with food. A few dozen Harleys were parked on the grassy area. The kinsmen who owned them clapped each other hard on the back in greeting. The brothers generously passed around joints, ice cold bottles of beer, and flasks filled with Johnny or Jack.

A sea of big-breasted, tattooed, barely-dressed women flanked the outlaw men. Or they stood elsewhere, depending on where they fell in the rank and file of biker babes. The pecking order, which I had grown to understand, still made me not quite comfortable. I knew that the Saints were not the only club where the men frequently exchanged the women in their beds. The order of rank seemed to be wives, old ladies, club Band-Aids, and straight-up professional whores. I knew that "bitch swapping" was a practiced tradition in the hardcore biker clubs otherwise known as outlaw nations. The Hells Saints fully embraced that tradition and in my opinion, raised it a couple of notches.

How they managed to keep it all straight and not kill each other in the process fascinated me.

It was a complicated system and one in which these women took their roles very seriously. They worked hard to get their men, harder to keep them, and had a handful of hell ready to deliver to any woman who had a mind to take them.

Yikes.

My girls and I had learned the hard way that it was much, *much* better to be off that particular radar.

We were about twenty seconds into a good time when Jules, the Hells Saints version of a Viking god, whisked Glory away to wherever it is that Vikings whisk their women away. I wondered, for the millionth time, what the deal was with those two. And judging from the looks of green-eyed jealousy being flung in Glory's general direction, I was not the only one.

I loved Glory, I did. We all did. But sometimes she made me want to scream.

Even after all this time, getting any personal information out of her was like nailing jelly to a tree. But I had not given up hope that one day Glory would open up. And I had absolutely no doubt in my mind that when that day came, it would definitely be worth the wait.

Alone now, I made my way to the kitchen house looking for my sister. The kitchen house was the largest structure on the compound. It had a big industrial kitchen and two wings of private housing for the club members' private use. The local brotherhood had their own set of accommodations, and there was also a string of rooms kept at the ready for any visiting club members who might want to make use of them.

Raine wasn't there yet, but Diego was. By way of greeting, my brother-in-law tossed me a beer. He and I sat down on the worn, comfy couch and threw back a couple of cold ones.

"You look a whole lot better, little sister. You're still too goddamn skinny, and you're still sporting that blue under your eyes. But I am glad to see you don't look like something that I scraped off the bottom of my boots anymore."

"Jesus, is that supposed to be a compliment?" I took a hit off my beer.

"Yeah, Claire, it actually is. For too long, little sister, you have been barely *there*. Everyone has been fucking worried about you. Now, it looks like you've been sleeping a little more. Yeah?"

"Yeah. Things are better, D. Just learning to live with the decisions I've made." I looked at him.

Then, thinking of Reno, I added, "And the decisions that have been made for me."

"Ain't we all, little sister. Ain't we all." He nodded his head. Diego reached for the flask that sat on the table and splashed something strong into two shot glasses.

He handed one to me, lifted his own and said, "To figuring shit out."

I raised my glass in answer. "To figuring shit out."

We sat quietly for a few minutes, at ease with one another and deep in our own thoughts.

"So, what's next?" Diego was first to break that comfortable silence. He nodded a greeting at Crow as he passed by.

"Next?" I looked at him. I was feeling relaxed from the little somethin' somethin' settling in my belly. I reached for my beer chaser.

"Yeah, next," Diego answered, taking another pull from the frosty bottle. "Raine's got the baby, and she's still doing that accounting shit for Ruby Reds. Glory's got her fishing, and from what I hear, a full-time addiction to the Home Shopping Network." He grinned.

I grinned back. "She cooks and bakes too. Bakes up a freaking storm."

Then I patted my brother-in-law's flat stomach.

"And don't you go telling me that you haven't been sampling some of those goodies yourself, big brother."

He looked at me in mock horror. "Man's got to have a little meat on him. Besides, that's pure muscle you're handling right there."

He was not wrong.

"Yeah, yeah, yeah," I teased him. Then I grew thoughtful. "Hey, Diego?" I looked at him with wariness. I had been quietly harboring this idea for a while.

"Yeah, Claire?" Diego gave me his full attention.

I pulled at the wet label on my frosty bottle. I was suddenly shy to say the words out loud.

Diego waited me out.

"What do you think about me going to school?" I looked up at him, suddenly.

"School? What kind of school?" Diego arched his eyebrow.

"College kind of school," I said softly.

He was still staring at me, so I went on.

"I have been thinking about it for a while. I always liked school. I got pretty good grades in high school. I was thinking about maybe starting off with some basic intro classes. If that goes well, I could look into choosing a major in business management or something like that. Before things got all messed up, before *I* got all messed up, I was on the management team at the bank. They liked me, and I think that I did a pretty good job for them. Maybe I can use what I learn to help out the club, like Raine does."

I said the words in one quick breath, desperate to get it all out before I lost my nerve.

Diego just sat there with one eye squinting at me. So I continued. But more slowly this time.

"I know I might be kind of old to start something like that . . ." My voice fluttered and trailed off in embarrassment. I figured most people my age had it all figured out by now. But then again, I really had no idea what normal was.

Diego looked at me thoughtfully.

"You know, little sister, I like it. It's a good idea. Right now, the club has three bars including Ruby Reds. Gianni and his crew are looking to put up two hotels in our territory. If all goes as planned, there's going to be plenty of legit work down the road. Only makes sense that we are going to need people who know their shit. College kind of shit," Diego said.

"So, you think I should do it?" I asked, after a pause.

"Oh, hell, yeah. As a matter of fact, I am sitting here wondering why you ain't done it already, sweetheart."

When Diego smiled at me, the lines around his eyes crinkled out like rays of sunshine. My brother-in-law didn't smile often, but when he did, it was worth noticing.

"Really?" I mirrored his smile with one of relief. Because the more I had thought about it, the more I really wanted to do it.

Diego nodded. And then to celebrate, Diego and I clinked our beers together.

Crow came over and leaned in. "What's up?"

"Claire is going to be a college fucking student," Diego said.

"No shit, babe?" Crow's beautiful emerald eyes glittered. He looked impressed.

"No shit," I confirmed, feeling a little impressed myself.

"So what's that going to look like?" Crow was interested.

"I really have no idea where to even start," I shrugged. "But I guess I will find out soon enough. Maybe I will put a call into that college in the valley and make an appointment next week to go and talk to somebody."

"Bring your car in before you head down there. I'll have the boys look at it," Crow said.

Then he turned to Diego. "Heap of shit she's driving needs new tires at the least. That fan belt could possibly be on its way out too. Replaced the water pump last time it was in. My guess is the fuel pump is next. Can't have her taking that trip every day without checking that shit out first."

"Yeah, that's for sure." Diego nodded in agreement. "That thing's been on its last legs for a while now."

"It'll make it," I said with a sinking feeling. What they said made sense. But I couldn't afford a new car. Even the tires would be stretching it.

"Yeah, Claire. It'll make it, maybe twice. But after that, who knows? Don't want you breaking down on that thruway, little sister. That shit's too far to come tow you back every other day."

I sighed.

Well, there goes that idea, I thought to myself. Diego and Crow were right. My car was a little shit box. In the past month I'd gotten it towed twice. I knew I needed a new car, but I couldn't swing classes and a loan.

"Well, maybe I could take the bus." I sighed.

Crow snorted. "Darlin', you ain't taking no bus. We'll figure that shit out."

Diego stood up, reached into his pocket and threw a set of car keys at me.

"What's this?" I reached high to catch them.

"That's me figuring shit out." Diego took another hit off his beer. "Brother's right, if you're serious about this school thing, then you're going to need something reliable to get there in. That piece of shit you've been driving saw its last day about a hundred years ago."

"You're giving me the Jeep?" I couldn't believe it.

Diego nodded.

"Do you think that Raine is going to be good with this?" I eyed him.

"I think that Raine is going to be great with this," Diego answered.

"Minivan time?" I teased.

Pipe, a Hells Saints soldier, had been walking by and chimed in. "Yeah!" He gave a rebel yell. "Minivans fucking rule!"

Even Crow laughed at that. Which, by the way, was a rare and beautiful thing.

Diego was halfway toward the door, but he turned to give Pipe the finger.

"I just changed my mind. Give me those keys back," he growled at me.

But then he smiled. Big.

I smiled big right back at him.

Then, feeling the booze and the love and the happy, I let out a rebel yell myself. And just for the hell of it, I coupled it all with a hoot and a holler. To the delight of the three half-drunken fools watching me, I even did my very own silly version of a happy dance.

And, because I let that happy place reign supreme for all of about three little minutes, I did not hear the familiar footsteps as they beat a path toward the frame of the darkened doorway.

Me and my stupid little happy dance.

I did not look up when the shadow flitted against the scarred wooden floor.

But I wish I had.

I really, really *wish I had.*

CHAPTER 9

As Reno pulled in to the Hells Saints compound, he hit the throttle with a minute's worth of fury before easing it up and parking it next to the two dozen or so Harleys that littered the driveway. Making his way past the fire pits of roasting pigs, grills of sizzling steaks, and kegs of cold beer, Reno walked through the yard. Nodding to his brothers in greeting, he stopped to take a toke of an offered joint and to grab a hit off a flask.

It was good to be home.

After traveling for almost three straight days, Reno's nerves were coiled rattlesnake-tight. He had shown up at the airport determined to take the first plane out. The large amount of green he had to fork over for that ticket rewarded him with two long layovers before landing him in an airport almost three hours away from where he had taken off. After a long-ass expensive cab ride to pick up his Harley, Reno had traveled half the night before he hit a rainstorm that forced him under a bridge to wait it out.

Under a motherfucking bridge.

Feeling the mud and backwash from the highway seeping deep into his pores, he had pulled off the thruway and grabbed a motel room. Though only wanting to stay long enough to shower and change, he waited out the couple of hours that it took for the storm to ease.

Then he had hit the road again.

He had done all this to get home to Claire. Reno was not a man who made decisions lightly or quickly. Reno was the kind of guy who followed through. Like a dog with a bone, he could be persistent and aggressive. Once Reno decided he wanted something, he did not always play nice with others, and he didn't like to share.

Yeah, Reno wasn't a guy who made decisions lightly.

And he had made a decision about Claire.

Now, standing in the shadows of the doorway, he felt his taut muscles ease up when he finally saw her. But as he looked closer, concern lined his face. His girl had lost weight and she had tired circles under her eyes. Seeing Claire with Diego, deep in conversation, looking skinny and lost and like she hadn't slept in months, just about killed him.

It brought him back to the time that he had first seen her.

Raine's little sister.

Reno had nicknamed Raine the "golden snatch." He had not been able to stand her; he could not get past the upheaval that she caused by showing up at the MC. Because of her, his brothers Diego and Crow had gone at each other like two junkyard dogs. Uncle Prosper had gone dewy-eyed every time he laid eyes on the long-lost bitch. Reno had been disgusted with the whole thing.

Until he wasn't.

Until the day that Prosper had ordered Reno to play fucking chauffeur to Raine. His orders were to accompany Miss Golden Snatch to pick up her little sister from her twenty-eight days in rehab. Reno had been more than a little pissed. He had seriously not been looking forward to it. Not a short trip either, six hours there and six more back. He had just wanted to get it over with. So much so that he'd made Raine practically beg him to stop the car just so she could take a piss.

Then, when they finally got there, Reno had waited with his arms folded in front of that rehab building. He had stood like stone, covered in attitude, meaning to intimidate Raine into hurrying the hell up.

Yep, Reno had seen his share of skanky, dull-eyed blow-bags. He was sure as shit not looking forward to accompanying one all the way back home.

When Reno saw Claire coming down the stairs toward him, he knew she was not that.

No, siree. Claire was not even close to that.

As a matter of fact, she was so far from that that Reno felt certain that Raine Winston's little sister had just spent her twenty-eight in the wrong place.

The sight of Claire, even at a distance, had pulled Reno in like quicksand. Seeing her up close had made his balls ache: sky blue eyes, long hair as dark as night, clear smooth skin that glistened like warm copper, high cheek bones, full lips. A smoking-hot body made for lying under a man.

Seeing her for the first time had made his dick twitch, no question. But really, it was her reaction to him that had caught his interest. Claire had burst through the doors of that drab building like a jewel-box ballerina whose lid had just been opened. Reno watched her happily bouncing her way down those long front steps.

Yep. She had bounced all right, until her gaze had crashed and burned into his.

Then Claire had stopped dead, narrowed her baby blues and hid behind her big sister. *She had tried to hide from him.* Reno couldn't believe it. Not letting that even come close to stopping him, Reno had moved in to get a better look.

Jesus.

Those Winston sisters sure had it in the looks department.

Raine was a whole truckload of beautiful. Even when Reno was hating on her, he could not deny that.

But her little sister.

Damn adorable.

Claire's freckles had sealed the deal for Reno. Dancing like little stars across the bridge of her nose. None of that spackle shit that some women wore on their faces to cover them up.

Claire was a natural beauty.

Reno had wanted to be up in that the minute he saw her.

Then, a few short hours later, he had almost gotten her killed.

Christ.

That day had been a disaster of epic proportions.

Crow liked to refer to it as the "nap" incident.

Asshole.

But Reno couldn't deny that those forty winks had almost cost three women their lives. And those three women had manned up in ways that some men would not have had the balls to do. The girls had held their shit together long enough for Reno to get them all home safe and sound.

Then crazy Ellie and shit-for-brains Rieldo had kidnapped and tried to kill Raine and Claire.

The two fools had tried to off the Winston sisters.

Yeah, Reno grinned in spite of himself, *good luck with that*.

When Prosper called him into the meet to tell him about Claire being taken, Reno had lost his shit. Lost it. Reining it in to let Prosper handle it took everything that Reno had. But then again, Reno had spent a lot of time reining it in on Claire's behalf.

Really, too much damn time.

He knew that she had been working her twelve-step bullshit. It turned out that she had been trying to stay away not only from substances, but from the bad men who brought her to that point.

Reno didn't think he was a bad man. He had known worse. But he knew, sure as shit knew, that he wasn't a good one either.

Reno knew exactly what Claire saw when she looked at him. She saw what most good citizens saw—a whole lot of badass. He hadn't wanted to scare her off. So he had waited and watched. Reno did what he could do not to punch his fist bloody into every road-block that she threw in his way.

Night and day for what had seemed like forever, Reno had done his best to be where Claire was. And that hadn't been easy because where Claire was, her girl posse followed.

Jesus, he had never seen three closer women in his life. They were a three-girl army when it came to protecting each other. And evidently, they had decided that Claire needed protection. From him.

And that would have been enough for Reno to stay away. He wasn't some desperate stalker. That was just creepy. Reno never had been and never would be that guy.

No, what kept Reno in the game was Claire.

It was in the way that she looked at him when she thought that he didn't see. In the way her eyes danced over every dude in the room, anxiously seeking him out, and breathing the smallest sigh of relief when she saw him. In the way she lowered her face when she was close to him, but then looked up at him from behind those thick long lashes of hers. In the way she colored that adorable shade of pink, all over, when he winked at her.

Those were the things that had kept Reno in it.

Jesus, it had taken him almost a whole year to get her to the point where she could have a conversation with him without turning herself inside out. Then, when he was finally in, when he had all that beauty in his bed, when they had finally gotten to a place where they could start working on that forever kind of shit, she had left him.

And that had been it for him.

Well, fuck her, he had thought. *Fuck you, Claire, and your issues.*

That's how Reno had felt about Claire when he left. He had tried to stay away, but he couldn't.

Because Reno loved Claire.

A lot.

Yeah, it had taken him a while to get there, but when he did, he felt it like a shot to his gut. With that, he had packed his shit up, took the first plane out, and drove through a rainstorm to get home. He had gone to the lake house for her first. Then not finding Claire there, Reno had driven straight to the compound.

He was one hundred percent in for the happily ever after with her.

Whatever it took.

But no more waiting.

He was all done with the waiting game. If he was right about the way Claire felt about him, then she had been just as miserable without him as he was without her. And remembering the way Claire had come to him that first night, Reno knew that he was right about the way that she felt.

Jesus, that sweet thing had been all over him. Unleashed. He hadn't known that shy little beauty had it in her. When he had moved to take her out of that hospital after the good news of the baby being born, she had practically jumped on the back of his bike. She had hung on tight to him all the way home, her heavy tits pressed hard against his back, her sleek, muscled legs clutched against his leather-covered thighs, and best of all, her arms holding on tight around him.

Claire had started in on him the moment his foot slammed the door shut. Almost frantically, she had pulled off his cut, then his T-shirt. When she moved to unhook his belt, he had stopped her and started to do some undressing of his own.

When he had her down to her tiny silk panties he had pushed her back on his bed and tongued her. All over. Soft little licks that made her whimper. Long gentle pulls that made her nipples harden and swell. When he finally pulled her legs wide apart and slung them over his shoulders, her back was arched so high that she was practically crawling with a need to take it.

Hours of that. Reno had given it to Claire for hours. And Claire had given it right back. Stretched out like a cat full of cream, she had purred and clawed for two straight days.

Best two goddamn days of his whole miserable life. Then those days had turned into more days, and longer nights. First it was all hot, hard, wet sex. They couldn't get enough of each other. It seemed they couldn't be around one another without wanting it. They were like two cats in heat, and Reno was all over that.

But he wanted more.

Reno always felt like Claire was holding back. Not physically. Physically she was pretty much game with whatever he wanted to do to her. That had surprised him. But Reno had been gentle and loving with Claire. Maybe that was why. He read her body like a book. He was careful with her and did his best to satisfy her and give her what he thought that she needed.

Thing was, that sometimes it seemed like the more he got to know her body, the less he got to know her. It had occurred to Reno more than once that Claire was hiding behind all that heat. Reno was never the *let's talk* kind of guy, but he had found himself wanting to get to know Claire. He wanted to know what she was thinking. Shit, he cared about her hopes and goddamn dreams.

He didn't want her to be his fuck buddy. He wanted much more than that.

So he worked on that too.

Claire had been a lot of work.

And then came the night when it was all worth it. She had opened up to him like a morning glory.

She had talked and talked and talked. Once those floodgates had opened, she couldn't seem to stop herself. They had stayed up all night talking. She had told him everything. They talked about the death of her mother and her time at the lake house with Prosper. She had shared what it was like growing up with Jack Winston.

41

With some prodding, Claire even opened up about her days with Jamie and her month in rehab.

The one thing she didn't talk about was the whole Manny thing. But as a member of the brotherhood, Reno already knew about that. He wasn't sure if Claire knew that he knew, but that didn't matter.

Claire came to him with everything else that night. Everything.

When there was no more left to tell, she had fallen asleep cradled in his arms. Reno had held Claire close and thought about everything she had told him. Nothing she had said put him off. As a matter of fact, everything that she had been through just made her seem stronger and more beautiful in his eyes. He fell asleep holding her tight with a goddamn smile on his face.

In the morning when he turned to reach for her, she was gone.

Just. Like. That.

Yeah, it had just about broken his hard heart to wake up and find her not there. He just could not go back to that cat-and-mouse game with her again.

Even thinking about it made him feel sick inside.

Worse than that, it made him feel weak.

And men like Reno were not made to feel weak.

She hadn't left for long. Claire had shown up at his door later that day. But he had been too drunk and high and pissed off by that time to hear her.

"Sorry. Blah. Blah. Blah."

"Scared. Blah. Blah. Blah."

Then the best of all . . . time.

Really? The bitch needed time?

Because he had not given her enough damn time already for her to work through whatever it was that kept her from going there with him?

Done. He had been done.

When Reno had learned the club had some business to settle on the West Coast he had volunteered to do the job. It was all good. Hot dry air. Endless roads of nothing but flat horizon and desert. Spending time with his brothers. Drunken nights, higher days, lots of unfamiliar, uncomplicated pussy.

Guzzling, snorting, and sexing Claire off his mind.

He thought it had worked. He really had. Stupid sonofabitch that he was, he thought it had worked.

But in the end, it had just made Reno miss Claire more.

Looking at her now, the sight of her burned into his chest. She looked about half the size she was when he left. How was that even possible? From where he stood in the shadows, he could see the deep hollows under her big blue eyes. The way her jeans hung on her hips told him she hadn't been eating much.

And was that a tattoo he saw peeking out under her belly button? What the hell? When he had left her, her body had been smooth and clear.

If she was going to wear anyone's ink, it was going to be his.

He never should have left her alone. Alone to get skinny and sleepless and marked with some meaningless shit on her body forever.

He started toward her.

Then he saw Diego throw her his set of keys. She looked down at her hand, said something to him, and then she smiled. But Claire did not just smile, she filled up with goddamn glee. Even from his place in the shadows Reno could see it, the transformation was amazing. Claire was jumping up and down like Diego had just given her the keys that opened the goddamn stairway to heaven. Crow, who smiled maybe twice a year, was grinning like a madman. Pipe had somehow joined the party and he could not keep his eyes off her. When Reno looked back at Claire, she was actually dancing a jig.

Sonofabitch.

Is that all it took for her?

He had just gone through months of self-destructive agony trying to kill the misery of being away from her. He hadn't had one happy thought since the day he had left.

And not only that. All this time, he had imagined that Claire had been just as unhappy and miserable without him.

Now he could see it was all a lie. It was all bullshit. He had been fooling himself. Maybe she was skinny and tired-looking but who wasn't? She couldn't have been nearly as miserable as he had selfishly hoped she had been. Not if all it took for her to laugh and shout out with goddamn glee were the keys to a three-year-old Jeep.

And there it was. Right then and there.

Because he was flawed and fragile in the face of what he felt for her, right then and there, Reno got pissed off at Claire all over again.

CHAPTER 10

"Well, look who finally made it the hell home." Jules looked up from the card game as Reno pulled out a chair, turned it backwards, and plopped down at the table.

Pipe, Riker, and a prospect were already seated and nodded to him.

"Good to see you, Brother." Jules slid the bottle over toward Reno.

"Yeah, not too sorry to see your ugly ass either." Reno took a long grateful hit off the whiskey. "Just saw Glory. Your woman is looking pretty goddamn fine. How come you're in here laying down a hand with these sorry looking boys 'stead of bedding her down, Brother?"

Jules took a long hard look at Reno, then he looked harder.

"You speaking about my woman, Reno?"

Reno rubbed the back of his neck. "Yeah, sorry man. Long ride."

Jules nodded.

"She talking to anybody?" Jules tried for the casual.

"Who you talking about?" Reno was looking toward the door.

Jules growled.

Reno looked back at his brother. "Talking? Nope. Woman wasn't saying a word. When I saw Glory, she was heading toward the rooms with one of the Point brothers. Her hand on his ass was doing all of the talking for her."

Reno grinned at Jules. The brothers at the table all nodded appreciatively.

"Very fucking funny." Jules did not look amused.

"Jesus, what do you think? That beauty hasn't talked to anybody but you, Prosper, and her girls since the day she came here. Barely nods to me, and I saved her life," Reno said.

"Yeah, well she ain't so quiet any more. Especially when she's pissed off at me," Jules said miserably.

"Yeah, got that." Reno nodded in commiseration.

He slid the bottle back toward his brother.

"You in?" Pipe was dealing.

"I'm in." The last thing that Reno felt like doing was playing cards. But, in what he saw as a strategic and conciliatory move, he had parked his bike in a visible location. It shouldn't be long before Claire saw it and came looking for him. His Irish temper had cooled down enough to want her to seek him out, but not enough for him to go looking for her again.

A little while later, Reno was about three hundred bucks down. He was still alone and getting more pissed off by the minute. He hadn't had his eyes off the entrance for more than five straight seconds. Nobody worth anything had come through those doors.

"Just go get her, man," Jules sighed.

"Don't know what the hell you are talking about, Brother," Reno snarled. "And really, man? You sitting there holding a losing hand when you could be holding your woman and you think you can give me fucking advice?"

"He's got a point." Pipe nodded.

"Can we stop with the soap opera shit and just play the goddamn game?" Riker picked up the cards to deal. All of a sudden, Reno decided he'd had enough. He threw down his hand and folded.

"I'm done here." Reno took the bottle off the table and headed for the door. "You coming?" He turned around and nodded to Cherry, a regular who just happened to be there

"You making a big mistake grabbing a bar whore 'stead of doing what you came for. Think this through, Brother." Jules gave it one more shot.

Reno flashed Jules the finger and headed to the door with Cherry draped eagerly around him. Jules gave a nod to Pipe.

Pipe glanced in Reno's direction, then turned back to Jules.

"Brother, you have got to be fucking kidding me."

"I look like I'm kidding you?"

Jules had leaned forward. "He's not the only one. Rebel brought in some West Coast porn girls last night, and shit-for-brains drove 'em over here a couple of hours ago. The girls ain't shy about what they want, and the boys have been drooling over the chance to get at them all night. All of the old ladies are just about done. They have been shooting daggers at 'em for hours. Bad goddamn mix. Rebel just made it harder for everyone. You're here and you're half sober, so that puts you on deck. We gotta contain this now, before it gets damn ugly. No one needs a bitch beat-down tonight. You don't like it, you take it up with Reb, who should have known better."

$\sim$

Reno headed toward his room to do what he had been doing for way too long. He went to drink and sex the woman he loved off his mind. But goddammit, if the same shit didn't start for him all over again. A few minutes into having a random woman in his bed, the only thing Reno could think about was Claire, the only thing he wanted was Claire. He was about two minutes into what should have been a good time when he felt himself pulling away. Reno felt his body tense with the shock of disappointment. Redoubling his efforts, he closed his eyes and willed himself not to think about Claire.

But it was no use.

Even with all that booze and reefer raging through his system, Reno felt it. Maybe his dick couldn't tell the difference, but what was left of his heart sure as hell could.

Revenge-fucking was definitely the wrong way to go.

Time to put his pride aside, man up, and go get his woman.

But as luck would have it, as always seemed to be the case with him and her, fate stepped in and Claire found Reno first.

CHAPTER 11

I was feeling *it*.

And the *it* was happy. I went out into the starry night smiling, the keys to the Jeep jingling in my pocket.

It had been a good night. I had spent some time talking with Dolly, then I had caught up with my sister and together we went and delivered Pinky's birthday present to her. Raine and I had searched high and low for just the right gift for the woman who meant so much to us. We finally found the perfect present in a small antique store in the valley. We bought Pinky an intricately engraved antique locket. The delicate clasp opened to reveal two miniature pictures. One was of Raine and me from that long ago summer that we had spent at the lake, and the other was of Willow.

Pinky loved it and put it on right away.

Seeing the locket around Pinky's neck made me feel like I had finally come full circle. For the first time in a long time, I felt hopeful. I couldn't remember the last time that I had felt that—like I had a fighting chance at normal. Like I had a plan.

I was still feeling that when I walked toward the kitchen house and saw Reno's bike parked with all the others.

So he was back.

Reno had been gone for months.

I sighed. Just like with everything else in my life, I had avoided thinking about him.

Reno and me.

A year ago, when I had walked out of Willows Point rehab and had seen Reno leaning against the car waiting, I knew that the gods were messing with me.

Totally messing with me.

I had just spent the previous four weeks of my life explaining and examining bad boys, and exorcising them from my mind, and I had not been even five minutes out of that serious gray building. Not even five minutes out of that place of repentance, resolve, and "God grant me" prayers, when he stood before me. A beacon of black leather and badass.

Not even five minutes out.

And I tried. Lord knows, I tried to stay away from Reno McCabe.

But he did not try to stay away from me.

I had spent my first few months at the compound navigating the choppy waters of recovery and resolve. I had been determined to find my way through to the other side of the shark-infested waters of addiction. And there Reno had stood shining out, right smack in the middle of it all. A big, bad lighthouse of temptation, beckoning me forward, calling me closer, and illuminating the way.

After a whole lot of stops and gos and I can'ts and I won'ts and a bunch of *I really, really need to waits*, we had gotten to that place.

Reno and I.

And it had been a beautiful thing. Full of light and lust and full-on everything goes, no-holds-barred hot.

The first time I was in his bed, I had turned to him out of pure exhaustion, lust, and need. I had not let myself think beyond that. He had been all hands and mouth and lots and lots of hard. And it had been incredible. God, the man paid attention. I could not get enough of his hot, hard body.

In the months that followed, it had gotten even better. Jesus. That man wore me out. When I was with him, when I felt his body slip into mine, I forgot everything. Being close to him, touched by him, kissed by him just made everything better. Being with Reno made me forget all the fear and the pain and the violence that haunted my dreams.

That's what he had meant to me at first.

Then slowly things began to change. To change because Reno changed them. He was so loving when we were together. Caring and gentle. Patient. Reno was everything I needed and nothing I had expected. Turns out that despite the leather and the gun and the outlaw tendencies, Reno wasn't the kind of guy that my therapist, Dolores, had warned me to stay away from.

I started to look at him differently, and to need him in a way that I had never needed anyone before. I never felt completely whole unless I was with him.

And that scared me.

And not just a little.

Then came the night when I took a chance. At first I only meant to tell him a little bit about my past. He had a plate of cookies on his nightstand that Pinky had made for him. Taking a bite of one of those cookies had brought back a flood of memories for me. Once I started talking, I couldn't stop. I didn't want to. I told him everything there was to tell about myself. My childhood, my years with Jamie, my time in rehab. I told him about it all.

Everything.

Well, almost everything.

I knew that night would change things for us. I knew that it could be the beginning of something pretty wonderful. Feeling that, I fell asleep in his arms. Despite all the full-on hot we had been having, I had never spent a whole night with him.

Until that night.

And then, when the morning came, I had left his bed while he was sleeping.

Which, honestly, did not seem to me the big, huge, insulting deal that it had obviously been to him.

I had needed a minute. I had needed a minute to gather the courage it took for me to acknowledge the love that I felt for this man.

This badass biker who I knew I probably shouldn't love.

But who I had grown to love.

And did love. A lot.

But that minute, those few friggin' tick tocks, had been too much for Reno.

And when I thought about it, I guess I didn't blame him.

I got that, for Reno, me leaving his bed the way I did meant something different to him than it did to me.

And in a very big way.

I got it. I just got it a little too late.

And now after months and months of being gone, Reno was back.

Because I was feeling happy, hopeful, and excited about my future, I let myself feel optimistic about what that could mean.

Silly me.

CHAPTER 12

I snatched a bottle of wine off the bar as I made my way to the kitchen house. I had looked for Reno outside in the sea of black leather, but I hadn't seen him. Thinking that he must be at the house, I headed in that direction.

"Hey, Claire." Pipe was somehow standing in front of me.

"Hey, Pipe." I nodded absently to him.

"Where to?" He wasn't moving.

"Where to?" I repeated, confused by the question.

"Yeah. Where you heading, sweetheart?"

I didn't really know Pipe all that well. He had been out to the lake house a couple of times to do some repair work on the deck. Aside from a vague wave in my direction, he had pretty much left me alone, and I had pretty much returned the favor. Except for tonight. Tonight he was standing in my way.

"I thought I'd head down to Reno's room. I heard that he's back, and I haven't seen him in a while."

Which, by the way, is absolutely none of your business, I thought to myself.

Pipe nodded. He took me in slowly from head to toe. As far as I was concerned, his gaze lingered much too long on my breasts.

"Brother's a lucky man." Pipe smirked. "But as far as I know, you ain't been invited, Claire."

Really?

"Far as I know, I don't answer to you, Pipe." I narrowed my eyes at him.

Pipe stood about six feet three. Looking at him now, it crossed my mind that the members of the Hells Saints seemed born and bred to it. Really, they were all as big as redwoods.

Pipe was blond, blue eyed, and square jawed. His tousled hair was worn short and was made lighter in parts by the sun. His lips were naturally full and he was clean shaven. He was the only brother who didn't have any tattoos. Not even one. A fact that even I found kind of strange. Pipe had underwear-model good looks, but there was a hardness in his eyes that I did not trust. He was definitely drool material for just about every woman with a pulse. But I really had never bothered to look at him long enough to see him that way. Now that I took the time, I still wasn't interested.

"Just looking out for the club, little girl," Pipe came back at me.

I made myself ignore the little girl part.

"Yeah, how's that?" I asked.

"Lots of strange tail hanging around tonight. Brothers' rooms are by invitation only. You know that."

"I look like *strange tail* to you, Pipe?"

He was still standing in front of me in a way that didn't make sense.

Yeah, Pipe standing in front of me in an effort to keep me from going to Reno's room made no sense at all.

Unless . . .

"Get out of my way, Pipe," I said quietly.

"Probably not a good idea, babe." Pipe remained where he was, blocking my way.

"Are you seriously going to make me find a way to go through you?" I asked him.

"I might enjoy that." He smirked.

I put my hands on my hips and held my ground. He chuckled heartily, but when I nudged past him again, he moved out of the way.

"Tell him I tried to keep you outta there," he yelled after me.

Without turning around, I flipped Pipe the middle finger.

His laughter followed me down the hallway.

Feeling oddly compelled, I walked toward Reno's room. Then, having reached it, my brain waged a battle with my heart. Both of them were wreaking havoc on my already-heightened senses.

I gave myself a minute to think this through.

Self-preservation was screaming at me not to knock on Reno's door. Every instinct I had was telling me that opening that door would be bad for me, bad for him, and bad for any chance we had toward working things out for the better. The more I thought about it, the more I knew that for lots of reasons, this was a very bad idea.

I turned and moved to walk away. Just as I did, a very drunk Saint came careening toward me with an equally drunk blonde squealing with delight at being hoisted over his shoulder. She rode ass-up with her stilettos waving dangerously in the air. I had to flatten myself quickly against the door to avoid having my eye poked out.

Unfortunately, at that exact moment, they slammed into me. The door to Reno's room swung open under the forced, quick pressure. The two lovebirds managed to right themselves again and move on, only to leave me to stumble hard and headlong into the very bad idea.

CHAPTER 13

It took a second for my eyes to adjust, and then what I saw made me feel sick. I inhaled sharply, trying to catch my breath, but that only made it worse. The stench of Jack Daniels, reefer, and cheap perfume hit me like a bucketful of cold, dirty water.

Moonlight cast an eerie glow on the large broken-winged angel tattooed on Reno's back. The hard muscles of Reno's denim-covered ass moved rhythmically to the squeals of the loudly orgasmic woman in his bed. Hypnotized, I watched as long, blood-red fingernails clawed their way into Reno's back. A pair of six-inch heels pointed straight up into the air.

"What the fuck?" Reno snarled. Reaching for the piece he had laid down on the nightstand, he twisted his body to seek out the intrusion.

I needed to get out of there.

Fast.

As I turned to hurry back out the door, the wine bottle slipped through my sweaty palms. Falling hard, it shattered all over the floor. Crimson-coated shards of glass pierced me like fine needles.

I felt that sting everywhere.

"Christ, Claire." Reno pulled himself off the woman and rolled over onto his side. "Is that you?"

Paralyzed now, I stood stupidly in the dark doorway. I was covered in glass, cheap merlot, and shattered pride.

"What's going on?" the redhead on the bed called out. She looked from Reno to me and pouted. She didn't bother to cover herself.

Reno didn't even glance her way.

He left the bed and he started to walk toward me, as the bulge in the front of his unbuttoned jeans cried out in protest.

"What are you doing in here, Claire?" Reno was closer now, and the smell of Jack Daniels came off him in waves.

I shook my head and started to back out the door. Humiliation had a dark hold on me, and it squeezed at my chest.

Reno just kept on coming at me.

I moved away from him until I felt the wall press hard and unyielding against my back. There I stood helplessly as Reno moved in on me.

With one quick sweep he settled himself between my legs and put his hands on either side of my head. In less than a minute, Reno had caged me in. Tight.

"Claire, what are you doing in here?" He drew so close I could feel his breath on my lips.

"I heard you were back," I managed to squeak out. My knees were suddenly jelly and my heart was doing this thing where it would beat fast and then stop dead, before it picked up that rapid pace again. I thought I might be dying.

His beautiful amber eyes melted into mine. His long deep caramel-colored hair fell over his face.

"Yeah, baby. I'm back. But that still doesn't tell me what you're doing in my room," he said.

The shadows covered us and beams of moonlight danced on the darkened room behind us.

"I . . . I . . . I wanted . . . I wanted to . . ." I tried with all I had to fight my way back from the brink.

Jesus.

Like some dark sorcerer's spell, the sound of his voice held me hypnotized.

I couldn't speak. I couldn't move. I couldn't look away. Reno pressed me deeper in the shadowed corner alcove. Darkness and light swirled like jeweled pieces of kaleidoscope glass around us.

My words were stuck between worlds.

"What, baby? You wanted what? Tell me what you want, Claire." His hips, hard and inviting, pushed against my core.

"I . . . I . . . wanted to say . . . uh . . ." My mind went blank.

His thumb brushed my lips.

"You wanted to say what, Claire?"

Then his eyes left mine and moved to my mouth. Reno's hand moved leisurely past the hollow of my throat, down to my breast. The back of his hand skimmed lightly up and down over me.

"What is it that you came in here to say, baby?"

Oh, God, his other hand was moving to the back of my neck, cupping it. Holding it tight.

"I came to say . . ."

Reno's heated gaze paralyzed me. He tweaked my nipple.

Oh, my God.

I tried again.

"Just came to say hello, Reno," I finished lamely.

Reno let out a deep feral sigh.

"Hello there, Claire." His tongue moved over his lower lip, like he was getting ready to eat.

Then he leaned in until the side of his cheek touched mine, and as he ran his fingers up and down the back of my neck, he whispered into my hair, "What took you so long?"

When his mouth dropped to just below the curve of my ear and he softly sucked on the lobe, I felt a shot of moisture soak through to my panties.

"Reno, you've been drinking." I fought to keep myself steady.

"Yeah, baby, I have. I've been whoring too. Been drinking and whoring you off my mind for too long now." His forehead touched mine, then I felt his whole body sigh against me.

Oh, boy.

My knees turned to jelly and my mouth went dry. On its own, my tongue reached out and wet my lips. When Reno touched the tip of his tongue to mine, I flooded. Again. I felt my nipples swell and push against the soft lace of my bra, as if reaching toward him. In a soft whimper, I found my breath. The heat of his amber eyes turned my own into a sea of liquid blue. I began to crest on a long, high wave. In answer, Reno hardened and ground into me. He felt the want in me. How could he not? Every cell in my body was crying out to him.

His hands buried themselves deeper into my hair. As he captured the soft masses in his big rough palms he tugged on the long strands and pulled my head back.

Then Reno's mouth touched me everywhere.

I came undone.

I arched toward him as I felt his soft lingering kisses rain all over me. The rough stubble of his jawline chafed deliciously against the curve of my cheek. Traces of wet cascaded down my neck, then back up again. Reno's mouth enveloped me in a salty sea of smoothness. Gently probing, I felt his warm mouth press against mine. His tongue parted my lips until it was moving inside, pushing and thrusting.

Long. Hard. Deep.

My whole being emptied then and filled with a kind of time and space where only the two of us existed. I was more aware of Reno than I had ever been of anything in my life. He was a part of me, and I was a part of him. The darkening of his hooded eyes, the scruffy stubble on his hard jaw, the thin scar that hit his cheek midcenter, there was nothing I did not see, nothing I did not want. Nothing I would not give.

I groaned against his mouth as I felt his tongue leave mine, disappointment sending shockwaves through to my soul. Then it was back, gliding over my lips. When he bit and tugged on my lower lip, I pulsed and tightened. I moved into him then. Rubbing against him, trying to ease the pain of wanting him. I was like a cat, caught in the rhapsody and confusion of that first heat.

Desperate.

Aching.

Primal.

The smoldering fire, which had started the minute I had first laid eyes on this man, rose up and ignited. Panting, I opened to him. I was lost. Deep swirling sparks of heat pulled at my every nerve ending. Reno's hands moved all over me. His strong fingers lingered and pulled against my swollen nipples. Over and over again he plundered, stopping only after he had drawn them into hard peaks. Satisfied, his hands rode up to the back of my neck and pulled my mouth to his again. Reno kissed me again and again until I thought our lips would fuse together in the heat. With a groan, his lips left mine to move down the soft cotton of my T-shirt. Biting gently, his mouth made small, wet circles on the thin fabric. I wrapped my hands in his hair and arched my back, pulling him toward me.

With easy strength he lifted me up against the wall and held me there.

Breathing heavily, Reno's husky voice was heavy with tender violence. "Baby, wrap your legs around me. Yeah, darlin', that's right. I've got you, baby."

When I felt Reno's hand dip inside my panties and push against me, I moaned into his neck. Moving my hips, I thrust hard against his fingers. He pulled at the swollen nub, rubbing and gliding into the wet, intimate folds. Reno played with me like that, on and on, creating currents of tortured pleasure throughout my body.

I needed release.

My body was begging for release.

When I bore down on him in frustration, Reno whispered against my hair, "Relax, baby, I got you. Let it happen. I'm not gonna stop. I fucking love this. I'm not gonna stop, baby. Until you come for me. I'm not gonna stop."

Those words released a deep hard spasm that I felt everywhere.

Reno let out a throaty sigh, cupped me gently one last time and slowly pulled his hand away from my hot center.

"That's it, baby. Feel that. Feel that and remember how good we are together," he murmured soothingly.

We rested against each other, feeling our hearts beating together and our breath slowly returning to normal. Reno carefully lowered me down to the ground and cradled the back of my neck. He drew me to him.

"Baby, I missed you," he said.

"Me too. Reno, I missed you too," I groaned. I never wanted to let him go. Not ever. Not ever again.

Before another minute passed, I wanted more. I wanted to feel him inside of me. I needed to feel the heat of his bare skin against mine. I wanted to run my tongue over the beautiful intricate lines of his inked body. I wanted to trace over the smooth, bumpy ridges of each warrior scar.

I wanted all of him.

These stolen minutes weren't enough, and I knew it was not enough for him. He was still rock hard against me. I wanted to give him back what he had so expertly given me.

Sliding my tongue into his mouth, I kissed him hard. Reno groaned and moved both of his hands to the sides of my head. I felt a clenching deep in my belly as I began to build again. Then I felt something inside of me burst wide open.

I whimpered in total surrender.

Because I loved this man.

I loved him. I loved him. I loved him.

That thought fluttered all around me, like a swarm of brightly colored butterflies, waiting for their chance to land gently in his heart.

I opened myself up to catch those words and give them to him.

And that's when I heard her.

CHAPTER 14

Y ou want some play, beautiful? Plenty of room in his bed for the three of us. My name is Cherry, but you can call me anything you want, sugar."

Snap.

Spell. Broken.

Just. Like. That.

Those words came crashing in, pulling me out of that magic place and into a vat of cheap perfume. I felt myself fall back to earth and land hard.

I love yous lay all around me, broken-winged on the floor.

Cherry was still talking.

"I don't mind sharing, sugar. Reno and me, we've been to that party before. Haven't we, honey?" Her tone sounded honest, sincere, and completely devoid of jealousy or malice. For Cherry, it was just a way of life.

I felt sick.

In an attempt to move away from Reno, I pulled against the tight bicep that held me prisoner. He loosened his grip, but still held on. His gaze spun to the woman on his bed, then pivoted back to me. He didn't say anything, but his hold tightened.

The hard, lean planes of Reno's face tensed and a muscle clenched near his jaw. His gaze volleyed back to her.

"Cherry," he growled in warning.

Undeterred, she glanced at Reno and waved her hand at him. "What do you say, beautiful?" She smiled at me.

Oh. My. God.

Back with my two feet on the ground, I somehow managed to shake my head.

"No? Too bad. Maybe another time, then." She raised her shoulder in a casual shrug. Then still naked and still on the bed, Cherry went back to checking the messages on her cell.

This was just so many shades of wrong.

And the wrong was mostly directed at me. Because who was I kidding? I was no better than she was.

I wasn't.

Had I lost my mind?

How had I gotten so caught up at seeing Reno again that I had let myself go wildly orgasmic, not fifteen feet away from her? Not fifteen lousy feet away from the woman who Reno surely would have been nine inches deep in had I not come stumbling into the room.

And even though we had been in the shadows, and I knew that Reno had been careful to shield my body from view with his own, the fact remained that we were all in that same room. No getting around that. And even if she couldn't quite see, she sure as hell could hear.

Yep, while I was getting off with Reno's hand down my pants, Cherry was on his bed watching.

The whole time.

That reality hit me like a bucket of cold, dirty wash water.

Slut, I hissed to myself.

Reno watched me carefully, and when I put my hands against his chest to push him from me, he was ready.

He countered with a push of his own, trapping me back in again.

His face moved to the side of mine. "It's just me and you, Babe," he said into my hair. "I want you. You want me. I think we just proved that. You know it, I know it. No more waiting, no more doubts. We are in this. But this time, you're going to stay, Claire. If I have to handcuff, blindfold, and tie you to my bed, baby, this time you're going to stay."

Wow.

Despite the way I had just beaten myself up about being weak when it came to this man, I flushed again with a deep yearning. My insides were still dewy and pulsing from his touch. I had missed him so very much. Being handcuffed, blindfolded, and tied to Reno's bed wasn't the worst thing I could think of.

Oh, boy.

Slut, I hissed again to myself. But this time with a little less conviction.

Just then Cherry's phone began to vibrate, and as she moved to get it her perfect breasts swayed provocatively against the rumpled sheets. She caught my eye and winked.

And that did it.

Reno followed my gaze and then he looked back at me. Waiting.

I stared into his eyes, fighting my way back from the haze of love that, maybe, was blinding me.

Reno saw that shift. Reno recognized that shift. And because sooner or later we always seemed to find ourselves at this messed-up familiar place, Reno shifted right along with it.

Then he said this. And he shouldn't have.

Because despite it all, despite everything we had been through together, there was still a part of me that remained optimistic. I had somehow managed to maintain this ridiculous, tiny shred of hope that Reno and I might still have a fighting chance at something good. Maybe it was insane, but there it was.

What Reno said next ruined everything.

"Or, you can take Cherry here up on her offer. She's right. Her and me, we've taken a ride on the three-way freeway before. And it's always a good time. Yeah, baby, Cherry and I can sure as shit show you a real good time."

I felt Reno's whole body tense. He leaned in, his eyes glittered, and his mouth was drawn into a hard line.

"Then when you've had enough play, Claire, you can do what you always do. You can run away and hide. You can leave *again*. Sneak out in the middle of the night *again*. No worries. She'll keep your place warm for you. Cherry and me, we'll just wait, keeping each other occupied and ready until the next time you feel the need to play your own little fucked-up version of Now You See Me, Now You Don't." He roared that last part.

I felt the blood drain from my face and my legs give way under me.

Months.

I had waited for Reno to come back for months.

Between the nightmares and the fear, I had cried in my pillow missing him.

I had spent countless days imagining him roaring up the hill to the lake house on that damn bike of his. I had spent countless nights sitting out on the dock, looking up at the stars and wondering if he would ever come home or if he ever thought of me. I dreamed about what I would say to him, how he would look, what it would feel like to be in his arms again. I had spent months anticipating a reunion with Reno McCabe.

I had dreamed of it.

But in my dreams it was never like this.

My wildest imaginings didn't even come close to include being propositioned by a naked stripper in his bed. Nor did they include me clawing my way to a wild orgasm within easy earshot of that same stripper.

But maybe they should have.

How could something that had felt so right go so wrong? And so fast? Months of agony had turned into minutes of pleasure then back to agony again.

I was tired of dreaming and hoping that Reno and I would find our way.

Screw the wishbone.

"I think I'll pass on the threesome, Reno. But you go right ahead. I am sure you will find a ton of willing women just waiting for the chance. Have. At. It," I said, punctuating every word. "And if not, I'm guessing Miss Two Shows a Night is probably up to giving you a good enough time all on her own."

I crossed my arms and glared.

So we're back there again, Claire? Reno's amber eyes glittered angrily.

Apparently so, Reno. My eyes narrowed back at him.

For a moment, I saw something that might have been frustration and disappointment cross his face, but it was gone just as quickly, and then it was replaced with something primal and undefined.

He took one longer, sweeping look at me. Then he took up the challenge.

Game on then, Claire.

Reno glanced over his shoulder.

"You a stripper, darling?" he called to the mostly naked woman texting from his bed.

"Exotic dancer." She looked up with a proud smile.

"See?" Reno leaned in again and smirked at me. "Not a stripper."

Asshole.

"Oh, sorry, I didn't realize there was a difference." I glared at him. Then I turned to go. "I'll leave you to it, Reno. Knock yourself out."

But he was not done.

"Not so fast, baby. You're the one came bursting in on a closed door." Reno hooked his finger under the band of the jeans that sat low on my hips and pulled me toward him. "Whose ink you sporting, Claire?"

CHAPTER 15

"What?" I asked him, looking down at the fingers that he had trapped in my jeans.

"The ink, Claire. Whose mark were you so hot to have on your belly that you got it like a minute after I left?"

"What?" My dazed mind could not focus on what he was saying.

"*The ink*," he pulled away from me and roared.

Evidently, he couldn't see well enough to answer his own stupid question, because Reno moved me away from the darkness of the alcove and into the light of the hallway. Then, to further illustrate his very messed up point, he tugged my pants downward almost to the tops of my thighs.

So now, courtesy of Reno, I was pinned under a light in the clubhouse hallway, while he raved on and on and pointed to the tattoo that peeked out from the top of my very small panties.

Yep. Right there in the public passageway of the Hells Saints MC clubhouse.

Me and my pubic bone.

Really? *Really?*

"Damn it, Reno." I pushed at his thickly muscled shoulders with my palms.

Jules appeared from out of nowhere.

"Brother, you are solidly going to regret this in the morning." Jules leaned in and around him. He grabbed me by the arm, and led me away from Reno and that bright light. I hitched up my pants and shot a look of thanks at Jules. Then I glared at his brother.

Reno's bloodshot eyes met mine. He stood a little straighter and blocked our way.

"Stay out of this, Jules." Reno turned and growled at him. "I got a right to know."

"Yeah, Brother? And what exactly is it that you think you got a right to know? What the hell is wrong with you, man? You don't push Prosper's own out here in the hallway, giving every degenerate in this clubhouse a free pass to eye-fuck her. I thought she was yours? And even if she ain't that anymore, you have got to respect that shit for what it was," Jules growled right back at him.

Reno moved in on him, and tried to reach around to grab back at me. Jules placed himself solidly in front of me.

"Reno, you stupid sonofabitch. Take a minute before this takes you somewhere you sure as shit do not want to go. Last time, I am telling you. Right now it's between you and her. One more minute of this bullshit, and it's going to be between you and me. Let it fucking go. Conversation for another time, Brother."

Reno faced off with Jules, but he didn't move toward me again.

"Fuck you, *Brother*. You'd do the same thing. Bitch spent her whole life ink-free. I come back to my brothers, to my club, and find my girl is bearing someone else's mark? You tellin' me that if the situation was reversed and it was Glory sporting that ink that you'd be down with that? Bullshit you would. Conversation is gonna happen right fucking now if I have to go through you to have it. And that's the last fucking time I am telling *you*."

Did he just call me a bitch? His girl? Someone else's mark? Just another prime example of why my relationship with Reno was so confusing, infuriating and . . . basically messed up.

The last thing I wanted, the very last thing I needed, was these two apes fighting over this. Over me. A short time ago I was having

70

one of the nicest, most uncomplicated and peaceful nights that I had had in a very long time and now this. How did this happen? Typical. So typical.

I had started this and I had to end it.

"It's no one's mark, Reno. Stop this. No one has marked me." I put my hand on the arm that was barring my way out. His bicep knotted and tensed.

Reno didn't move. Not one bit.

Jules sighed deeply and ran his hand through his hair.

"It's a tree, man," he surprised me by answering. "Her sister's got one too."

"What kind of a fucking tree?" Reno eyed him with suspicion.

A movement caught my eye through the doorway to Reno's room. Apparently Cherry was done with her text messages and had gotten tired of the wait. When I glanced her way, she had already gotten halfway across the room. She was naked except for a candy-apple-red thong, two nipple rings shaped like fire, and a pair of six-inch ruby-sequined stilettos.

I had no intention of sticking around for a closer look.

"Willow." I turned my attention back to him and answered quickly.

"What are you talking about, Claire?" Reno's eyes moved up from the intricately inked tattoo on my stomach.

"It's a willow tree," I said. "In honor of the baby. Tree of life. Baby Willow . . . get it? Willow. Tree."

My heart clattered against my rib cage, and blood pounded in my ears. I felt dizzy and light-headed. I needed to get out of there. Enough.

As he stood in front of me, looking big and bad and barring me from the only way out, I could see it. I watched Reno's face as he fought through the haze of the booze and the reefer and the anger to make sense out of what I was telling him.

Having no other choice, I crossed my arms, willed my heart to stop racing, and waited for the light of understanding to dawn behind his bloodshot eyes.

One . . . two . . . three . . . and there it was.

"Shit." Reno looked at me.

Humph.

"Claire, baby, I'm . . ." He frowned.

Reno lifted his hand to touch my face, but I pulled away so fast my head slammed against the wall.

I felt so dirty and crazy and unsteady.

The lights were suddenly too bright, the riot of color they cast against the wall was making me sick.

I needed out.

Now.

From the corner of my eye, I saw Jules grab the quickly approaching Cherry, throw something over her naked shoulders, and drag her off.

It was too late to matter.

"Get out of my way, Reno." I fought to stay on my feet.

"No."

"No? Jesus. Just let me go." I needed to leave, like right now.

"No. Babe, you're not going anywhere," he said with solemnness. The look on my face had sobered him up fast.

"Not a request, Reno. Get out of my way. I'm going home."

"Not when you look like that, baby." His eyes skimmed me.

I looked down to see the remnants of small shards of glass and big wet spots of red wine soaked through my pants like spiderwebs of glittering blood. Funny, I didn't feel a thing.

Reno followed my gaze.

"I don't mean your clothes, Claire. I mean the look on your face. I know that look. You always look like that just before you do something extreme."

Something extreme? Was he kidding? My whole life had been an experiment in the extreme.

I was so very, very tired. Bone tired. I felt like I had never been so tired in my whole life. But I had been, I had been this kind of tired lots and lots of times before. And every time I felt myself reaching this *extreme* level, it took a little more from me. The only place, *the only place* I wanted to be was someplace that was not here.

Having years of experience with this particular kind of weariness, I waited for that familiar surge of contradictory power to course through my veins: fight or flight, the sympathetic nervous system's inherent response to danger. My body released adrenaline in such large quantities I could probably bottle it and sell it.

Escape when threatened.

Fight when cornered.

Really, it would be better for everyone if Reno just got the hell out of my way.

I tried one more time to move past him and when he stopped me, I let him have it.

"Extreme? Yeah. Well, that's me, Reno. Miss Extreme. I *always* do something extreme. Jesus, from the time I was four years old I have found myself in situations where I have had to do something *extreme*. And you know what? I've survived those things. All of them. Every single last one of them. And you know what else I survived? I survived you walking out on me. Yeah, I said it. *You* walked out on *me,* Reno, and why? Because I needed a minute? If I hadn't gone back to you that very same day and practically begged for you to understand, I wouldn't blame you. But you took everything I said, everything I gave, and you left anyway. So get away from me, Reno. Just get away from me, I don't need you anymore. I don't want you anymore."

And then I looked pointedly in the direction that Jules had taken Cherry and said "And I don't care who you take to your bed, just as long as it isn't me."

Reno looked at me like I had shot him.

Too bad.

I pushed past him with as much dignity as I could muster and didn't stop until I was in my car and almost home.

Then I pulled over and threw up.

CHAPTER 16

"Geez, do you have any idea how much Madagascar Bourbon Vanilla or Pernigotti Cocoa Powder is going for these days?" Glory stared at her laptop screen.

"No clue," I said and squinted at my own computer in outrage.

"Well, it's a lot," she moaned.

As I sat across the table from Glory, I did my own set of calculations. The Pay Less Buy More website for used college textbooks had been a real eye opener. If this was the *less*, I'd hate to see the *more*.

Glory and I were spending a laid-back Sunday at home together. The cool rain, which had started in the early morning, had lasted all day. A pearl gray veil of mist had settled on the lake, wrapped around the house, and made everything feel cozy and peaceful. Glory had proclaimed these kinds of days Sweatpants Sundays.

Sweatpants Sundays came with a very serious set of rules. Old sweats and T-shirts, no makeup, hair in loose ponytails, underwear optional, big fluffy socks, and an exclusive diet of carbs.

Sweatpants Sundays totally rocked.

As I sipped the perfectly brewed coffee and munched on wild berry scones drizzled with Tupelo honey, I checked the list of required reading for the third time.

Then I groaned.

"I am up to four hundred bucks, and I still have two classes to go."

Glory didn't look up.

"I thought you were going to check the used-book site," she murmured around the pencil in her mouth.

"This *is* the used-book site."

Glory sighed and nodded in sympathy while I punched in some numbers on my calculator.

My roommate was busy furiously scratching down some numbers of her own on a yellow legal pad.

"Shit, at this point I'm going to just about break even for this catering job. Maybe I can skip the truffle oil and use something else," she said thoughtfully. Glory's ponytail had slipped off the top of her head and her T-shirt rode one smooth shoulder. Her brows were knit together, as she chewed absently on the end of a pencil.

"Five books? Five books? You have got to be kidding me. One course and there's five books for it?" I began to punch in more numbers.

"I wonder if it'll make a big difference if I use portobello instead of shiitake," Glory murmured.

"I can't believe this! Damn! The books for the last two classes aren't selling used." I groaned.

Glory and I parallel-played with each other like that all afternoon. Each of us was lost in our own world.

Neither of us heard the car pull in, but we both looked up when we heard the screen door open and then slam shut. My sister stood dripping wet in the middle of the living room. She had the baby in one arm and a suitcase in the other.

Uh-oh.

"Diego left," she blurted out. "Can I stay here?"

So much for happily ever after, I thought.

Glory and I moved into action. She grabbed Willow, and I put my arm around my sister.

"Oh, Raine! Sure you can, honey. You know you can always stay here." I began to fuss like an old hen.

"Your old room's just the way you left it," Glory sang out reassuringly. Her ice blue eyes warmed in sympathy.

"Here, let me take the baby," I said while Glory steered Raine to the couch.

"I'll put on a nice cup of tea." I smiled into Willow's sleepy eyes and kissed her head as she curled to my shoulder and stuck a thumb in her mouth. Then I started toward the kitchen.

"What?" Raine let herself be guided, but she kept looking over her shoulder at me. Then she stopped and pivoted.

"What is wrong with the two of you?" Raine volleyed a look from me to Glory and then back again.

"You two are acting like . . . Oh my God! You think that Diego and I? Really? Geez!" Her eyes went wide with sudden understanding.

Then she put her hands on her hips and shook her head at us.

"I didn't mean he left *me*! Prosper sent some of the boys up to the north county this weekend on club business. I called him from my cell last night and begged him to send Diego along with them."

"Why would you do that?" Glory asked.

"Let's just say that the man is driving me crazy. When he isn't jumping at every tiny noise that Willow makes, he's all over me."

Then she paused dramatically. "Look at this," Raine said with disgust written all over her face.

Then my sister jerked open her jacket to reveal a soft blue T-shirt, and some impressive breasts. It was evident that Raine's naturally thin body had filled out with the birth of the baby. Now front and center with her post-baby body, I had to admit it, Raine's breasts were at least twice the size that they were pre-Willow. And that was sort of saying a lot, because small breasts did not exactly run in our family.

"Look at them! They are *huge*. And they *leak*. It's ridiculous. And Diego. Jesus. You would think that man has never seen a pair of tits before. He can't keep his eyes off me. He is like a kid in a candy store."

Just then Willow started to cry, and two small wet spots began to appear like voodoo magic on the front of Raine's shirt.

She kept talking, and I couldn't help it. I kept staring right at those growing spots.

I could kind of understand Diego's fascination.

"Claire? Claire! I am talking to you." My sister's eyes followed my gaze and looked down at her shirt. Then she blushed a deep rose and sighed.

She grabbed the baby and stomped up the stairs to her former bedroom.

Glory glared at me, and although I tried to look contrite, I just couldn't pull it off. Glory tried to keep that glare steady, but she couldn't do it either.

I started to giggle and then she did too.

Before we knew it, we were both knee-slapping like two drunken nuns.

"I can hear you two, you know," Raine shouted from upstairs, which of course just sent Glory and me into gales and gales of barely controlled laughter.

Minutes later, when we heard Raine pound her way back down the stairs, we did our best to compose ourselves. When she saw us, she threw the stained T-shirt at me. It landed straight on my face, and the wet made it stick right to my nose. That sent us off on another riot of hilarity. Raine held out as long as she could, then she laughed longer and harder than either of us.

CHAPTER 17

While Willow slept peacefully in the portable crib we kept for her upstairs, I watched Raine check the baby monitor every five seconds when she thought we weren't looking. I smiled to myself. She could glue it to her thigh, I didn't care. I was just glad to have my sister and my sweet little niece with us for a couple of days.

After having a light supper, Raine, Glory, and I worked together to clean up the kitchen. The heavy pressure system that had been bearing down on us all day had now turned into a full-blown storm. Gusts of wind blew in from the lake and forced the rain to beat angrily against the windowpanes. Glory and I had taken up cozy residence on the couch. Two glasses and a half-empty bottle of the good wine sat on the coffee table in front of us. Raine was curled up on the loveseat. Her hands were wrapped around a mug of steaming peppermint tea. And there the three of us sat, warmed by quilts, fluffy socks, and sisterhood.

"So exactly who did Prosper send up north?" I tried for a casual tone.

"I heard that Crow went, and I think that Pipe did too," Glory volunteered.

"Crow? Really? I saw him a while ago at the clubhouse but aside from that, I hadn't seen him in forever," I pointed out.

"Pinky told me that she overheard Crow and Prosper talking. Word is that Crow is thinking about going nomad for a while," Glory answered.

"Pinky overheard?" I smiled. "You mean Dolly and Pinky had a glass up against the door with their ears glued to it."

Glory smiled, but Raine let out a small sigh. My roommate and I exchanged a wary look. Then the three of us sat in silence for a minute, each of us lost in our own thoughts.

Crow.

Now there was an interesting guy. Aside from working on his bike at the compound once in a while, or helping Diego out with the house, he really wasn't around much anymore. And it was kind of too bad, because I liked looking at him. Who didn't? Crow was a beautiful Apache man—a head-turning, drop-dead-gorgeous, emerald-eyed god with a body just made for sin. I had to admit, when he was around, even I paid attention.

My gaze wandered over to my sister. And for about the hundredth time, I wondered how she really felt about Crow. Diego was her husband, the father of her child, and I knew that she loved him totally and without reservation. I also knew, without a doubt, that he returned that love. That all anyone had to do was to look at the two of them together to know that they shared something that was true and lasting.

But, I also knew that a woman could love two men. I knew that a woman could make a home with one man and keep a corner of her heart for another. Our mother had been living proof of that.

It was common knowledge that while Raine and Diego were still in the *trying to figure it out* phase of their relationship, Crow and my sister had shared a brief something together. I knew that it had happened close to the time when Raine first arrived at the compound, but I wasn't too clear on the details.

When Raine came to pick me up from rehab, she had filled me in on everything compound-related, and that included her brief, confusing time with Crow. Shame on me, because I had been too self-involved to pay much attention. At the time, he had been nothing more than a name to me. But the minute that I put that name to a face, I regretted not having listened to the story more closely.

I had tried to coax the whole sordid tale out of her again and again.

But Raine was strangely protective where Crow was concerned and after that first time, she refused to talk about him.

From what I remembered, Crow had expressed an interest in Raine almost immediately. He knew that Diego had laid claim to her but he had bided his time. And it had paid off. Because while Diego was otherwise occupied with batshit-crazy Ellie, Crow had stepped up and taken his shot. And my sister, being confused, hurt, and otherwise pissed off about Diego, had given Crow that shot.

Honestly, I would have given him that shot too. I don't think there are a lot of women who would have refused Crow's attentions. When I thought about it, the attraction between the two of them made sense. Raine and Crow had a shared heritage. At a time when my sister was alone in a strange place and trying to figure it all out, it must have been a comfort for her to be able to share that part of herself with someone. The only thing I remembered for sure was how it had ended between them—with Crow telling my sister that he had a wife somewhere and a marriage that was not quite over. When Raine heard that, she did not want to hear anymore. Shortly after that, Diego and Raine found their way back to each other.

Pinky told me once that Diego and Crow had gone at each other like two jungle animals over that brief something. She said that it had been a good thing that the two of them had worked through that before Prosper had to step in.

Brothers before, they were now brothers again.

Good for them.

Except . . .

A few weeks after Willow came home from the hospital, I had driven up to visit Raine. The house was still in the planning stages then and Diego had enlisted Crow's help with some of the surveying. As luck would have it, he happened to be just finishing up when I pulled in. As Crow and I walked toward the trailer together, we turned the corner to find Raine sitting under a tree nursing her new baby girl. A field of flowers surrounded her and sunlight dappled the ground through the leaves.

The scene was picture perfect. Serene, simplistic, and so innocently sensual that even my heart skipped a beat.

My sister's pretty white eyelet sundress had been unbuttoned, and her breast was fully exposed except for where the baby pulled on her dark, engorged nipple. The wind had picked up the soft tendrils of Raine's hair and settled them back down in wild disarray. At the sound of our footsteps my sister had looked up. The smile on her face faded into something tender and unknowable when Crow's eyes burned into hers. I heard something catch in Crow's throat and a minute later he was on his bike, speeding down that hill like demons were chasing him.

And maybe they were.

My sister's eyes lingered on Crow until he was long out of sight.

As I watched her, I couldn't help but think of our own mother. At that precise moment, the resemblance between Raine and Maggie just about broke my heart.

Yeah, I had a pretty good idea why Crow was not around much anymore.

~

"Anyone else hanging here?" I was the first one to break the silence.

Raine raised an eyebrow. "Reno and most of the other guys are staying, honey."

Then.

"You going to talk to him again? Ever?" Glory opened another bottle of wine.

I sat on in stubborn silence.

I had, of course, shared with my girls the whole embarrassing, infuriating, stumbling-headlong-into-Reno's-room incident.

After a lot of *no he didn't*s, and *what did you do then*s, and *what are you gonna do now*s, I had proclaimed the subject off-limits, at least for the time being. Because there were no easy answers.

Had I seen Reno?

Yeah, I had seen him.

From a distance.

He had been at the compound working on his bike. I had glared at him and he had glared right back at me.

That about summed it up.

"What's all this?" Changing the subject, Raine reached for the sheets of paper on the table. On those pages sat the numbers that Glory and I had spent most of the day trying to tally, and most of the evening trying to forget.

"It's the high cost of attempting to make something of one's life," Glory sighed poetically.

"Glory got her first catering job," I added.

"And Claire is starting school soon." Glory smiled at me.

"And we're both going to be drowning in a shitload of debt trying to make it all happen," I grumbled.

Raine, ever a numbers girl, looked over the lists.

"Wow, eight hundred bucks for ingredients and a couple of pans?" She arched her eyebrows and looked at Glory. "Think that might be overkill?"

"No. It's start-up money. I want to use the best ingredients, otherwise what's the point? And if I buy in bulk, I won't have to order again for a while. But, you're right, it does seem like a lot for me to spend right now." Glory took the list and looked at it again. "And to think I used to make that in an hour."

I sputtered the wine I was drinking back into the glass. When I looked up, I saw Raine's eyes water from downing a gulp of hot tea.

"An hour?" Raine and I managed to croak out together.

Then Glory looked up at us. "Oh yeah. That was the average. Sometimes a little more, sometimes a little less, but it wasn't unusual for me to make a couple thousand a night when I worked the room."

Glory had been a nude showgirl in Vegas. She had mostly danced in elaborately costumed and professionally choreographed stage shows. As extravagant as they were, the costumes had consisted solely of tassels, bejeweled headdresses, and sparkling stilettos. Mostly, she had been separated from the customers by theatrical lights and raised platforms.

Except when she worked the private rooms by request.

With Glory's white-blond hair, glacial blue eyes, smooth alabaster skin, and the best set of real tits that I personally had ever seen, I was not surprised when she told me that she was requested a lot. Glory was a perfect combination of Grace Kelly and Tassel Sally. Cool and unapproachable when it suited her to be, but ballsy, funny, and a whole lot of kick-ass, once you got to know her.

Glory continued.

"Don't get me wrong, I'm not glamorizing it or anything. I hated being so close to those sweaty suits."

Then she took a thoughtful sip of her wine and added, "Although, there was this one guy. Always had an entourage with him. Security, personal assistants, and God knows what else. 'Beck and call boys' we used to call them. Anyway, I think he was the prince of some little country. Luxembourg, maybe? He came into town about every couple of months or so. He would play big at the tables and then book the room. That prince was the kind of client every nude dancer dreams of." Glory grinned wickedly at us. "Win big, lose big, the guy always

84

tipped big. Not a bad-looking man either. He wore these dark sunglasses, so I never really knew where his eyes were hitting me. At first it kind of freaked me out, but after working the room a bit, and having the beady little eyes of all those drunken fools ogling me, it was a relief. In a weird kind of way, wearing those sunglasses was almost a gentlemanly thing to do. Anyway, I'm not sure whatever happened to him, I suppose he kept going to the club after I left. I kind of wonder sometimes if he ever asked about me. Could sure use the fifteen hundred bucks he used to tip for an hour of seeing me strutting in front of him now, I tell ya." Glory twirled her blond hair, lost in thought.

Raine and I leaned forward with our mouths hanging open.

Glory was spilling.

And I was right, it was worth the wait. Every single minute of it.

She looked at the two of us. Then she smiled like the cat who had just bagged the canary.

She leaned in, "And you two have been just dying to know where all that money went, and why I showed my bits for good old Benjamin Franklins in the first place."

Raine and I both nodded, transfixed.

Glory sighed softly.

"I'm afraid after all this time, the story isn't going to live up to your expectations. Actually, it's so common, it's clichéd. Living in Vegas like we did, lots of kids grew up chasing it. Bright lights, fast money, tons of action. You know the deal. All the little boys hanging around the back doors of the casinos, wanting to grow up to be the big man, the one with the juice. Maybe one in a million make it, the rest of them either wind up dead, in jail, or owing very big to some very bad men who they can't pay. My brother fell into that last category. Which, by the way, is how I met that bastard Gino. Between what my brother sent Gino's cousin, Vincenzo, what I made, and the little we got for inheritance, it still took a couple of years to pay off the debt that Hal owed him."

Glory took another sip of her wine then looked at Raine.

"During my time in Vegas I got to know that smooth-talking snake better. Gino was back and forth from here to the casino a lot. He made me all kinds of promises. I think now that he must have been making lots of those promises to me and you at the same time."

Glory looked at Raine. "Does that make sense?"

Raine nodded. "Yeah, that makes a lot of sense."

Gino and Raine had never made sense to me, but then again, neither had Gino and Glory. Those bad Gino memories were something that my sister and my best friend had in common. They had both made the colossal mistake of being in a relationship with that psychopath. I had a few bad Gino memories myself, but those mainly consisted of seeing his brain matter splattered against my sister's T-shirt.

I shuddered just thinking about it.

"Anyway," Glory continued. "Long story short, I ended up striking a deal to dance at the club to pay off my brother's debt. See? The whole thing is a stupid cliché."

Glory shrugged her shoulders, but her eyes got damp when she did. That could not have been an easy time for our friend. No wonder it had taken her this long to share.

Raine's eyes met mine.

"There's nothing clichéd about what you did, Glory. I think it was an unselfish act that took a lot of love and courage. Your brother's a lucky guy to have you." Raine squeezed her hand.

I nodded in agreement.

"Anyway, it took me a long time, but I paid them up. And here I am." Glory smiled a little then.

"Where's your brother now?" I asked.

"He's in the military. The Marines. I made a deal with him. I would pay up if he joined up. It was the only way I could think to keep him out of trouble. Maybe not the safest solution, but better than the alternative. He's doing great! He's already gotten a couple of promotions and now he is with some special operations division, I think. But, he puts half the money he earns in an account that he set up just for me, so he's trying to make it right. I didn't ask him to do that, but he's doing it and honestly it helps." Glory shrugged.

"So that's that. The mystery of Glory Thomas solved." She smiled at us.

"Somehow I doubt that," I answered ruefully, grinning at her. "Somehow, I think the prince of Luxembourg and the gambling Marine are just teasers. They are just the tip of the iceberg of the mystery that is you."

Glory laughed then. The effects of being kidnapped, tied up for several days, and beaten savagely by Gino had wrought havoc on Glory's vocal chords.

Screaming in fear and pain for a very long time can do that.

Most of the damage from that nightmare had been mended by time, love, and sisterhood. But the harm to Glory's vocal chords had remained. The result had left Glory with a low, throaty rasp to her voice. It made her sound like she was always just getting out of bed. Diego had once told Raine that the sound of Glory's voice gave all the brothers instant hard-ons. I had to admit, despite the horrible circumstances that led to the damage, Glory's voice was as sexy as hell.

But her laughter was a gift.

Sadly, tonight, it also heralded the end of the spilling.

Raine and I both knew it would do no good to ask questions; we both had tried and failed that route before.

"Night, all." She waved at us. Then she winked at our open-mouthed stares.

Just like that. Glory stopped sharing just as quickly as she had started and left us hungry for more. Apparently the show-stopping side of our friend had not been left in that flashy casino.

Raine and I looked at each other and smiled.

Because we knew that there would be more to come. The mystery of our very own Vegas showgirl, our Glory, would absolutely be solved.

And it would all be worth the wait.

I didn't know about Raine, but speaking strictly for myself, I went to bed that night dreaming of swinging tassels, million-dollar payoffs and handsome princes smiling behind dark sunglasses.

CHAPTER 18

Reno told himself he was moving on.

Oh. Yes. He. Was.

He hadn't seen Claire since the night he came back from the West Coast, and he didn't give a shit if he ever saw that woman again.

Or at least, that's what he kept telling himself. And it was easy to tell himself that because she was not there. At least not anywhere he was. Or was going to be, or had been in the recent past.

And that was just fine with him. Yep. He was golden with it. Just fine.

Reno knew that Claire was about to start school soon. He knew that she was going to be taking courses at some fancy college down in the valley.

Not that he had asked.

Nope. Nobody could say he had asked one damn thing about her.

But he couldn't help it if he had somehow managed to overhear every single drop of information coming out of Pinky or Prosper or Raine's mouth regarding Claire.

It wasn't as if he was eavesdropping. Not at all. It wasn't as if he stored every single bit of information regarding Claire. It wasn't as if he had to physically stop himself from showing up at the lake house, throwing her over his shoulder, taking her to his bed, and slamming some sense into her. Nah. It wasn't like that at all.

Reno pulled on the last of the smoke before he stomped his cigarette out and went back to working on his bike. *Sure it is.* He thought to himself. *It is exactly fucking like that.*

He was miserable.

The future stretched out in front of him like a long, dark tunnel. Thousands of nights without Claire.

Yeah, he could spend his time with lots of women, but none of them would be her.

And where would that leave Claire?

She would end up with someone that wasn't him. She could end up with some asshole who wouldn't get how shy she was with new people, or how she took forever to get to the point of what she was trying to say, or how she was always dropping things when she got nervous. She could end up with someone who didn't understand that she had absolutely no sense of direction.

She might end up with a guy who wouldn't know how easily she could get lost.

Yeah. She could wind up with somebody that was way worse than he was.

And she didn't deserve that guy.

No. Claire deserved better than that. She deserved the guy who loved her more than life itself.

Claire deserved the kind of love that only he could give her. She was his. And he was hers. That's just the way it was.

He could beat himself bloody, he could race across the country, he could sleep with a thousand other women, but the fact was and always would be that she belonged to him.

Now he just had to figure out how to get her to see it that way.

His whole body ached, but that was nothing, he realized, compared to his heart.

He gripped the tire and tried to get back to work. His hand was killing him. He was having trouble holding the wrench. Wincing in pain, he wiped the grease off his hands, and then he went into the kitchen house to grab a little somethin'.

The smell of cooked bacon hit him the minute he cleared the door and Reno felt his stomach roll over. He sat down at the counter and nodded to Jules, who was mopping up the bar.

"Eggs?" Jules looked up at Reno.

"Whiskey." Reno shot back.

Jules motioned toward the clock. "Little early to be drinking."

Reno looked at his knuckles and stretched them out painfully. He knew the pain showed on his face.

"Fuck you, Jules," Reno grimaced.

Jules poured Reno a cup of coffee and put a shot of Jack right next to it.

"With all the fighting, whoring, and drinking you've been doing lately, I'm surprised that you have any fuck-yous left, Brother."

Reno muttered something that, lucky for him, Jules chose to ignore.

Then, pouring the whiskey into the cup, the outlaw winced as he put his big paw around the mug and carefully brought it to his lips.

"There's a reason they banned bare-knuckle boxing, man." Jules nodded at Reno's swollen hand.

"Yeah, and what would that be?" Reno took another sip of the coffee and pushed it away.

"Coffee bad? Jesus, I just made it fresh." Jules turned around to look at the full pot.

"Naw, whiskey tastes like shit in it. Give me a fresh cup, Brother?" Reno asked.

Jules let out a sigh. "Glad to do it, man."

He poured Reno another cup of coffee, and put the bottle back under the counter. Then he reached over and shoved a plate of scrambled eggs at him.

"Eat up."

Reno grabbed a fork and stabbed at the eggs. Then he washed them down with gulps of hot, untainted coffee.

"Better?" Jules watched Reno down the hot brew. "Eggs good?"

Reno looked at Jules. "Eggs are eggs."

Jules arched an eyebrow and glared back at Reno.

"You're fucking welcome."

Reno took another hit of the coffee and looked at Jules over the rim of the cup.

"Everything tastes like shit to me lately."

"Really? I didn't notice," Jules snarled at him. Then he placed his arms on the bar and looked Reno in the eye. "When you gonna snap the fuck out of it? This *pissed off at the world* shit is getting old and I am getting sick of running interference for you. You know it's just a matter of time before Prosper calls you on it. You know that you don't want that coming down on you with whatever else you got on your plate."

Reno nodded. "Yeah, well, I got things on my mind. And right now, I am in some serious pain, so do me a favor and just shut the fuck up. And I don't remember asking you to run any kind of interference with me and the boss."

"Someone has to have your back, because you sure as shit ain't looking out for yourself. Like to think if the situation were reversed, you'd do the same." Jules's gaze left Reno's and he started to mop up the bar.

"You know I would, Brother," Reno said in contrition. Then he added, "Eggs are great, man."

Jules nodded to the swollen fist on the bar. "You want me to see to that hand?"

Jules's training as a medic in the Marine Corps had earned him the role of go-to guy for all the club's medical emergencies. That training, coupled with the fact that he had a surprisingly and suspiciously well-equipped clinic set up in the compound, made Jules a very handy guy to have around. So much so, that Reno had often wondered just who, in another life, Jules had actually been.

"You got a hard-on to play doctor, man? Sure, I'll bite."

Jules looked closer at Reno, who could feel his face drip with sweat from the pain.

"Okay, Brother, I got some stuff I need to be doing in the clinic anyway. Let's go."

Jules poured himself another cup of coffee and headed toward the door. For years now, he had been treating the boys for everything from gunshot wounds to the clap. Some of them were already half-dead by the time they got to him, and he hadn't lost one of the ungrateful motherfuckers yet. But, whether they came to him with a bullet lodged in their chest, or a splinter under their fingernail, they were all the same. They all acted like they were doing Jules a big, huge favor by allowing him to save their sorry asses. And then just like clockwork, every one of them would start screaming and moaning the minute that Jules had to take the needle and nylon to them.

Little bitch-ass mama's boys, every last one of them.

They entered the clinic waiting area.

"Grab a seat, Brother, the boys are just finishing up the addition. I'll take care of you here. Be right back. I'm going to go grab an ice pack and some pain pills." Jules disappeared into the next room. He came back with a vial of prescription drugs and two ice packs.

He dipped his head toward Reno's outstretched hand and began to slowly examine it. At least one finger was broken, and all the knuckles were swollen.

"Ouch!" Reno pulled his hand back as Jules applied pressure to the inflamed hand to check further for breaks. "Show a little tenderness will ya? That's my hand you're squeezing, not a goddamn tit."

Jules leaned back. "Really? You could have fooled me, because you sure the hell are screaming like a girl."

93

"Shut up," Reno growled. "Just fix the damn thing. It is killing me, Brother."

"Here, take these." Jules moved the pills toward him. "Eat three of those bad boys and you won't be feeling anything 'til tomorrow."

"Hate swallowing pills," Reno muttered.

"You're lucky you're not swallowing your own teeth. When are you going to cut this shit out? You ain't hurting anybody but yourself."

Reno gave him a shaky grin. "Yeah? Well you ain't seen the other guy."

Jules snorted.

"One of your fingers is broken. I have to splint it. I'll be right back."

Just then a shadow moved past the window and Jules grabbed the ice pack off Reno's swollen knuckles. Reno opened his mouth to begin a stream of profane protests.

"You can thank me later, Brother." Jules nodded to the doorway.

Reno twisted around to look in that direction.

"Claire." Jules called to her. "Can you help me out and make sure this ice stays on his hand?"

Then without waiting for a reply, he tossed the ice pack to her. Claire caught it in one hand, her eyes wide with surprise.

"Thanks, doll. I have to go grab a splint. Be right back." Jules held his grin until he turned away from the door.

"Hey, Claire." Reno fought hard for the casual tone.

"Hey, Reno." Claire fought too.

Silence followed as Claire moved toward Reno. She placed the ice pack gently on his swollen hand.

"Right here?" She did not meet his eyes.

"Yeah, baby. Right there is perfect. Thanks." He watched as the blush swept over her face.

She looked at him with clear blue eyes. "You're welcome."

Jules walked back in and let out a low appreciative whistle. "Wow, looking good, babe. What brings you by?"

Claire smiled prettily at him. Reno let out a low, feral growl that Claire and Jules both pretended not to hear.

Then Claire winced and raised her knee to show Jules a big, dirty, bleeding scrape.

"Ouch, darlin', how did you do that?" Jules moved closer to Claire and wrapped his arm around her knee. Then he pulled that knee slowly toward him.

Reno tensed beside him—he knew Jules was getting off on it just a little bit. When he ran his hand up and down Claire's smooth tanned leg and pretended to check it for damage, Reno almost lifted himself off the chair.

"I'm on my way out to help Glory with her catering gig. I stopped by the kitchen house to grab a couple of trays. I tried to carry too much at once, I guess. I tripped and fell on the gravel in the driveway. Took a chance you'd be out here. But if you're busy, Jules, I can just grab the first aid kit," she said.

"You came to the right place, honey. It's about time I got to treat something that doesn't have a year's worth of road dirt on it. Just do me a favor and keep that cold pack on my boy's hand. That knee of yours needs to be cleaned out." Jules disappeared again into the back room.

Claire pierced Reno with a questioning look.

Reno's chest puffed out just a little bit. "Been bare-fisted fighting."

"Sounds painful." Claire's eyes widened and she adjusted the ice pack.

"Yeah, some fucking things just hurt more than others," Reno countered.

Claire let out a soft sigh. "That's one thing that you and I can absolutely agree on, Reno." Then she turned her big beautiful blue eyes right on him.

Reno heated all over. He didn't move a muscle. Even though it fucking killed him not to reach out to her, he didn't do it. The next time they touched, it was going to have to come from her.

Claire busied herself with adjusting the ice pack across Reno's knuckles. She was close enough for him to smell her fresh, clean scent. When a lock of her long hair escaped and brushed softly against his arm, Reno couldn't help himself. He moved his free hand and tucked it back behind her ear.

Claire blushed a deep rose and let out a jagged sigh.

And on Reno's part, he got wood. Just like that.

"How have you been?" he asked.

"Good. Been okay, Reno," she said softly back.

"Well, uh, you look good." Reno's eyes were fixed on her face. Drinking her in.

Just as Jules walked into the room, Reno saw Claire blush hard, her pupils dilate, and her nipples pop out like meringue tips against that pretty white shirt of hers.

"So Glory's got a gig?" Jules was obviously trying to keep his tone even.

With feigned innocence Claire fixed her big blue eyes on his. Reno knew what this was about.

"Yeah, she does and she's really excited about it. I'm really proud of her," Claire said with enthusiasm.

"Gianni's crew again?"

"Ouch." Claire pulled back slightly under Jules's sudden increased pressure.

"Sorry, darlin'." Jules lessened that pressure instantly.

"So . . . Gianni's crew again?" he repeated.

"Yeah. Gianni's crew," she answered, then quickly added, "Haven't seen you around the house too much lately, Jules. We still have a fishing pole sitting in the corner with your name on it," Claire spoke softly to him. None of the brothers liked the idea of

Glory working for the mob. That point had been made loud and clear. But Claire was still hopeful that Jules would stop being so damn ridiculous about the whole thing. After all, Prosper was okay with it and he was the *boss* for chrissakes. Maybe Jules just needed a little help to get his head out of his ass.

Jules grunted and pressed a small antiseptic square against the open scrape on her leg.

Claire let out a sharp breath, then she bent way over and panted. Her soft breasts hit her thighs and her skirt rode way, way up on her smooth legs.

She looked up suddenly, and focused her wide blue eyes right at Jules. Then she said pointedly, "Little trick that Glory taught me. Blowing on it always makes it feel better."

"Gimme that damn Band-Aid." Reno grabbed it from Jules's hand and pressed it gently against Claire's knee.

Claire smiled brilliantly at both of them, now satisfied that Jules had all but forgotten being pissed at Glory for accepting the job for Gianni's boys, and had started remembering a few of the things that he loved about Glory. Claire decided she had better leave on a high note.

"Thanks, Jules. It feels better already. I need to get going. Do you want me to tell Glory that you'll be dropping by soon?"

When Claire reached the door she paused and looked back at Jules, whose mouth was *still* hanging open.

"Well?"

Jules hesitated only a fraction of a second, then called out, "Yeah, tell Glory I'll be around soon to . . . uh . . . to . . . uh . . . to take her fishing."

Claire nodded and flashed Reno a look of total triumph. She had gotten Jules to cave in. No one ever got Jules to cave in. Reno hadn't missed that and returned her look with such an expression of disbelief that she almost burst out laughing right on the spot. "I'll let her know," Claire called out to Jules, flashed him a bright smile, and sashayed right out the door.

Claire held her composure until she drove through the gates of the compound. Then she rolled down the window, turned up the tunes, and let the priceless expressions on the faces of two rough, tough outlaws dance through her mind.

As she sped down the highway, she laughed out loud.

CHAPTER 19

Reno's breath is warm against my bare skin. I arch slightly as his hands move up to my hair and bury themselves in the tangled mess. Tugging on the back of my head gently, he imprisons me. I tremble as his mouth moves over mine. I feel the heat of that kiss everywhere. His voice is a gentle rumble, whispering against my ear, "You're mine, baby . . ."

The jarring ring of the alarm clock woke me up and brought me back.

I didn't want to be back. I wanted to be where I had just been, in Reno's bed.

Oh God.

In Reno's bed.

It was the third night in a row that I had had that dream or an equally steamy variation of it. Running into Reno unexpectedly at the clinic had caught me off guard. For the following few days, all I could do was think about him. When the alarm woke me up, I stayed in bed for a few extra minutes and willed myself back to that delicious dream state. To my great disappointment, instead of drifting back to wonderland, I lay awake staring at the ceiling. Not only did I end up feeling pathetic and sorry for myself, but I had also managed to make myself ten minutes late starting my day.

The morning had just gone downhill from there.

Now, I was sitting in the driveway, kicking at the tires of the Jeep, swearing my head off, and cursing Diego and his damn gift. It really wasn't very fair, or very nice of me, and it didn't even make me feel any better, but I kept on kicking and swearing anyway.

Because really? Really? Goddammit! The stupid thing wouldn't start and I was going to be late. It was my first day of college, and I was as nervous as a mouse in a cat's house.

And I had just spent the entire morning filled with self-doubt.

Maybe I wasn't ready for this. Maybe I wasn't smart enough. I didn't even know what to pack for lunch. Did people even use brown bags anymore? What if I got lost on my way to class? Or worse, what if I sat down in a class, only to discover that I was in the wrong one?

On and on and on I went, just like that.

Doubts assailed me and I came dangerously close to losing my nerve. That Glory was not home only made matters worse. I had no one to bounce the fears off of. No one to tell me that I could do this. No one to give me an "Atta Girl."

And I really needed an "Atta Girl" right about now.

It was pretty safe to say I was losing my brave. And fast.

After managing to pull myself together for maybe a minute and a half, I made the colossal mistake of calling the college registrar's office with one single, simple question. Instead of just answering that one single, simple question, the very bitchy receptionist referred me to the class's online course syllabus.

And that was the worst thing of all, because . . . I had absolutely no idea what a syllabus was.

Then the Jeep wouldn't start.

But that was not all.

Nope, that was not all.

On this, my very first day of college, fate just had to step in and throw one more whammy at me. When I called the clubhouse for help with the Jeep, out of all the people who could have possibly picked up that phone, Reno just happened to be walking by.

Damn Prosper, and his stupid resistance to cell phones.

When I heard Reno's warm familiar voice, I felt those flood gates open. Feeling totally frustrated and overwhelmed, I started to heave and stutter. Reno, unable to make sense of the conversation, kept telling me to calm down, which everybody knows is the worst thing that you can say to a woman who is on the verge of hysteria. After about five rounds of, "Babe, you have got to rein it in," I was able to sputter out something that I hoped sounded like, "the Jeep won't start."

Reno seemed totally confused. And I couldn't blame him.

I had no idea what I was talking about.

I hung up the phone, slumped against the Jeep, and waited for somebody to send someone to fix this. It was no use to try and hold back the pity party any longer, so for the next five minutes I gave the tears full permission to run down my cheeks and drip off my nose.

Then I got into the Jeep and tried again. When I heard the click of that stupid engine, I collapsed in total defeat.

After what seemed like hours and hours, the club utility van pulled into the driveway, driven by a prospect I had seen once or twice before. When I turned my tear-stained face to him, he looked at me sheepishly through the windshield and motioned to the cable wires that he had in his hand. He wanted me to pop the hood.

I looked at my watch for the hundredth time, and felt sick with disappointment. I did not have time for this. I reached down and pulled up the release lever. Then I laid my head against the steering wheel and let the tears flow.

"Aw, baby, don't cry." The voice cut through my crying jag.

I looked up just as Reno reached through the open window and unlocked the door. Then he pulled me gently out of the car and into his arms.

I heaved and sniffed all over the front of his leather cut.

"Claire, honey. I can't help if you don't tell me what's going on," he said softly, rubbing my hair and patting my back.

I nodded into his chest, and wiped my nose noisily.

Still heaving, I managed to get the words out. "I . . . am . . . going . . . to . . . be . . . late . . . for . . . my . . . first . . . day . . . of . . . school."

I felt his chest rumble.

"It's not funny," I heaved and tried to pull away.

He pulled me tighter into him.

"No, Claire, it's not funny. It's great. You and this school shit."

Except for that one incident in the clinic and the other time when Reno and I had glared at each other from across the field, I hadn't seen him at all, and as far as I knew, he hadn't seen me.

"You do? You know?" I sniffled and looked up at him.

"Of course I know. Just because I've been acting like a dick doesn't mean I haven't been paying attention." He looked at me and ran his thumb down the curve of my cheek.

Then Reno said this: "Claire, I don't know why it took me this long to get what a prick I've been, but I'm there now, and it feels like shit knowing that I hurt you. I'm sorry, baby."

And there it was.

Maybe there was more to talk about between us, maybe there wasn't. Maybe there would someday be a Reno-and-me that made sense, maybe not. I just knew that I missed what we sometimes used to be.

"I'm sorry" is always a good start to finding your way back to something that you thought might have been lost forever.

I put my head against Reno's warm familiar chest and felt the rest of the tension in me release. And that last part had nothing to do with being late but everything to do with finding myself back in his arms.

"Let it out, baby, give it to me." Reno just kept rubbing and patting.

Then when my sputtering and heaving had died down to just small gulps, he pulled me away from him and brushed away my tears with the back of his hand.

"Alternator's gone, boss," the prospect called out to us. "Won't be able to do much with it today. Orders are to get the van right back and ready for a shipment."

Big heaving sigh. I shrugged my shoulders in resignation. "Well, that's it then, game over." I brushed away the rest of my tears and felt the corners of my mouth fall down. Disappointment streamed over me like a cold winter rain.

"Honey, the game hasn't even started yet." Reno grabbed my hand and led me to his bike. He must have followed behind the van. I had been too deep in my own pity party to hear the rumble of his pipes.

"What time do you have to be there, Claire?" He strapped the helmet on my head.

"Eleven o'clock." I looked at him with hope in my eyes.

"Plenty of time, baby. Just wrap your arms around me and hold on tight."

Then Reno started his engine.

And, having all the faith in the world that he would get me exactly where I needed to be and when I needed to be there, I did it.

And he got me there.

Not only on time.

But with a full ten minutes to spare.

CHAPTER 20

Once we pulled onto the campus, I got nervous all over again. Reno turned into the parking lot and killed the motor. I got off the bike and stared at the sight before me.

The central campus consisted of a few large brick-covered buildings and a grassy area called the quad.

I thought about the many scholars that had stood where I stood now, on the edge of something wonderful and terrifying. The structures themselves intimidated and impressed—aged, ivy-covered, and beautiful.

Damn.

After all the headaches, and fears, and self-doubts about doing this thing, a thing that was way, way out of my comfort zone, here I was.

I had really done it.

"Thank you for getting me here, Reno," I said formally.

"You are welcome, Claire. Happy to be of service," he said back to me, just as formally.

Then we grinned at each other.

"Reno?"

"Yeah, Claire?"

"Do you know what a syllabus is?" I pulled at the heavy backpack on my shoulder.

"Sure, Babe. Everyone . . ." He stopped when he saw the expression on my face.

"It's an outline of the important information of the class. It gives you shit like due dates, assignments, and other stuff you need to know," he finished and grabbed the backpack from me.

I nodded. That made sense.

"Do you know where your first class is?" he asked me.

I handed him everything that I had printed off the Internet.

He looked over the pages, then he looked up at the buildings facing us. Reno grabbed my hand and off we went through the pretty cement arches.

Reno walked me to the front of the building of my first class. My nerves did jumping jacks in the meantime.

"I can stay and see you through this." Reno stood close to me, his hand on the small of my back.

"Thanks, Reno, but I got this," I muttered. I eyed the four imposing structures before me. There was also a sign on the corner of the last building that I had not noticed before. It said "North Campus / South Campus Shuttle" and it had an arrow that pointed to a narrow alleyway.

So there was more. I sighed thinking I was never going to find my way.

"You got this, Claire?" Reno increased the pressure on my back.

I answered with a confidence that I came nowhere close to feeling, "Of course I do."

"Glad to hear it." Then he leaned in and whispered. "Where's your next class going to be?"

He had me there.

"I can ask someone, or go in the general direction," I said with more certainty than I felt.

Just then, the doors to three of the four buildings swung open wide and what seemed to be a million people poured out in a quickly streaming mass.

"Okay, Babe. Check it out. Ask someone." Reno folded his inked biceps.

I tried. But nothing came out. I just stood there in the middle of it all, ridiculously opening and closing my mouth like a baby bird.

Reno let that go on for about a minute and a half.

"Hey man, can you tell me where this is?" He placed himself in front of the dreadlocked guy who was about to walk past us.

Without completely stopping, the guy glanced at the printout and said, "Uh, I think it's over in North Campus somewhere. Not sure. You might hafta take the shuttle. Wish I could help, but I got maybe two seconds to piss and grab a smoke before my ass needs to be sitting in World Lit. Good luck, man."

Then he disappeared into the sea of scholars.

Reno arched an eyebrow at me.

I took another look at the imposing buildings and the crowds. Then I thought about the ten minutes between classes, and the braided guy who seemed to know what he was doing, but still didn't have enough time to pee, smoke, and help me out.

I looked back at Reno then. Dark aviator glasses hid his eyes. He stood a head taller than the crowd hurrying past us. His biceps stretched and strained out of the MC cut, its leather branding him a Hells Saints outlaw. He stood out like a column of fire in a deep pool of water, beautiful and burning bright.

"Reno, don't go," I said suddenly. As the edge of panic closed in on me again, I tugged on his arm and held on for dear life.

He hesitated for only a second. Then he said, "Babe, you have to get moving. You're running out of clock. You're on the second floor, room number 25B. I'm going to wait for you right here and you'll be out in about forty-five." Reno untangled himself from me. Then he actually shoved me toward the building.

Geez.

I looked back at him one more time before the pressing crowd pushed me through the door.

Reno smiled at me.

Then he winked.

Taking that smile and that wink with me, I headed into my next big thing.

CHAPTER 21

"What the hell were you thinking?" I asked myself for about the millionth time. It had been a few weeks since that first day of school and I was swimming against the academic tide.

And that was on a good day.

On a bad day I was drowning in it.

I looked through bleary eyes at the pile of reference books before me. I had been in the college library all morning and had made little progress. The big red D slashed against my first psychology research paper glared back at me in reproach.

"Hope springs eternal."

I almost laughed out loud when I saw the quote from Alexander Pope flash across the laptop screen. Thank you, Mr. Pope, and whoever had the foresight to program in those inspiring words as a stock screensaver. I shook my head, closed the computer, and reached for the bottle of pain-reliever that I kept in my school bag. The new laptop had cost me a small fortune. I had bought it straight from the college bookstore. It came with all the right software, a faux leather bag, and a kick-ass sleeve. It also came with unlimited tech support and a generous warranty.

Even more important than all those great features came the sense of promise and belonging that had filled me when I opened the computer and placed it on a desk for the very first time. Having it had made me feel like I fit in.

Lately when I opened the laptop I just felt dumb.

This is what you wanted, I reminded myself. I was officially a college student, and I was trying my best.

But there were definitely times when my best was not good enough.

I had to remind myself that all this was still relatively new to me and that I had had small triumphs along the way. There were times when I did not feel like a complete idiot and not all of my grades had been Ds. As a matter of fact, most of my grades were not Ds.

But they were not As either.

I was determined to keep trying my best. On the days when everything came together, I was filled with a sense of happiness and pride that I had never experienced on this level before. And really, I was learning so much. Attending these classes had also helped me turn a negative into a positive. In order to survive a childhood with the perpetually depressed and barely there Jack Winston, Raine and I had had to be organized, skilled at observations, and filled with a fierce determination to succeed. It turned out that these qualities were exactly what I needed to rock the college world. Unfortunately a strong academic background was also needed to rock the college world.

Although I was mostly doing okay, there were definite gaps in my learning that put me at a disadvantage. In my child development class, I had recently read that childhood crisis takes up to ninety percent of working memory.

That explained a lot.

But I was not going to give myself a pass. What's done was done. I told myself if I could do it then, I certainly could do it now.

I had this.

Just not today. I didn't have it today.

Today was a pain in my ass.

I sighed as I looked at the mountain of work ahead of me, and took another look at my watch. The tutor I had hired from a poster in the bookstore was five minutes late and I was paying by the hour.

Then I looked at my phone buzzing with a text message. It was Reno telling me he might be late.

Reno.

Hope springs eternal.

Reno had been as good as his word. Even after that first day he had continued to give me rides back and forth to school.

While my vehicle sat waiting for the alternator, Reno had told me it was a good idea for the Jeep to have a tune-up. Once I consented to the tune-up, the boys found a whole lot of other things that needed to be replaced or repaired. The Jeep was only a few years old, and Diego had loved it. Since I had firsthand knowledge of just how well my brother-in-law took care of the things that he loved, I was kind of confused at the growing list of replacements and repairs that kept my ride away from me and on the back of Reno's bike.

But then again a lot about Reno and me was confusing.

For the last few weeks, Reno and I had been on what I guessed you could call a learning curve. We were learning to get back to a place where we had never been before. It was new, strange, and at times oddly frustrating—a place where we were careful with one another. I wasn't even sure how we had gotten here. Or how long it would last.

From that first ride to class, Reno never brought me right home after school. We would run errands together, go out for lunch, or just take a ride through parts of the area that I had never been to before. On the weekends, if I had a shift to do at Reds, he would pick me up and hang out for a sandwich or a beer. Then he would be there to bring me home.

Reno didn't spend all of his time with me though; our nights were our own. I spent my nights knee-deep in books. I had no idea who or what Reno spent his nights knee-deep in.

I couldn't get the scene of him and Cherry out of my mind. As hard as I tried, I couldn't. It hurt me every time I thought about it. The fact that I knew Cherry was a permanent fixture around the club didn't help much.

And for Reno's part, he did nothing to ease my mind. He never asked for my nights and when he dropped me off, he didn't linger. When we were on the bike, he never leaned into me or let his hand casually brush against my leg like he used to. And apart from that first day, he never held my hand when he walked me to class.

Reno never touched me anymore, even by accident.

CHAPTER 22

"Claire?"

I looked up from my studies and recognized the guy with the dreads Reno had asked for directions from my first day on the campus. He was standing by the table. I'd lost five minutes to thoughts of Reno?

I nodded. "Yep, that's me. Are you my tutor?"

The guy smiled and held out his hand. "Sure am. My name is Julian."

As we shook hands, he looked at me closely. "Hey, I think I ran into you a while back with some big dude, yeah?"

I nodded.

"How's it going? You finding your way around okay?"

I shrugged. "I still get confused sometimes."

"It's a jungle out there." He nodded in agreement, then flashed me a smile.

I smiled back. Julian was younger than I was, but not by much. On the skinny side, he sported a full head of light brown dreadlocks, eyes the color of Christmas coal, and skin like warm cinnamon. His wrist bore an array of hemp bracelets, and his shirt read, "I can't keep calm. I'm a Jamaican."

"Are you originally from Jamaica?" I asked.

"Yah, mahn." He grinned. "*Mi baan a Jamaican Yardi,*" he said in a perfect accent.

I arched an eyebrow and grinned back.

"I was born in Jamaica, but moved here with my mom when I was a kid. I still have family there and go back between semesters," he said in perfect English.

"And apparently you go back and forth between accents too," I teased him.

He shrugged. "Yah, mahn." Then he winked. "It gets me the girls."

Julian changed his focus to the paper on the table, skimmed through it, and then looked at the comments on the last page.

He glanced up at me. "Dr. Charto's a raving bitch. I had her last semester. I got her gig down. I can definitely help you with this. I got Bob Marley tied up outside. You mind if we sit on the quad and do this?"

"I'm guessing Bob Marley is your dog?" I asked.

He just looked at me with that bright white smile again. I shook my head and wondered what I had gotten myself into. But I let Julian help me pack up my stuff and I followed him outside where I was introduced to Bob Marley, who was tied up just outside the door. He was an adorable chocolate lab puppy who wagged his tail ferociously at the sight of his owner.

Julian and I sat out on one of the picnic tables that littered the main lawn of the college and I showed him all my notes and the research I had done. "Do you think you can help me get where I need to be?"

He concentrated for a minute then looked at me and nodded. "No worries. You actually got all the facts you need right here. We can make this work. We gonna mash this shit up."

I had no idea what that meant, but it sounded optimistic. Julian and I spent the better part of the next hour "mashing it up," which evidently meant working our asses off.

To my great relief, Julian really seemed to know what he was talking about. Once into it, he lost his Jamaican *yah, mahn* swagger and took his tutoring job seriously. But he tempered that seriousness with a great sense of humor. Just listening to him make jokes about what a pain in the ass some of the professors were made me feel better about myself as a student. He was charging me twenty bucks an hour, and as far as I was concerned, he was worth twice that.

"Yeah. See this paragraph here? Move it about three down and the flow is better. Then you want to throw that statistic table in somewhere near the bottom." Julian was focused on my laptop screen.

I pointed at the screen. "Right there?"

"No. Right there." He grabbed my index finger and slid it down to the bottom of the screen. We were shoulder to shoulder. "Now right here you want to stick in a pie chart. That bitch loves the pie charts for real. Pie chart will get you a couple of extra points. Bar graph will just piss her off. That's it. Now add some color and you're good to go." Julian let go of my hand, but leaned in close as we both watched the program work its magic.

At Julian's instruction I manipulated some more things in the document. Then I paused and looked at him.

"Go for it." He nodded.

I pressed the send button and grinned with relief. Julian gave me a high five.

"See? You totally rock this." Julian grinned at me. "*And* you got a great smile. Listen, don't worry about this shit. You catch on quick. And if you need more help after today, I'm just a phone call away."

"Thanks, I feel much better." I started digging in my wallet for the money to pay him.

"Feel better about what?" I looked up surprised to find Reno looking down at me.

"Hey." I smiled up at him from the picnic table and looked at my watch. "Wow. Is it that time already?'

"Yeah, it's that time." Reno had a tone.

I smiled tentatively at him.

He didn't smile back. Geesh.

"What's she feeling so much better about?" he asked again, but this time his focus was on my tutor. The glare in Reno's eyes said, "Who the fuck is this?" but thank God his mouth remained in a tight line.

"Hey, man. I'm Julian. I'm Claire's tutor." Julian stuck out his hand. "I just helped her tweak a few things in her assignment."

Reno looked at Julian for a minute. Then he stuck out his hand too.

I watched as Reno's man paw engulfed Julian's hand. He winced just before Reno let go.

"Hey, man. I'm just the hired help. No need to crush it." Julian grinned as he held up his hands in surrender. "But I get it." He nodded and then looked at me. "I totally get it."

I felt my face color with embarrassment.

"How much she owe you?" Reno growled.

"Nah. We're good. It's cool. She can get me next time." Julian made himself busy stuffing his things in his backpack.

Reno reached past him and stuffed a bill in his bag. Julian looked at the bill, then looked back at Reno.

"Seriously, dude, it was only about an hour. That's wayyy too much green." He looked at me. "Claire, seriously, you can get me next time."

Before I could answer Reno answered for me.

"There won't be a next time. But *seriously* thanks for your help, *dude.*" Reno crossed his arms. "Now I'm guessing you got somewhere else you need to be."

I watched my tutor, and probably my only chance of ever getting an A, untie his dog and skedaddle away from me as fast as he could. Despite his protests, I knew how tight money was for a college student. He was probably afraid that Reno was going to change his mind and take back whatever exorbitant payoff he had just slipped into his bag. Or he was afraid that Reno was going to the beat the shit out of him.

I turned from the rapidly exiting Julian to the firmly planted Reno. "Really?" I hissed. "What was that?"

"You get what you need from that guy?" Reno stood with his arms still folded and flexed against his chest.

"From my *tutor*, you mean?"

"Okay, you want to call him that, we'll call him that. You get what you need?"

"Yeah. I got what I need." I glared at him.

"Then there's not a problem."

"Yeah. Okay. Not a problem." I collected my work papers, while I fought back both tears threatening and my need to scratch out Reno's eyes.

"What's the deal here, Claire?" Reno's voice rumbled close to my ear.

I went nose to nose with him. "The deal here, Reno, is that there *is* a problem. A big one. You just scared off my tutor. And I needed him."

"They got women for that," he growled.

"What?" I pulled back and looked at him, stunned.

Oh no. He. Did. Not.

"They got women for that," Reno repeated.

I just stared at him. "I heard what you said, I just can't believe you said it," I hissed. I grabbed my bag and started walking away from him.

"Bike's over this way, Claire," Reno called out to me.

"I'm taking the bus, Reno," I spat back.

All of a sudden he was walking beside me.

"Don't you have someone else you need to go scare today?" I snarled.

"Babe," he said.

"No? Well, too bad. Let's see if I can help you out with that. I'm going to the grocery store later. The bag boy sometimes brings the heavy stuff out to my car. You could probably rough him up a little bit," I said.

"Very funny," Reno said.

I stopped and swung around then to look at him.

"Actually, it's not funny. There is nothing funny about it. I am drowning here, Reno. I am paying thousands of dollars for just this semester alone, and I am not even a month in and I am drowning."

"You're smart, Babe, you'll get there. Shit. They let you in, didn't they?" He looked at me warily.

"Yeah, they let me in. Doesn't mean they are gonna let me *stay* in. There are academic standards." I narrowed my eyes at him.

I threw my book bag down, rifled through it, and found the source of my shame and frustration.

"And *this* does not meet those standards." I fisted the paper and waved it in his face. "It's a *D*. Not an *A* or a *B* or even a goddamn *C*. It's a *D*. And the worst part is I don't even know what I did wrong. Julian knows what he is doing and he agreed to help me. He is a tutor, for chrissakes. That's what he does. As a matter of fact, I was lucky that I could get him. You just messed that up for me."

"Well you can just get him back, then. He said you could call him." Reno squinted and he rubbed the back of his neck.

"Yeah. And you think he's gonna come running knowing my big bad boyfriend is waiting around the corner to break the bones in his hand and pay him off to stay away?" I snarled. "Just forget it."

"Your boyfriend?" Reno grinned.

"I didn't say *boyfriend*." I looked at him, startled.

"Yeah, Babe. You did. You said *boyfriend*."

"Oh, shut up." I started to walk away again.

"Okay, so maybe I overreacted a little. But he had his hands all over you." He was walking beside me.

I rolled my eyes and kept walking.

"If you really need his help. I'll call him for you. He won't say no to me," Reno continued.

"Yeah. Good idea. That'll work," I snarled.

"Come on, Babe. You know you aren't getting on that bus." Reno was in front of me now, walking backwards.

"Watch me." I kept walking.

"Hey, you hungry?"

I glared at him. Then my stomach growled.

"Yeah, you're hungry." He smirked.

"The only thing I am hungry for is knowledge," I huffed with deliberate drama.

Reno stopped short in front of me, and when I almost bumped into him, he grabbed me by the arms.

"Knowledge. That's good. That's real good, Babe." He smirked again. "I get it. I can do knowledge. Call a truce long enough to get your ass on my bike and let me take you out for a sandwich, okay? And if you are a real good girl, I'll teach ya a few things on the way."

I just shook my head. Because really, that was kind of funny, and despite the very frustrating and embarrassing thing that had just happened with Julian, I needed a laugh, a sandwich, and a few minutes to stop worrying about school. So I gave in; after all, a girl has got to eat.

CHAPTER 23

"I'm fucking starving." Reno grabbed the waitress by the elbow and ordered a couple of sandwiches and two coffees for the two of us.

She served the coffees right away and dimpled at him. I took a minute to see him through her eyes and I didn't blame her. Being mad at him didn't change the fact that he was one seriously good-looking guy.

Then, because I needed something to do other than look at him, I took a gulp of the scalding hot coffee.

My eyes went bright with the effort it took to force it down.

"Hot?" Reno's eyes smiled at me.

"Just a little." I frowned.

He held my eyes for a minute, then picked up one of my General Psychology books. To my surprise, Reno began to thumb through it.

"So how's it going, so far? Do you think these books are going to help you figure shit out?" He looked from the book to me.

Reno was familiar with my quest for the normal.

"It's not like that." I waved at the book. "It's just an entry-level course."

"Really? Let's take a look. Yeah, I see what you mean, but, hey, chapter thirteen looks kind of interesting. There's a whole section here on stimulus. You a little foggy on what stimulation is, Claire?" He grinned.

"Very funny. Give it to me, Reno."

As I reached for the textbook, Reno held it up and away from me. His eyes twinkled and his tone turned teasing. Annoyed, I reached up to take the book back from him. When I did, he surprised me by putting his hand against my cheek and drawing me to him.

Then with his mouth against my ear, he whispered.

"Just say the word, Claire. And I'll be happy to give it to you."

And there it was. The tingle that set my whole body on edge. Damn it.

I made another swipe for the book.

"Stop it Reno. Stimulus and stimulation are two entirely different things and you know it. You know it's not the same." I grabbed the book, exasperated.

"Yeah, Babe, it's not the same for me either." He looked hard at me.

"Well, you could have fooled me." Despite all my good intentions not to let him bait me, I let him bait me.

"What?" Reno asked.

"Cherry still hanging out at the clubhouse?" I asked. If the tutor was fair game, then so was the stripper.

"Who?" Reno honestly looked confused.

I looked around quickly to make sure no one else was watching us, then I pointed to my nipples and made small circular motions with my index fingers.

"You know, Miss Flame Thrower," I snarled.

Reno stared at me for a minute, then burst out laughing.

"Baby, you know what that was."

"No, *baby,* actually I don't. But I'd like to know, I really would," I huffed, because really when it came down to it, I had no idea where Reno and Cherry stood. Or where Reno and I stood.

Reno stopped smiling and he looked at me. "You would, huh?"

"No, just forget it, Reno," I said with exasperation. "Let's just keep on pretending at whatever this is."

"Pretending at whatever this is?" He narrowed his eyes at me. "Really? That's how you see this?" Reno's eyes met mine for what seemed to be forever. He threw a twenty down on the table and pulled me up from my seat.

"What are you doing, Reno?"

He picked up the books and shoved them hard in my bag.

"We are leaving, Claire." Then he grabbed my hand and dragged me out the door. "I am not doing this here."

I was barely on the back of the bike before he tore out of the parking lot.

Jesus. A few short weeks of a happy Reno and me gone.

~

After miles and miles of just trying to stay seated on the rumbling bike with minimum contact, we pulled up in front of the club-house. Today there would be no lunch, or errands, or rides through pretty, winding country roads. Today Reno brought me straight to the compound. I guessed, sadly, that he brought me here to pick up my Jeep.

Free ride time was over.

I sat for a minute after Reno killed the engine.

"Getting off any time soon, Claire?" The minute I did, he tore the helmet from my head and threw it on the ground. Then he grabbed me by the hand and led me into the building. He surprised me by dragging me down the hallway to his room.

The last time I had been in Reno's room was the *last time I had been in Reno's room.* Wincing at the memory, I pulled back just slightly. He pulled me forward with such force that if he wasn't there to catch me, I would have fallen flat.

Then without another word, he slammed the door shut with his foot.

"Reno, I . . ." I started to stutter and began to sweat. Now that I started this, I wasn't sure I wanted to finish it. I just didn't know why we always had to be so complicated. I knew Reno was feeling that too. Because in spite of everything that was still left unsettled between us, Reno had been helpful and supportive in a way that I knew was far out of his comfort zone. I knew what kind of women usually drew a brother's eye. Not many of the boys strayed too far from club offerings and I think it was pretty safe to assume that when a woman in the club bent her head, it was not toward a book.

So yeah, I would have to be a fool not to see how hard Reno was trying. But despite some pretty strong effort on both our parts, here we were again. One step forward, three steps back.

I just didn't know if we would ever get past this place. The fact that Cherry was still hanging around the club didn't help matters.

Earlier that morning I had gone with Glory to help her return some stuff to the kitchen house. While I was making my way back to the car, I had run straight into Cherry. I knew her not only from *that night,* of course, but also from reputation. Cherry was a stripper, exotic dancer, club favorite, whatever you wanted to call her. But I also knew, that unlike some of the other club band-aids, she was pretty well liked by most of the old ladies. She didn't get in anyone's way and she seemed to know her place in the messed-up ladder of Saints' women. I had heard a while ago that she had a couple of kids and that one of them had special needs. I had also heard that the money Cherry made from her dancing mostly went to the private residential school that her son was in.

So really, Cherry was just another overwhelmed, overworked woman who was doing what she had to do to ensure her future and the well-being of those that she loved. And in the meantime, she was looking for love in all the wrong places.

She was really not so very different from me except that, despite the fact that Cherry handed it out for free, she was also drop-dead gorgeous in a way I would never be. She was also sexy, funny, and pretty easygoing. In the land of old-school reruns, she was Ginger to my Mary Ann.

Yeah, Cherry still being at the club did not help matters at all.

I watched Reno as he prowled around the room. He stopped, scrubbed his hand over his face, and looked at me. He tore off his cut and pulled his T-shirt over his head. He sat on his bed and began to kick off his black leather biker boots.

"Reno, we need to . . ."

"We need to what?" Reno had both of his boots off now and he was sitting on a freshly made bed with what looked like new bed coverings.

I took a look around the rest of the room then, and I noticed that it was spotless. Reno's room was one of the nicer ones in the compound. It was large and it had its own bathroom. I had been here a lot, but I had never seen it look anywhere near as tidy.

Who had cleaned Reno's room? My eyes narrowed and the green-eyed snake curled again deep in my belly and waited to strike.

Sometimes, this man just brought out the worst in me.

"Why is your room clean, Reno?" I glared at him.

In bare feet, Reno walked over to the windows and adjusted the blinds down before he turned to look at me.

"Claire, are you seriously getting pissed off because this place is clean? I got new sheets and one of those comforter things too, is that going to send you into a rage, Babe?"

Now I was totally confused. Reno had shoved me out of the coffee shop, onto his bike, and into the compound. Once we cleared the gate, he had practically dragged me to his room. Now he stood in front of me half naked, in a clean room, adjusting the shades.

Wow.

I started to get what this was.

Maybe.

Then he took something out of his back pocket and gave it to me.

"What's this?" I looked at the folded piece of paper in my hand.

"The reason I was late today, Claire." Reno nodded to the paper.

I had no idea what it could be, and I was really not in the mood for another surprise today.

Every ounce of self-preservation screamed at me to give that paper back unfolded and unread.

"Read it, Claire."

With unsteady hands, I unfolded the white sheet. It was some sort of spreadsheet with Reno's name at the top of it. There were a whole bunch of lines with names of things that I didn't recognize, medical terms maybe. At the end of the words were negative signs. The heading read "Main Street Lab and Clinic."

This was a medical report.

I sat for a minute and tried to make sense of what I was seeing.

Reno had gotten tested.

For me.

Reno had cleaned his place.

For me.

Reno had bought clean sheets and a "comforter thing."

For me.

Oh, boy.

In an effort to slow down what I thought this might be, I made one more attempt to hold on to the bitch train that I had been riding. Not that I didn't get hot at the possibility of another steamy bout with Reno, but, really, I wasn't sure where this all would lead.

If we were going to be taking that trip together again, I thought it was important to get it all out there.

"I saw Cherry today. Here. On Saints property. Last time I saw her, she was with you, Reno," I blurted out. Then I waited.

"Yeah, Babe, and since then she's been with half a dozen other guys. I can't go grab a beer without running into a brother that she's given it to. I already told you what that was. I am not going to explain again." He folded his arms across his massive chest.

"Come here, baby." Reno's tone suddenly softened and his eyes were warm. "It's over with Cherry. That's done. And it was never even close to what we had . . . have. Not even on the same planet and you know that."

I did know that.

"I just don't think we should be doing this," I said softly.

"Why not?"

"It's not a good idea."

"Baby, it's a fucking great idea."

"I'm afraid that it is just gonna confuse everything even more than it already is," I answered honestly.

"I'm not confused," Reno said.

I shook my head. "I'm not sure . . ."

Reno looked at me. "Door's right behind you. You can walk out anytime you want. I'm not gonna force you, Babe. But I really hope you stay."

"Why? Reno, why do you want me to stay," I whispered.

Then he moved in closer. "Baby, you know why I want you to stay."

"Reno . . ."

He was on me now, his whole body pushed up against mine. He was whispering soft and low in my ear.

"Baby, just say you'll stay."

"Okay," I breathed. "I'll . . ."

"Fucking finally, Claire." He smiled against my ear.

CHAPTER 24

Reno took my hand in his and led me to the bed. He sat down on the edge of it and pulled me down on his lap. For a minute, he just dropped his head in the crook of my neck and breathed.

Reno was inhaling me.

His long hair brushed my collarbone and I could feel his sigh against the sensitive spot right underneath my earlobe.

As he pulled me slowly toward him, his hands moved gently up and down my back. Then he reached up and buried his hands into my hair. He grasped big soft clouds of it and pulled it gently away from my face. When he pressed his mouth to mine, he took my breath away. I grew hot and cold all over.

His lips felt soft and full. His hands, callused and rough, drew through my hair. He smelled like tobacco, coffee, clean air, and fresh winds.

Reno smelled incredible.

But he tasted even better.

He kissed me until my lips were swollen and the taste of him poured like molten lava straight to my heart.

I twisted in Reno's lap until I straddled him. My sundress edged itself up high around my thighs. The thin straps fell off my shoulders. I took my time, and did some kissing of my own, raining soft, wet touches along his jawline. My lips found that sensitive spot right under his ear. The soft, velvety skin of that beautiful lobe was a gift after the hard stubble of his chin. I sucked softly on it, bit it gently and pulled at it with my teeth.

I moved my hands to Reno's arms. From his shoulder to his wrists, I felt each hard muscle, each pulsing vein, every raised scar. Intricate woven lines of rich, dark ink marked my man as a warrior, Hells Saints soldier, and beautiful bad man.

I slipped my tongue along the Celtic knot on his bicep and traced it, leaving a trail of myself, wet and lingering on his skin. I took my time. I heard something catch in Reno's throat and he let out a feral growl. Then he put both of his hands on my ass, picked me up, dropped me gently to the floor, and stood in front of me. His eyes touched me like fire, everywhere.

"Pretty dress, Babe."

I smiled at him.

"Now take it off."

My eyes widened as his darkened.

"Take off the dress, Claire," Reno repeated.

I hesitated and was suddenly shy.

"No more hiding, Claire. Not from me."

My hands shook as I slipped the sundress off my shoulders. I felt my body heat, and the slight cool of the room harden my nipples as the fabric fell smoothly past my hips and to the floor.

When I tagged my thumbs under my panties, my man growled.

"No, baby, not yet. I like those. Those little silky white panties with those pink little flowers on the sides. Damn sexy."

"They are called rosettes," I managed to breathe out.

Reno just looked at me and smiled.

I stood still. Resisting the urge to cover myself.

Reno moved to me. "Open up for me, baby," he whispered.

I parted my legs slightly and felt the warm palm of his hand cup and gently tease the soft silk of my panties.

Reno rested his forehead against mine and groaned. I moved against the soft rhythmic rubbing of his fingers.

When he pulled away, a small sigh of need escaped me. I flushed as I felt my panties slip off and float softly to my feet. Reno lifted me and put me on the bed. As he moved away, I watched him quickly unzip his jeans and pull them off in one fluid move.

Everything about Reno screamed primal. His long hair fell around his face, tousled and wild. A muscle jumped in his hard jawline. He watched me with dark, hungry eyes. When he leaned onto the bed, I moved against the wall. Spanning the width between us, he crawled toward me. A panther homing in on his prey. The muscles of his powerful arms pulled him forward. His actions beautiful, sleek, and deliberate.

Reno kept coming at me.

Slowly.

A shiver passed through my body and paralyzed me. I felt my heart rate slow and my muscles freeze, like prey before a predator I stilled and waited.

My every instinct cried out for flight; I made a small movement. I must have. Maybe my eyes shifted or my breath caught in my throat. I just knew that I barely moved, and Reno was on me.

"Fuck, baby, with your back up against the wall like that, and you looking all scared like I'm something that's going to eat you, it makes me want to tie you down." Then he wound his hand in my hair and pulled me toward him. Slowly, slowly his mouth opened mine until his tongue found me.

"I'd never hurt you, baby," he murmured. Then Reno kissed me again.

My arms wrapped around him and pulled him closer. He moved away then and smiled into my eyes.

"Fucking beautiful. You are so fucking beautiful."

I was so wet and ready that I ached. My legs moved by themselves to wrap around him.

Reno pulled away. Teasing me, fighting me for that control. I pulled him back. "Reno, please."

I moved to position myself under him.

"Fuck, baby, when your eyes get all big like that, only thing I want to do is be inside of you."

"Hurry." I was ready, just at the sound of his voice. Jesus, if he didn't enter me soon, I was going to have to seal the deal on my own. I was ready to combust.

Reno caught my hand. I whimpered. "I'm going to take my time. And, woman, you are going to wait while I do that."

I moaned softly—dangerously close to begging.

Reno's eyes darkened and he shifted over my body. Slowly. He bared his teeth, and nipped and pulled at the tips of my breasts until they were dark pink and swollen. I arched my back to meet each gentle pull. I was slick and wet and almost crazy with need.

Reno moaned, then he imprisoned my hand between us as it moved to pause him. Pressing heavy against me, he began to work his way between my legs.

Oh. My. God.

Reno's fingers slid up and down, teasing the soft, moist folds. His touch left trails of fire before he finally settled. When the rough callus of his thumb hit my soft, swollen nub, I bit the inside of my cheek to stop myself from screaming in pleasure.

Reno tapped the sensitive bud gently, then he pressed, and swirled. His finger made soft insistent circles while my body arched and stretched against his hand.

Expertly, Reno kept me on the edge.

I felt my eyes go wide, and my mouth open with soft little puffs of air.

"Ahhh, that's it, baby. We are going to get to know each other all over again and real slow. I want to see the light in your eyes when I touch you like this . . ." Reno had turned on his side and was watching my face as he touched me.

"And like that." His finger dipped inside of me.

Oh. My. God.

"Baby, you are so wet for me. Nice."

"That thing, Reno . . ." I breathed. "That thing you just did, do it again."

"This thing, baby?"

Yep. That thing. That exact thing.

I fought to wrap my legs around him, to draw him closer. When I arched my back, Reno pushed me back down.

I writhed against his hand in frustration.

When he grabbed my hands and captured them over my head with one of his big ones, I felt another exquisite shock of wet pulsate through me.

Then Reno grinned at me and kissed me tenderly. When I felt his hard body cover mine, I almost screamed in relief. The hot insistent length of him prodded against me. Reno's body slowly began to fill my own empty, aching need. Then with one last steady motion he was inside of me.

Holy. Holy. Wow.

His hand worked me between my legs, while his hardness slid slowly in and out of me.

I was burning alive with the heat of my own body.

My whole body pushed against him, drawing him in. He let me hold him there, deep inside of me.

Then Reno withdrew his length from me again.

I beat at him with my fists in sheer and frantic frustration.

"You are so fucking beautiful." Reno captured my nipple again just long enough to whisper against my skin. His breath shot sparks of heat against the wet swollen tips before he entered me again. I felt him plunge deep inside me. I clenched and spasmed around him. Over and over again meeting his desire with my own until we came together in an explosion of tangled limbs and breathless murmurings.

I felt unhinged at the hips, and hot, sensitive, and swollen. My nipples were chapped. My inner thigh muscles screamed from being stretched wonderfully beyond their limits. My cheeks were chafed where the rough stubble of Reno's face had rubbed against me.

Yep, I was sore, all right. Sore in a deliciously, decadent, totally dirty girl sort of way. And it felt great.

"Rest up, beautiful." My man pulled me close into his arms. And as I lay in Reno's arms and waited for sleep to come take me, I pushed all the doubts and questions to the far recesses of my mind.

Then I snuggled closer to my man and fell into a deep and dreamless sleep.

CHAPTER 25

Oh, my God.

Not again.

I had just come back from a very long day at Ruby Reds. One of the waitresses had a sick kid so I had picked up both her weekend shifts. One weekend shift was hard enough, but two was brutal, and if they hadn't been incredibly shorthanded, I never would have agreed to it.

I smelled like fried onions, beer, and the pickle juice that had splattered all over me when I had tried to open the jar. My head pounded from the constant piped-in music and my back hurt from all the bending and stretching.

Prosper had sent Reno and some of the boys away again on club business and Reno texted and called whenever he could. While the sound of Reno's voice never failed to leave me blushing and breathless, I knew there was still much to be settled between us and I welcomed the short reprieve. Midterms were right around the corner and I knew I had to focus on my schoolwork.

What I needed was a glass of wine, a hot bath, and a quiet night with my studies.

What I got was Glory and Jules arguing.

Again.

In the serene lakefront setting, Jules's loud voice shattered the silence. The strains of his worn-out argument reached me as I drove up the driveway.

Great. Just great.

After a long day on my feet, I was not feeling the love or the patience I would need to referee this new round in their old argument. Besides, I was totally on Glory's side.

To everyone's surprise, Glory's little venture had taken off big time. Having said that, it had not gone unnoticed by anyone that the rise of Glory's star could be credited mostly to the mob. Glory's first big break came from catering Gianni's niece's sweet sixteen party and she had gotten several jobs from that one successful gig.

The boys, Reno included, weren't thrilled with one of their own women serving the "dago wops" as they called them, but Prosper had decided that there was no harm in it. Prosper also knew, like anyone with any sort of sense would know, that it would be a huge insult to the Italians to refuse the opportunity they had extended in Glory's direction. As long as things continued to go smoothly, it was all good with the president of the MC.

But Jules hated the idea.

Hated it.

And he had made it very clear to Glory, that as far as he was concerned, Glory's first job for the Italians would be her last. Glory was frustrated and confused by Jules's attitude, but I got it. When Jules first met Glory, she had still been shell-shocked. Although it had taken us all a while to recuperate from that horrible day, it had taken Glory the longest. And that was because, while it had been one terrifying day for Raine and me, it had been much longer than that for Glory. Glory had been kidnapped by Gino, the bastard, and survived that and God knew what else. It had taken Glory literally months before she could even drum up the courage or desire to leave the relative safety of the home she had made with us.

While I would never want to think that Jules preferred Glory to remain a scared little shut-in, even I had to admit that Glory's unwillingness to leave the house had made it pretty convenient for Jules to make his play. She had never been unavailable to him in all that time, nor had she put her beautiful self out there to be available to anyone else. For a long time now, Jules had had Glory exactly where he wanted her. Under his thumb.

This new Glory, he wasn't so sure about.

I grabbed my stuff and headed toward the war zone, hoping to skip by unnoticed and whisk up the back steps to the bathroom.

Luck was not on my side.

∾

"Oh, no, you are fucking not." Jules's voice came booming around the corner.

"Fuck you, I'm not!" Glory yelled at Jules.

"Calm your ass down, Glory, or I fucking swear . . ."

"What? You fucking swear what, Jules? You're not going to stop me from doing this, so don't even try. As a matter of fact, I have peppers to chop and you're in my way, so I want you to leave." Glory waved her new ninety-dollar ceramic chef's knife in the air. Then, she pointed it toward the door.

Jules didn't move.

Glory stabbed the air with the knife. "Get out!"

Whoa. Apparently, our beautiful soft-spoken Glory had found her voice.

It was about time too.

Because how dare Jules try to stop her from doing something that made her happy?

And even though I strongly suspected that Jules had the bad luck of being the straw that had finally broken that proverbial camel's back, Glory's rage was just about the most beautiful rage that I had ever seen.

Good for her.

Glory had put too much into her business to stop just because, as she said, the brothers had a stick up their asses about it. I had to hand it to her. My best friend had taken her love of cooking and baking from an enjoyable pastime to a successful business.

And she loved it.

So what if her first big break came from feeding an internationally known mob boss? Everyone had to start somewhere, right?

And it had to be said, the Italians didn't mind throwing their money around. I didn't know what they were into, but they had our boys beat by half. Gianni's top crew seemed to be rolling in it. Their places were all five-bedroom, five-bath mansions. These houses boasted marble everything, carefully groomed lawns, and alabaster stone fountains. Their wives dressed in Versace, and accessorized in Giuseppe Zanotti. From what I heard, their mistresses or goomahs, as I guess they were called, all had their own apartments.

The differences between the MC world and the mob world hit us like a cold shower whenever we worked one of those events. Raven-haired, dark-eyed, handsome men in Armani suits kissed each other's cheeks in greeting. Thick envelopes created an endless parade of offerings at the christenings of their sons and even more at the weddings of their daughters. Each shake of the hand left their palms full of green.

The Italians wanted only the best. No open pits for the mob. They wanted their pork cut into thin tender strips steeped in marinara sauce, their tables laden with fresh fruit and the best cheeses, their table wine served in thick crystal goblets.

Glory joked, "Give them cheese, garlic, and olive oil, and they will come."

She was not wrong.

Gianni paid well. Strangely enough, some of his crew paid even better. The girls and I had talked about it, and we had noticed Gianni was never far away when we were getting our very own envelopes of cash. We all had the feeling that he had, as they say, put the squeeze on his boys to make sure that they paid us well. They always added at least half to the fee that Glory charged. Because of that and a host of other reasons, Dolly and I helped Glory out with the parties as often as we could, and even I enjoyed working them.

I loved our boys. I did. The Saints were all big and gorgeous in that bad boy kind of way—muscled, tattooed, and born to be wild. Every woman knew that draw, felt that pull, at least once in her life. Every good girl dreamed of being loved at least once by an outlaw man. Every bad girl lived for it. Rugged, surly, dangerous outlaws in leather taking what they wanted and riding with thunder between their legs.

A lot could be said about the good ol' red-blooded American male.

But the Italians wove a pretty hot man-web of their own.

Just as big. Just as muscled. Just as dangerous.

But instead of custom Harleys, they drove sleek black Cadillacs. Instead of hand-stitched leathers and silver skulls, they wore custom-made suits and eighteen-karat gold rings. Best of all, they spoke a different language.

Yeah, the Italians definitely cast their own spell.

They appreciated good-tasting food, good-looking women, and they liked to throw their money around.

Nothing wrong with that, Glory had said. More than once.

∾

Glory moved quickly past me with Jules hot on her heels.

"Hey, Claire," she managed as she walked by.

Jules looked at me and snarled.

Nice.

"Get back here and sit the fuck down, Glory. I am not leaving this house until we have talked this food fucking serving shit out." Jules crossed his huge arms over his chest, ready to do battle.

"Food fucking serving shit? Food fucking serving shit? Are you referring to *my business*?"

"Babe, throwing together a couple of cupcakes, whipping up some goddamn Rice-A-Roni, and serving it to some fucking mobsters who are downing it, while staring at your tits, is not a *business*."

Glory's blue eyes narrowed and glinted like ice.

"You big, dumb moron. How dare you? *How dare you*? You wouldn't know good food if it bit you in your ass! Rice-A-Roni? Did you just call my creamy wild mushroom risotto, *my signature dish*, Rice-A-Roni?"

"Yeah, I said it." Jules stood his ground and roared even louder than before. "And I don't care if you are serving solid gold goose shit under goddamn crystal domes. My woman is not going to be serving anything to some oily-haired, dago wops. I mean it, Glory. The boys don't like it and neither do I."

"Oh really? Really, Jules? You and your boys don't like how I make my money? Well, guess what? I don't give two shits what you and your boys like. Last time I looked, you and your boys weren't exactly standing in line to pay my bills."

She had a point.

"And what was that? Your woman? Am I your woman, now, Jules?" Glory swung around and advanced toward him.

Jules looked suddenly unsure of himself, and took a step back.

"And what exactly makes me your woman? The fact that we have been *doing it* for over a year now? Is that it? Is that what makes me your woman?"

"*Doing it?*" Jules still looked confused. "Yeah, if by *doing it* you mean me taking you to my bed, then yeah. I would say that, yeah, that makes you my woman."

"Yeah, well lucky me," Glory hissed.

Uh-oh.

Jules arched an eyebrow. "That ain't enough for you, woman? Because I sure as hell don't remember you ever complaining. I remember a lot of moaning and groaning and you screaming out my name loud enough to wake every brother from here to Texas, but complaining? Nah, don't recall any of that." He stood in front of her with a self-satisfied grin and his big arms crossed in front of him.

Glory narrowed her eyes.

I thought that would be a very good time to get the hell out of there and into that tub. I had just started toward the door when I saw Glory hold up her hand and waggle her ring finger in Jules's face.

Oh, boy.

"Do you see a ring on this finger?" Glory growled at him. "No? Well, neither do I, and where I come from, when a woman belongs to a man, she has his ring on her finger!"

"A ring? Is that what you want? You want to get married, Glory?" Jules roared back. "Love, honor, and *obey*? You ready for that, baby? Because it sure as hell does not look like it."

Jules could roar all he wanted.

He could stomp and yell and pace.

But there was no covering it up.

When Glory had flung that ring finger in his face, he'd turned an immediate and unmistakable ghostly shade of pale despite his bluster. A sheen of sweat appeared instantly on his forehead. If

Glory had suddenly sprouted wings and flew over the guy's head, he could not have looked more stunned.

Glory did not miss that. "Did I ever say that, Jules? Have I even once said that I wanted to get married? Did you ever, *ever* hear me even mention the word?"

Then she moved toward him and pushed one long elegant finger into the leather-covered steel that was his chest.

"No, you haven't. Because if I did, if I ever wanted to get married, why would I want to marry a gigantic ass like you, who does not know a good thing when he has it?"

Jules looked down at that finger. Even I could see that Glory meant business.

"Baby, I know a good thing. Course I do," Jules growled. "And if you need green, you know that I got you covered. Whatever you need, baby. You know, I got you."

Way to try and save it, Jules. I cheered to myself, until he added the next bit . . .

"But, Jesus, Glory, you ain't serious about that marriage shit, are you? You are not standing there telling me that you want to get . . . uh . . ." Jules scrubbed his hand over his face and looked totally ill at ease.

Jules's confusion just seemed to add fuel to Glory's fire. I had never seen anything even close to this side of her, and despite the awkwardness of the situation, I had to admit I was totally fascinated.

"Oh, just forget it, Jules. Why would I want to marry a man who I had to tell that I wanted to get married? A man who is too damn stupid to think of it on his own is no one, *no one* I would even consider marrying. Ever!" Glory turned to walk away.

"Woman, what the fuck are you talking about?" Jules followed her. "Damn woman, how the hell did we get from your goddamn *signature dish* to me putting a ring on your finger? Where is this coming from?" He looked so confused, I almost felt sorry for him.

Then Jules arched one perfectly formed blond eyebrow and said, "Babe, you on the rag?"

He ducked just in time.

"Woman, you throw one more of those dishes at . . ."

Glory kept on throwing things at him until Jules was out the door.

When he was gone, she snapped the lock noisily behind him.

My best friend leaned against the door and took a minute to pull herself together.

Then she looked at me. And I knew, I just knew, that she was going to ask me if I thought Jules was the marrying kind.

I had no idea what I should say to her. Because while I didn't want to hurt my friend, I really did not think Jules had the first idea of what it took to be that guy.

"Can I ask you something and will you answer me truthfully?" My girl's light blue eyes looked sunken in her pale face. Her eyes shimmered with unshed tears.

I moved to place my arm around her and whispered, "Of course."

She turned to me, one teardrop spilling over onto her smooth cheek. She sighed and put her head on my shoulder. "My whole future depends on this, Claire. So please, please tell me what you really think."

Oh, boy. I prepared a careful answer in my head.

"My creamy wild mushroom risotto . . ." Glory's lips trembled.

Her creamy wild mushroom risotto?

"Do you think Jules was right? Do you think it tastes like Rice-A-Roni?" Glory sputtered those last words out like she was trying to rid poison from her blood stream.

I heaved a sigh of relief. This question I could answer with one hundred percent honesty.

"Not even close, honey," I answered and hugged her tight.

CHAPTER 26

By the time I got back from class at midday, Glory was home putting on the final touches for the catering job that she had booked for tomorrow. The screen door was wedged open and I could hear Bono singing through the open windows. As I walked toward the house, the mouth-watering scent of perfectly seasoned sausage, onions, and peppers wafted through the air.

I glanced at my phone to find a text from Reno. He and the rest of the brothers had been home about a week now. Since their return the air had been charged with tension. The rumble of exhaust pipes had been echoing through the compound for days. Chief officers from the surrounding chapters been called in for a meet, and it was safe to assume that whatever business was keeping the outlaw men behind closed doors was risky, dangerous, and illegal.

It wasn't the first time I had felt that wave of secrecy and surge of violent urgency wash over the compound. It all came with the territory. Raine had learned to navigate these times, but I knew they scared her just as they scared me. I knew that Reno expected the same of me. I just didn't know if I could do it. Or if I even wanted to. A part of me still yearned for that normal everyday kind of life.

The kind of life that I knew loving a man like Reno could not provide.

Sometimes I felt like he and I were just a big puzzle to be solved and every time I got close to solving it, I discovered a new piece that just didn't seem to quite fit.

I sighed and turned my attention to my roommate. I stood in the doorway for a minute and watched Glory work her magic. I had to hand it to her, it had been a few weeks now since that scene with Jules and undeterred by his ultimatum, our girl had cut her losses and moved on. While I knew that letting go wasn't easy for her, I was once again impressed by Glory's strong will and strength of character. At times it even made me a little envious. While Glory was enjoying enormous success with her business, I was still struggling with my course work. While Glory was busy getting on with the Life After Jules, I was still busy figuring out Reno and me.

Standing in the doorway watching her now, I thought for the millionth time that I could learn a lot from Glory.

Besides, Glory in the kitchen was a thing of beauty. Blond hair flying, blue eyes flashing, and long limbs swinging, Glory was like a one-man band. Only instead of crashing the cymbals, beating the drums, and humming into a harmonica, Glory got her groove on by stirring, melting, and sifting.

My best buddy was feeling the happy. Most days. Most days Glory was feeling the happy.

But as always in life, at least in our lives, everything was a trade-off. Every grain of happiness had its price.

That last huge disagreement between Glory and Jules turned out to be the *last* huge disagreement between Glory and Jules.

Reno had heard from Jules that things had gone bad between him and Glory. And even though I had been careful not to divulge any of the particulars Glory shared with me, Reno knew how deep our friendship went. He took as much of my ranting and worrying as he could before he said, "Babe, if it don't involve me or you, I honestly don't give two shits about it. Now get your sweet self over here and I will show you exactly what I do care about."

I stopped talking about Glory and Jules as much after that, but I never stopped fretting. I hoped for a happy outcome. Glory seemed content to wait it out, and I thought that might be a good sign. Then Jules did something really stupid.

In a very poorly played, typical Hells Saints fashion, Jules started to pay a lot of attention to Bambi. Bambi was a twenty-five-year-old club whore with bottle-blond hair, skinny legs, huge tits, and eager eyes, and her only ambition was to snag a brother.

The first time Glory saw them together, Jules had stared hard at her. His eyes issued a challenge, his body language smugly signaled his ultimatum.

Glory took one look at Bambi pulled tight to her man's side, and decided to let him go for good.

When she turned and walked out that door, there was such a look of utter disbelief on Jules's face that I almost felt sorry for him.

Almost.

But mostly, I felt sorry for Glory, because I knew just what turning away from the man that she loved had cost her. I knew because in the days that followed, Glory reverted back to a lesser version of herself. I knew standing her ground wasn't easy for her. Glory gave herself a few weeks after the final blow to learn how to live without him.

Then she rallied, like I knew she would, and bravely kept on keeping on.

My girl had this.

And we had her back.

CHAPTER 27

It had been a long night, but another smash hit for Glory Days Catering. The booking had been the wedding of Julio "Little Finger" Pagnatellio and Antonia Baccalaria, the daughter of Anthony Baccalaria, a well-known, high-profile attorney and reported consigliere for the Bonzini family. Raine, Glory, and I were all in a great mood.

We had been one of three catering services chosen for the extremely lavish celebration. Glory Days would make and serve the hors d'oeuvres at the extended cocktail hour. Glory had spent the last couple of days preparing prosciutto and fig wraps, Italian fried olives, paper thin slices of Calabrese salami, and provolone wrapped in a flaky crust, steakhouse crostini, grilled mussels, and a huge antipasto platter.

All the way home, Glory chattered away like a happy little songbird. "I think that went well. Don't you? And those girls from the college, they did a great job. There was a couple of times when I thought that tall one was going to drop the crostini, and the one with all that hair, next time I will have to make sure she puts it up. But I think we should use them again. What do you think?"

"I . . . uh." Glory had been talking at such a nonstop rate that I had been taken totally by surprise when she actually directed a question at me. But, I shouldn't have worried, because the question was strictly rhetorical.

"Of course," Glory continued without missing a beat, "Dolly and Pinky get right of first refusal on every job, but I know how much they love looking after Willow. Not sure why it takes two of them, though. Gianni asked for her a couple of times . . . hm . . . really hadn't thought much about that at the time. But do you think? Dolly and Gianni? Oh God, if the boys had a hard time accepting me working for the Italians, can you imagine if Dolly and Gianni . . . Oh, boy, can you just imagine that?" Glory paused for a moment to consider the possibility.

Not in my wildest dreams.

I couldn't imagine the sister-in-law of the president of the Hells Saints MC having any sort of romantic entanglement with the purported front boss of the Bonzini crime family.

Talk about complicated. Disaster would not even begin to define it.

But Glory was right. Tonight, Gianni had definitely expressed concern about Dolly's absence. I suddenly wondered if all the jobs being thrown in Glory's direction had less to do with her and more to do with the fact that Gianni seemed to like having Dolly around. Not to take anything away from the bang-up job that Glory always did. But still, Gianni did seem to hover whenever Dolly joined our little serving crew.

I pushed that thought aside and concentrated on how good it was just to see Glory happy. And she was right, the girls had done a great job helping out. Donna and Linda were classmates of mine. I knew that they had previous experience waitressing. When Glory told me that we were going to be short some help, I had asked them if they were interested in earning a few extra bucks. I think that they said yes before the offer was fully out of my mouth. And I didn't blame them. I knew firsthand that the cliché about perpetually broke college students was true, and I had assured them that Glory would make it worth their while.

Usually when Raine worked for Glory, Diego stayed home with Willow. But today he had had business to take care of, so Pinky and Dolly had happily stepped up. Diego knew how Jules and some of his brothers felt about the Hells Saints women serving it up to the mob, but he never gave us any shit about it. I thought that was very, very cool of him. Even though D and I had a rocky start, I had not only grown to respect the man that my sister had married, I had grown to love him.

No question about it, Diego Montesalto had his outlaw ways. But I knew that he would totally support my sister in whatever she wanted to do. I knew it by the way he had supported me when I told him that I wanted to go back to school. I knew it by the way that he had stepped up to help Glory pick out the used van that she had decided she needed for the business.

Diego took care of his girls, and he did not feel the need to offer up his opinion at every opportunity.

Unlike Jules. Who, even though he had ended things with Glory, still felt the need to express his very strong opinions each time Glory's business was mentioned.

Jules was still doing that shit.

Which is why it took us by surprise when we pulled into our driveway at well past midnight, and we saw Jules's bike parked in its old spot. As we drove the van closer to the lake house we noticed more bikes.

Then we crested the hill and saw the boys.

Their shadows cast an eerie glow against the pale light of the crescent moon.

I felt my sister tense beside me and I knew that her first thought was for Willow. Whatever had brought the boys out in force like this could not be good.

Diego, Reno, Crow, Pipe, and Riker stood with their backs to us, forming a tight circle some yards from the front door. They stood on the lawn with their guns trained on whatever it was that was in the middle of that circle. Tension split the air. Not one of the brothers looked up as our van slowly made its approach. Every move they made was deliberate, focused, and primed.

Raine opened the van door before we came to a complete stop. My sister bolted past whatever was happening in the yard and ran toward the brightly lit cabin.

Her baby was in that house.

I saw Diego lift his shoulders slightly as his wife ran past him, but he kept his eyes focused in front of him.

Glory and I stepped out of the van, but stood quietly next to it.

My eyes were trained on my man. I didn't like this one bit. I didn't care that a circle of his brothers stood side by side with Reno. Weapons had been drawn and that single act terrified me. I knew firsthand that advantage could turn to disadvantage very quickly when deadly force was on the table.

"Claire?" Reno called out to me without turning around. "I want you to get back in the van. Now."

A thick cloud moved across the dim light of the moon, making it even harder to see. A flash of lightning split the distant sky and I automatically began to count the seconds and wait for the crash of thunder. The large broken-angel emblem on the back of Reno's leather cut stood out in sharp relief.

I stood frozen to the spot.

"Claire, get in the goddamn van," Reno snarled the command again. I had only heard him use that tone once before with me. And that was the night that Gino had died.

Not only did I haul myself into the van, I pulled Glory in with me. Once back inside the safety of the paneled walls, Glory and I sat stone still and completely silent. No one wanted to startle five men with drawn weapons.

We had no idea who or what was on the inside of that circle.

"This can't be good," Glory whispered to me. "I don't see Jules. Do you see him?"

I shook my head.

Just then I heard the loud rumble of thunder and a flash of lightning split through the black sky. The bright light tore a jagged hole through the leather-covered, heavily booted legs of the brothers. The violent light blazed through the circle and illuminated two silhouettes.

"Oh, my God. Is that him?" Glory leaned toward the windshield. "Look! There on the ground. Claire, is that Jules?"

"I think it might be." I leaned in too.

"Holy shit. What is happening?" Glory whispered.

"I don't know," I whispered back.

From where we sat, Jules's face was barely recognizable. He lay with his cheek to the ground while the heel of a worn, brown leather boot sat pressed against his throat. Jules's eyes had opened wide with the pressure of bursting capillaries, and his face was a grotesque shade of eggplant. His arm was being pulled taut, his wrist bent forward in a bone-shattering hold.

"Claire, whoever that guy is, he is going to kill Jules." Glory choked back a sob. She put her hand on the door release.

I stopped her.

"Don't you dare," I warned my friend. "You'll only make things worse. Let the boys handle this. Reno won't let anything happen to Jules."

Glory nodded mutely. Then she put her hands back in her lap. We waited.

In the heavy stillness of the dark night, the strains of a calm voice crackled through the air. Despite the circle of 9mm trained on him, whoever this guy was, he meant business.

I rolled down my window just enough to be able to hear what was being said.

Glory leaned in. "What are they saying?"

"Shh," I whispered back and placed my ear to the open window.

That same low, soft voice laced with controlled violence drifted toward me on the cool night air.

"The way I see it, motherfucker, is we both live to have a conversation about why you snuck up behind me and cocked a fucking piece to the back of my head, or we both go to hell never knowing why. But I got to tell you, my arm is getting pretty goddamn tired of keeping this hold, and I'm thinking it's only a matter of time before one of these boys gets trigger-happy. I am not sure who is in charge here, but whoever is better listen up. Either I'm gonna ease up and these assholes are gonna stand down, or I'm gonna lean in and snap your boy's neck. I really don't want to kill him, and I sure as shit don't want to die in the middle of nowhere. But you have got to know, if I meet the boatman tonight, I am not crossing that river alone."

I held my breath and waited.

After what seemed like an eternity, Diego came to a decision. He slowly stretched out his right hand and gave a silent command. The boys immediately withdrew their weapons. In response, the booted foot visibly eased up on Jules's neck. The color returned to his face, but the boot remained in place.

Glory and I breathed a sigh of relief.

In one weird fluid movement, the boys disengaged their handguns and immediately returned their pieces to the back of their waistbands. The response was quick. Whoever had Jules's neck under his boot drew back entirely. Then he eased up on the crippling grip he had on his arm and hoisted Jules up.

Nobody moved.

Nobody spoke.

The boys stood ready to have at the stranger. They were just waiting for Diego's slightest command. But they kept their hands close to their sides. Even from where I sat, I could see the tense lines of their faces and the clenched balls of their fists.

The shift in the circle had increased my visibility. I could see him now. And the man I saw looked every bit as badass as the ones who were facing him. He was tall enough to meet Jules's murderous stare head-on. He had on an olive-green T-shirt and a pair of camouflage-type cargo pants. At first glance, he looked bald. But in the sometimes light of the drifting moon, I caught a glimpse of cropped white-blond hair. Mumbled strains of conversation traveled toward us. Glory and I held our breath as the stranger turned to Diego as if asking permission for something.

Apparently permission had been granted. Because, in a slow and precise move, the stranger clutched at his neck and reached inside his shirt to release what must have been some sort of chain.

Moonlight flashed off a pair of thin metal dog tags.

The stranger moved back slowly then, away from the circle of brothers, and raised his arms to shoulder level. Then in the universal gesture of surrender, he made his hands clearly visible in midair. His eyes locked on Jules's face, and he was speaking directly to him.

I rolled down the window all the way so I could hear.

"I don't know who the fuck you are, man. But I know what you're thinking. And before you go for your piece or you have one of your brothers go for theirs, put yourself in my goddamn place. I don't know what business you have with me, but while that USMC tattoo on your arm tells me you're my brother, your actions tell me a whole different story."

He paused and looked around at the rest of the boys.

"I didn't survive three tours to be shanghaied in my own country with a gun to the back of my skull. Now you want to tell me who you motherfuckers are?"

That single gesture of surrender, coupled with the honestly

delivered words, cut the tension by half. The boys were no longer standing ramrod straight with itchy fingers at their hips and murder in their eyes. Still wary, their postures got more relaxed. The Saints now looked at the stranger with something more like curiosity and less like intent to kill.

Thank God.

After that initial flash of lightning, Glory pretty much had to depend on me to tell her what was going on. Because of the tree angle, she couldn't see through the passenger side. Evidently the blow-by-blow I was giving her was not quite up to par, because suddenly she squeezed herself between me and the steering wheel. Then she shoved her head sideways out the window.

"Roll it down all the way," she whispered. "My head is going to get stuck."

"You're leaning on my arms," I hissed back. "I can't move. And it's moved as far down as it goes."

Just then another strike of lightning split the sky, and its bright white light fully illuminated the scene before us. The faces of all the players were spotlighted in that quick flash.

Glory gasped loudly beside me.

"Oh, my God," she cried out. She extricated herself from the small space, slid over to the passenger side and opened the door. "Oh, my God. Oh, my God. Oh, my God."

I watched through the windshield as my roommate ran straight toward the mayhem.

"Glory, get back here!" I yelled to her through the open window.

"It's okay, Claire, come on." Glory turned around and motioned me forward. Then she started running again.

I looked immediately to my left and met Reno's glare from across the yard. When he saw Glory start to rush toward him, he shifted his body forward and made a jabbing pointed motion to me.

A motion that clearly said, "Stay in the van."

I immediately answered his silent command. By getting right out of the van and going after Glory.

Because really what choice did I have? I couldn't leave my friend alone to deal with the maniac inside the circle, could I?

Besides, I was curious as hell.

I was hot on Glory's heels when she shoved her way through a small opening in the circle of men.

"Jesus, Claire. Did you not just see me tell you to stay put?" Reno intercepted me and pulled me to him.

"I saw you, Reno. I did. I just didn't do it," I answered.

My man just shook his head.

I leaned in closer to him. "Who is this guy anyway?"

"No idea, Babe, but it sure looks like Glory knows." He pointed his chin beyond me. I followed his gesture.

Yep. It sure did.

CHAPTER 28

Fearlessly, my friend had taken her place right in front of the dangerous stranger. For what seemed like forever, the two of them just stared at each other.

When the big guy made his move toward Glory, I gasped and turned to Reno in alarm.

My man moved forward.

All of a sudden, Glory released a cry of such complete and utter happiness that no one could mistake that sound for anything other than what it was.

Pure joy.

Then Glory pulled Jules's would-be assassin close to her, and hugged him.

Hard.

He answered by wrapping his arms around her and lifting her clear off her feet.

Glory giggled.

I looked at Reno, who had stopped. "This is just getting more and more bizarre."

My man kept his eyes trained on Glory and his arms around me.

"Can't make this shit up, Babe." He nodded in agreement.

Who was this guy?

I snuck a look at Jules, who had murder written all over his face. The rest of the guys just looked confused.

The heavily muscled man was busy extricating himself from Glory's arms. When he put her down gently, she turned to everybody and announced, "This is my brother, Master Sergeant Hallelujah Thomas, United States Marine Corps."

Oh, my God. This was Glory's brother?

The boys weren't feeling it. Jules, still sporting a face that was somewhat puce, definitely was not feeling it.

But Glory was feeling it.

Really, really, *feeling* it.

And that was good enough for me.

"Honey, let me go," I whispered to Reno. Reno arched an eyebrow, but he released me.

I pushed through the dispersing crowd of somewhat confused Saints and walked up to Master Sergeant Hallelujah Thomas. When he looked at me, I stuck out my hand and said "Glad to meet you, Master Sergeant Thomas. I'm Glory's roommate, Claire. Welcome home."

Glory's brother took my hand and smiled. Then he blushed.

"Thank you, ma'am." Hallelujah paused to give his sister a wink. "Actually, it's captain now. And you can call me Hal."

Glory beamed proudly.

"Captain now," Glory whispered and nudged me. "Did you hear that?"

"I sure did," I replied with a smile.

A dark shadow moved closer, and I looked to see that Diego had stepped up beside me. He nodded to the ink on the young captain's pumped bicep. There was an intricate seal tattooed into his arm with an insignia that I did not recognize. The large tattoo read, *Always Faithful, Always Forward.*

Diego asked him, "You Special Ops?"

"Yes, sir," Hal answered. "MARSOC."

Then Hal nodded at Jules.

"I'm a Marine, like my brother, here."

We all turned to look at Jules. The murderous look of barely contained violence had not left his face. A small muscle jumped in visible fury against the clenched line of his jaw. His eyes were narrowed and his mouth drew a grim line. Jules's body was primed and ready for a fight.

Hal did not miss that.

I doubted that Hal missed much of anything.

Glory's brother released a small sigh. A look of what might have been disappointment passed quickly over his face. Upping the ante, Hallelujah Thomas then met Jules's glare head-on.

Glory made a small sound of distress. The two warriors looked at her. When Jules made a small move toward her, Hal reached for his sister first. Then in a deliberate and defensive movement, Captain Thomas put himself directly in front of Glory. He put himself right between her and the rest the boys.

That move was not lost on any of us.

Out of the corner of my eye, I saw Jules's expression of outrage. Reno moved quickly and placed his hand firmly down on his brother's shoulder.

Then he muttered something to Jules that I did not hear.

Jules nodded. He left Reno's hand where it was, but he moved slightly forward.

"All my brothers are now wearing leather, *motherfucker*. And that woman you just put behind your back in some bullshit protective move? A while back, my boy Reno here saved her life." Then Jules paused and looked right at Glory. "And her and me, we ain't been exactly what you would call strangers."

Glory flushed so brightly that even her ears turned pink, but Hal did not seem to notice. After hearing Jules out, he still stayed right where he was.

And, he kept his sister right where *she* was.

"Yeah, well. Thing is, *motherfucker*, the woman that you 'ain't exactly been strangers with' is my blood. And right now she is standing behind me, and not beside you. And knowing my sister the way I do, I've got to think that there's a pretty good reason for that."

Tension filled the air and another crack of lightning split the sky. Thunder rolled and large raindrops splashed crimson in the eerie illumination of the garden lights.

All eyes were on Glory now. The color of my friend's face had deepened to the bright red of a newly burst watermelon. She was flushed everywhere and her eyes were wide.

Glory's joy at her brother's homecoming had quickly turned into something else entirely.

Reno stepped up.

"Claire, take Glory into the house."

"Good fucking idea," Jules chimed in.

Hal nodded.

I walked toward Glory, who quickly took my hand, and we headed toward the house together.

When we got to the heavy wooden steps, we paused to look back.

It seemed like Jules and Hal were not quite done with each other yet.

We watched as the young captain pulled out a fat blunt and wet the tip of it with his mouth. He lit up and took a deep pull on the cigar.

Then with all the calm of a brewing storm, he looked at Jules.

"I can see by those leathers that your *brothers* are wearing, you don't exactly run with choir boys. I also get that your boys got family in that house. It was never my intention to frighten your women. But I understand how me looking through those windows in the middle of the night brought that on. For that I apologize. I really should have fucking known better. I'm here to see my little sister and get to the bottom of exactly who put her through the hell I know that she's been through. So before I go in there and stir that shit up for her, I'm going to ask you nice. Who the fuck are you and what makes you think you got any claim on my sister?"

CHAPTER 29

Jules and Prosper sat at the table in Prosper's office. A week after the incident at the lake house, Prosper had returned from business down in South County. Diego had filled him in on what had happened, and now Jules was giving him his own version. In a few minutes, Hal would be knocking at the door. There were some decisions to be made, and before he made them, Prosper wanted to meet the marine.

"He put a fucking boot to my throat. You were me, you'd let that slide?" Jules sat forward with his elbows on the scarred wood. He looked at his president with fury in his eyes.

"Yeah, after you cocked a nine to the back of his head. What the fuck did you think he was gonna do?" Prosper leaned back in his chair and regarded his sergeant at arms.

Jules was seriously pissed.

And Prosper knew it took a lot for Jules to get pissed.

Come to think of it, Prosper thought to himself, it took a whole boatload of shit for Jules to show much of any emotion at all.

Jules and goddamn Crow. Right there you had two stoic sons of bitches. Not like him. If he didn't smash a chair to bits at least once a week, his wife stuck a goddamn thermometer in his mouth.

"Pinky called and said someone was sneaking around the house, looking in windows and shit. What the fuck was I supposed to think? Why didn't the asshole just ring the doorbell like anybody else?"

Really? This again?

"'Cause it was one o'clock in the morning. Stupid fucker thought that it would be better to see if someone was up. He explained all that shit."

"Yeah. Explained, my ass," Jules muttered underneath his breath.

"Look," Prosper growled. "If you want to put a decorated Special Forces Marine to ground because he bested you, that's your own damn business. But you keep the brothers out of it. This is your deal and you do it alone, without the backing of this club and without my goddamn blessings. The last thing we need is the military crawling up our asses looking for their officer."

"He didn't fucking best me," Jules spat.

"Yeah, he did, Brother. The motherfucker held you with his boot at your throat and your wrist close to breaking. And that's what got you pissed off more than anything. Jules, I don't blame you. If it was me, I'd want to kill the sonofabitch too. But there's more to it than that, and you fucking know it. He didn't know what he was going to run into out there. So really, he showed remarkable restraint by not crushing your larynx from the get-go. And as for him, a man doesn't usually get a chance to hear that click at the back of his head twice. You were both goddamn lucky. You didn't blow his head off and he didn't sever your windpipe. Seems like a draw to me. Now man the fuck up and get past it."

Prosper was right and deep down inside Jules knew it. It didn't make it go down any easier though.

Prosper lit a smoke and tried to pretend indifference. Man being held to the ground in front of his brothers goes down about as smooth as swallowing broken glass. Hard to take for any of them. But for a tough brother like Jules, Prosper knew it must have killed him. This shit had to be handled with diplomacy, but shit also had to be said.

Prosper sighed. "Look, Brother, put yourself in his place. First thing he finds out after being gone on some long damn mission is that his sister's been in some kind of trouble. He comes out here to see for himself what the deal is, and finds out that her last known address is a house in the middle of goddamn nowhere. *In the middle of goddamn nowhere.* For all he knew, someone had her chained up in the basement. He decides to scope that shit out before making a move and finds himself with one gun pushed to the back of his skull and another five cocked and pointed at him. You really want to put your woman's brother to ground over a fucking mistake? Jesus, you are the one voice of reason in this whole goddamn club. What the fuck is wrong with you lately?"

"She ain't my woman." Jules looked down at his hands.

So that is what this is about, Prosper thought to himself.

Prosper pushed his chair back and got up to swing the door open.

"Wife, we need some damn coffee in here!" Prosper knew that his woman would take one look at the brother's face and know exactly what to do about it.

Lovesick jerk-offs were not his thing.

In a matter of minutes Pinky appeared with a fresh pot and a plate of those cookies she was always baking. Seeing the look in Jules's eyes, she shot her husband a warning glance before she put the tray down in front of them.

"Yeah, well, you got time to fix that shit." Prosper didn't know what else to say.

"Don't know how to fix it." Jules leaned in to grab a cup of coffee.

"Fix what?" Pinky asked.

Jules put a fifth spoonful of sugar into his coffee.

"Is this about Glory?" Pinky prodded Jules gently.

Prosper sat back and lit up his smoke. Pinky was a genius at this stuff. Jules shifted uncomfortably.

"Yeah, it's about Glory." Jules looked miserable. "Gave her shit about working for Gianni's crew. I don't fucking like it."

"What about it exactly don't you like, sweetheart?" Pinky asked. She poured herself a cup of coffee, seated herself next to him, and adopted a casual tone. "It appears to me that they treat her right and pay her well. You know, I've been on a couple of those jobs myself and I don't see anything wrong there." Pinky looked at her husband for help.

"Seems if I'm okay with that shit, you should be too, Brother," Prosper said gruffly.

Jules was quiet for a while. "Not just that, Boss."

"Then what the fuck is it?" Prosper did not have the time for this bullshit.

Pinky shot him another warning look.

"I'm going to go take a leak." Prosper got up.

"Jules, what is it?" Pinky really wanted to help.

Jules shrugged his shoulders, and sat silently. Then he lit up a smoke.

Pinky watched him carefully. "You know, Jules, when you met Glory, she was in a bad way. I know you don't want her to stay all scared and lost like that for the rest of her life. It's good that she found this, and her finding this doesn't mean that you have to lose her. But, if you keep messing things up and fooling around like you have been, then you will lose her. You will lose that sweet, pretty, little thing for good." Pinky put her hand over his.

Jules grunted.

"Just think about it, sweetheart." Pinky reached over and gave him a kiss on the cheek. Jules stood up and wrapped his arms around her.

Prosper watched from the door, once again totally amazed at his woman. "Get your goddamn hands off my wife," he yelled.

"She's too fucking good for you and you know it, Boss." Jules let Pinky go with a kiss on the cheek.

"Yeah, been knowing that shit for years," Prosper growled. "Now are you going to get your ass in here and watch the game or what?"

Jules downed the rest of the hot coffee, snatched half a dozen cookies off the plate and headed to the door.

"I'm taking a two-point spread!" Jules said. Then he stopped and grabbed a beer on the way to the living room.

"Fuck that you are," Prosper replied and grabbed a beer of his own. But before he hit the media room, he also stopped to grab his woman's ass.

~

Hal hit the door twice in rapid succession, then stopped. The woman he assumed was Prosper's wife answered.

"Sorry to bother you, ma'am. Your husband is expecting me," he said.

The blond woman smiled slightly and nodded. Then she moved away from the door to let him in. Hal had noticed the security cameras that were placed all along the perimeter of the property. They had seen him coming.

Hal's military training steered him even here—his eyes took in everything. The house was big, but built shotgun style with one long hallway down the middle and two easily accessed exits. Hal guessed that in a house this size there was a labyrinth of small corridors off the main hall as well. The house itself was set high, with its back abutting a stone ledge. The windows were long and narrow and while they let in a lot of natural light, they were set close to the roof and did not allow easy access to the outside. To the untrained eye, the house was an architectural dream of unique use of space and light. To someone who knew what to look for, it was a fortress.

Hal was not surprised when he was led into a back office. He was also not surprised to see that Jules was there with Prosper. He had hoped that he would be.

Prosper nodded to the seat next to him.

Hal took that seat with a silent greeting to both. He was not fooled at all by Jules's outward appearance of detachment.

Fucker had it down.

Hal was known to pull it out himself when he needed to. Every Marine mastered that stare before he even left boot camp. That focused blank one. The one that glared at each hopeful recruit from every damn enlistment poster. It was a look that was intended to represent years of time-honored tradition, and to scare the piss out of the enemy. Marines were taught to hold that focus no matter what. If a bee flew up their ass, or a snake slithered down their god-damn boot, their orders were to remain steady.

Yeah, Jules had it down.

And Hal threw it right back at him.

Prosper was the first to break the silence.

"If you boys are done with your pissing contest, I'd like to get this shit over with."

Hal turned his attention to Prosper. "You and me and your boy here, we got some unfinished business," Hal began.

"Ain't nobody's fucking boy," Jules snarled.

Hal sighed deeply then, and raised both of his hands in surrender.

"No disrespect intended. Never been good with words. You ask me whatever you want. And I got a few things to say. We talk this through until it's all good, then I'll be on my way." Hal's intent was to get this over with as soon as possible. Explaining himself to these two guys wasn't exactly how he wanted to spend his day. He got right to the point and spoke directly to Prosper. "Your VP and me had a talk about the shit that went down at the house. He said I'd have to see you, but as far as he went, we're good." Hal paused long enough to show Prosper the respect he knew was expected. "What do you say?"

Prosper took a minute.

Then he nodded. "Yeah, Diego filled me in, it sounds like a big-ass mix-up to me. And while I'm pretty sure that with a little god-damn forethought on your part, the whole thing could have been avoided, I'm down with D's assessment."

Jules snorted.

Prosper ignored him and continued. "But there is something that still don't add up to my way of thinking."

"Yeah, and what would that be?" Hal tensed. He wasn't used to his actions being questioned.

"It's obvious that you care a lot about Glory," Prosper said.

"Your point?" Hal's eyes grew hard. Hearing his sister's name roll so easily off the tongues of these guys didn't sit well.

"His point, motherfucker," Jules interrupted, "is that your sister's been through a boatload of shit. The kind of shit that could have gotten her dead. How the hell did that escape your attention for all this time?"

Hal scrubbed his hand on the back of his neck. It was a fair question and something he had asked himself about a lot. "Listen, I'm not denying that I fucked up six ways to Sunday. But it was a long time ago, and Glory didn't say anything, never said a word. And since it's just me and her, there was no one else to drop a dime on it either. I didn't know anything about what went down with Glory and Abbiati until just recently. Nothing would have kept me from coming home if I had known what kind of trouble she was in. I came back as soon as I found out. That shit in Vegas, man. I'm going to kill somebody for that."

"What shit in Vegas?" Jules said.

"You don't know?" Hal shot back, surprised

"What the fuck don't I know?" Jules countered.

Hal shook his head. He would not break his sister's confidence. "You're going to have to ask Glory about that. But for now, just know that I am taking care of it."

Jules scowled, but remained silent.

Hal turned to Prosper and forced his tone to remain even.

"I came here to ask you, that guy? That fucking Gino? Glory told me that the matter's been dealt with, but I want to hear it from you."

"The matter has been dealt with," Prosper said.

Hal took a minute to think about what that probably meant in the MC world and decided that he was good with it.

"Any chance of that coming back and landing at my sister's door?" he asked a final time.

Jules answered that for him. "No fucking chance."

Hal looked from Jules to Prosper and back again. While Hal still wasn't exactly sure what he was dealing with here, he knew that these men would be good for their word. And they seemed to care about his sister. For now, that was enough for him.

"I owe you. You and your crew."

"I'll keep that in mind," Prosper nodded.

"We good?" Hal asked.

Prosper nodded again. Hal turned his attention to Jules and nodded once.

Jules scraped back his chair and stood up. Hal did the same.

"You and me? I'd like to get this shit out of the way before I leave," said Hal. And because he knew there was no way of getting around this without bruising and bloodshed, he added, "You gotta know that I cannot go back with my face looking like a fucking punching bag. So when you go for it, you go for my torso. You good with that?"

"Fucking great with that," Jules growled.

"Let's do this, then," Hal ground out.

Prosper nodded. "You boys take it outside. One more thing gets busted in this room, my woman's going to bust my head."

It took only a few moments for Hal and Jules to reach the yard. When Jules pulled his shirt over his head and Hal saw the Marine flag inked over his heart, it gave him pause. Even here in the middle of Hells Saints territory, it went against his grain to fight with someone he considered a brother. But then Hal looked at the fire in Jules's eyes and knew that he didn't see it that way. Hal knew he owed him a fair fight.

Jules had clearly been waiting days for this. He was on Hal in a flash. He rammed his fist so hard into Hal's stomach that Hal swore that he felt his spine snap. Then Hal spun around, landed his foot midchest, and sent Jules flying back against the hard ground. Jules jumped up and charged after Hal. He landed a right, then a left square into his hard-muscled stomach. That move caught Hal by surprise and knocked the wind right out of him. Hal rallied and gave Jules two swift jabs to the kidneys. Jules countered and used the exact same move on Hal that Hal had used on him that night at the lake house. The fight ended with Jules's foot on Hal's neck and his arm stretched in a painful hold.

But Jules didn't apply the pressure to Hal's neck that they both knew he could have. He didn't apply nearly the same amount of weight that Hal, fighting for his life, had forced on Jules. Hal felt Jules hesitate just long enough to make sure that point was understood, then he eased up. When Jules reached down to offer his hand, Hal took it.

The pair eyed each other warily. Each sore, each breathing heavily, each wincing in pain with every intake of breath.

"Would have done the same in your shoes." Jules looked Hal in the eye, and conceded.

Hal leaned over, then, with one hand on each knee, trying to catch his breath. Jesus, the fucker could fight. Hal had no idea how he had gotten the drop on him in the first place.

Hal looked at Jules with a newfound respect. "I appreciate that. And if it had been my own in that house and some dick was hovering around under the windows, I would have done same as you," he managed to wheeze out.

～

Prosper, who had been watching from the deck, breathed a sigh of agitated relief. Sunday was supposed to be the damn day of rest, wasn't it?

"You two done with this shit now? Because I want to get back to the game." Prosper pulled himself out of the chair he had been sitting in.

"Game's still on?" Hal croaked out. "Glory won't let me watch it at her place. Mind if I watch the last half here?"

Jesus. The guy had nuts of steel. He looked at Jules, who was busy surveying the damage done to his ribs. Despite the fact that he had gotten his own back, Prosper didn't know if his boy was quite ready to play nice.

Jules answered for him.

"Yeah, shit. Stay. Have a beer. Then, maybe later, you can show me some more of those fucking moves. Been a long time, but I don't ever remember learning that shit. That thing that you did when you got me in the kidneys? Man, that almost brought me down. I have got to know how to do that."

Hal reached out and threw Jules's T-shirt at him.

"That's my best foot jab. Motherfucker, ain't it? First time someone threw that one at me, I lost my lunch. You are one tough sonofabitch. I'll show you that and a few others . . . It's all in the ankle snap."

Holy Christ Almighty. Prosper could not believe this shit.

Pinky, who always knew the exact time to make an entrance, hit the yard with two ice packs and a couple of cold beers.

Prosper was still out on the deck when Reno and Diego showed up a couple of hours later to catch the second game. They grabbed a couple of beers and watched the two former enemies playfully duking it out in the backyard. Jules and Hal had decided to spend the hour in between games showing each other flips, crosses, sways, clinches, uppercuts, defensive moves, offensive moves, and holds that were almost impossible to break.

After about fifteen minutes of watching them go at each other hard, Diego looked at Prosper. "You gonna explain this shit?"

"Would if I could, Brother." Prosper took a long pull on his beer and chuckled. Then he added, "Got to agree that is some weird fucking turn of events right there."

Reno nodded beside him and the three men lit up a smoke and watched on as Hal and Jules laid into each other.

"Game's gonna start in ten minutes!" Pinky called from the door.

"You hear that? Time to quit this shit, come on in and lay your money down," Prosper threw down his cigarette and called to Jules and Hal who were still in the yard.

Jules reached down and pulled Hal up off the ground. "I got a hundred says the Ravens take it."

"You're on. I'll take that, but I'm gonna need a two-point spread." Hal pulled his shirt gingerly over his head with a grimace.

Prosper just shook his head and went into the house smiling.

~

Hal had spent most of his leave time with his sister. He had tried his best to put together the pieces of what had happened. Hal had made some mistakes in his life and had done some stupid things, but he never would have agreed to a deal where his sister danced buck naked in front of strangers to bail him out. It hurt him deeply that his sister had thought he would have sold her out like that. Some scumbag used Glory's love for him and turned that around to demean her and profit. It took all Hal had in him not to hop on a plane and get some immediate justice for her.

But he also needed some time with her to figure out where her head was at after all she had been through. And to see if she really was as okay as she seemed to be. And this wasn't only about her. The last mission Hal had been on had been a tough one, worse than most. He had done things, seen things, ordered things to be done, that were the stuff of nightmares. He needed this time alone with the comfort of his sister and the serenity of the cool lake as much as he thought that his sister might need the time with him.

The two of them took some long walks and spent a lot of lazy days on the dock talking it all out. Hal had also spent a good amount of time checking out Jules and the rest of the Hells Saints. Most of them had done some hard time, the way they made their money was more than a little questionable, and their network of connections was as widespread and impressive as his own. But there was absolutely no record of any kind of child neglect or abuse from even one member of the club. And even though Hal didn't really get the whole free-thinking kind of thing the club had going on with their women, he really didn't see that as any of his business. No one seemed to be around the club that didn't want to be there. As long as Glory was safe and happy, he didn't give a shit about that. Besides, Hal had met Raine and Claire, and liked them.

As far as his sister and the club went, Hal owed them. Big time. He had no doubt that they would cash in that marker at some point. And that was fine with him. Anything that ended up with his sister alive was fine with him.

As far as what was going on with Glory and Jules, Hal now knew enough to leave that alone.

~

Hal rose before dawn the morning that he left. He brought his cup of coffee out onto the dock one last time and he sat for a while, just thinking. He wondered if he would ever see his sister again. He hoped that he would. He really, really hoped that he would. But if things didn't go that way in his deployment, he knew that at least she was in good hands. Before he left her, he was going to slip an envelope full of cash under his sister's pillow. It was repayment for the last of the money that she had worked so hard to pay off. That money was the reason that he hadn't come home between his tours before. He had used his time off to make use of the specific set of skills that he had acquired as Special Ops. He knew he had been taking a risk with his life and career by using his knowledge to be a hired gun in the private sector, but he had been willing to take that chance. And he could not live with himself, continuing to serve the country that he loved, with the debt to his sister hanging over his head. So he had done what he had to do to make the money to pay that up. Thank God, that was all behind him now.

Well, almost. It was almost behind him.

He had one last stop and then it was over. He was going to go see Vincenzo Abiatti, the sonofabitch who had told him that between what he sent and what his sister made working, he could make it all good. He was going to see the guy who had lied to him and told him that his sister could make it good serving up drinks.

With her clothes fully on. He was going to go and see the so-called man who had made his sister strut naked before horny, fucking lowlife degenerates.

And he was going to kill him.

Then, finally, he could put the sins of his past behind him and go back to the brotherhood that he loved. He could go back to defending the country that he loved. His move to Special Operations had been the proudest moment of his life. And he planned to spend the rest of that life as a Marine.

He just had no idea how long the rest of his life would be.

CHAPTER 30

It had been a couple of weeks since that whole weird surfacing of Glory's brother. Who named their kid *Hallelujah* anyway? The same person who named their daughter Glory, he supposed.

But it was all good.

As long as Claire was with him, it was all good. Claire was in his bed now more often than not, and she hadn't done her disappearing act in a while. While he was grateful that they seemed to be making small steps forward, he knew Claire was still holding back. Sometimes he would catch her looking at him with a measure of wariness in her eyes that he understood all too well. Claire was doing what she always did when things got too good between them—she was waiting for the other shoe to drop, for the bottom to fall out of the fragile happiness. Reno wished he could reassure her. He wished that he could tell her that she had nothing to fear from loving him. But he knew that his actions would show her more than his words ever could. He was determined to make her feel safe and secure in what he felt for her.

He knew that it would not be easy. Nothing between them ever was, he reminded himself. But he also knew that what they had was worth fighting for. Fighting for Claire wouldn't be the hard part. Getting her to stick around long enough for her to see how good they were together . . . that was another story.

Yeah, he and Claire were going to have that talk soon, but for now Reno was giving her the one thing that he said he was done giving, and that was time. But he had tried it the other way and he had realized that with or without Claire, time moved the fuck on. He also realized how miserable he was without her.

Reno looked down at the soft cloud of dark hair as it lay over his shoulder. His woman's hand rested small and trusting right there on his chest and over his heart.

"Reno?" Claire stirred next to him. She was stretched out like a new little kitten, all warm and soft and still groggy from sleep. Her breath blew out on his chest. His name slid from her mouth like warmed honey and exotic spices. Waking up to Claire was better than any wet dream that Reno had ever had.

"Right here, baby," he rumbled.

"Hmmm." Claire moved against him. Reno felt the tips of her nipples graze his own and almost shot his load like a horny thirteen-year-old.

When she slid her leg up and placed it high on his thigh, he felt her open, hot and warm to him. Her knee rubbed against his balls gently.

Claire in his bed. She reminded him of one of those colorful glass tubes his father had given his mother once. Dolly had kept it high on a shelf in the living room with her special things, but some-times she would take it down and let Reno look through it. It was a long cylinder with a glass marble at the end. When the sun caught it, the light shining through the mirrors inside created bright color-ful patterns. Pretty little thing.

Reno felt Claire press close against him. He shifted his weight and buried his hands in her hair.

Claire rained soft wet little kisses on his warm belly as her tongue dipped into the perfect circle of his belly button. He held his breath as he felt her tongue trace the tattoo on his hip. The little pink piece of heaven moved slowly down and center.

Reno moved his hip slightly toward her.

"Yeah, baby," he sighed softly.

When Claire's tongue began to move its way back up his body, he let out a soft growl of frustration.

"Little coward," he whispered.

Reno felt Claire tense and warm at his words. He pulled her up toward him and wrapped his arms around her tight.

"Jesus, baby," he said, "I think that we've been together long enough for you to go there. You're sure as hell not shy about anything else we do."

Then he paused, considering. "Unless you don't like that, honey. Then that's cool."

Claire buried her face in Reno's shoulder and mumbled something.

"Say again, Babe?"

When Claire pulled away to look at Reno, he saw that her face had blushed a hot pink.

"Reno . . . I've never . . . um," she stammered.

Reno arched his eyebrow.

"Never?"

If possible Claire colored even deeper. Then shook her head.

"Never ever?" Reno teased her.

"Reno, stop it." Claire stuck her face into his neck. Mortified.

Reno moved his hand to the back of her head and felt the silken strands tickle his palm.

"Just like licking a lollipop, honey," he whispered into her hair.

"You like *that*?" Claire muffled from the safety of the curve of his neck.

"*That*?" Reno's chest was rumbling. Screw the kaleidoscope. This morning his woman was like pure Cracker Jack Surprise. And the good kind. The kind where you got the spy ring instead of the stupid little plastic pony.

"Hmmm . . . if by *that* you mean *blow jobs*, honey, then, yeah, I like 'em."

Claire squirmed and peered up at him with one eye.

"But if by *that,* you are asking if I would like you, Claire Winston, to wrap your beautiful pink lips around my dick?" Reno paused then and looked out into the distance. "Like it? Nah."

"Oh." Claire's big blue eyes were on him. Her beautiful mouth frowned slightly.

Reno pulled Claire under him quickly, stretched his full length on her and grinned wickedly, "I would goddamn love it."

Then Reno's hands moved quickly to Claire's waist, tickling her mercilessly until she screamed with laughter for him to stop. Still grinning, Reno pulled Claire in to his side. The warm feeling of contentment, which always filled him when he held her, was dangerously close to the point of flooding. He felt himself grow hard with the need for her. Claire felt that same need as she pressed against him. Her hands danced lightly against the velvet steel of his chest, the bunched muscles of his arms, and his hard, flat stomach.

Then just when he thought he couldn't take it anymore, Claire whispered softly against his ear.

"Like a lollipop?"

"Yeah, baby, just like that." Just when Reno thought things could not possibly get any better, his woman lost that last tiny bit of reserve. It was obvious to Reno that Claire really had never done *that* before and the thought of him being her first made him want to stand up and cheer.

What Claire lacked in technique she made up for in the sheer desire to please him. He forced himself to lie perfectly still while his woman took her time. He moaned his encouragement as he felt her press soft little kisses along his most sensitive areas. He moved her gently, showing her what he liked, and when Reno felt Claire wrap her lips around him tight for the first time, it took all he had not to release hot and full into her mouth. Reno buried his hands in Claire's hair as she fed on him. Her soft pink mouth opened over him and slowly, softly, devoured him. He murmured words of encouragement as he felt her smooth, moist tongue run up and down the length of him. He held his breath until she got to his base. Reno groaned when she sucked gently on the soft sack, cupping him. He felt her long hair brush teasingly against his thickly muscled thighs. Then she was moving back up, her mouth leaving tiny wet kisses until it reached the tip of his cock, where she took him greedily and completely into her warm, wet mouth. Reno arched his back and moaned loudly. Over and over again, he felt Claire tenderly move her mouth over him. When he felt her tongue circle his rim, he became undone. Reno couldn't take any more. With one quick motion he twisted Claire until he was on top of her.

"Now, honey. Please, I want to feel you inside of me. Take me hard, baby," she whispered to him. Claire wrapped her legs around her man and pulled him closer. She was hot and wet and achingly empty.

Reno gave it to her. Hard.

His hands slid up and down her thighs and pulled her even closer. Then he grabbed her tight, round ass in his hands and ground into her. Shifting his hips, he lay balls deep in her soft, silky wetness.

"Damn, Claire, you're so wet, baby." Reno felt her pulse hard at his words.

He groaned and pushed himself deeper and deeper until he felt his dick hit her cervix. Claire reached up and grasped the headboard behind her until she started to build again. Reno felt it and in one long pulsing thrust he spilt hot inside of her.

When he moved to pull out of her, Claire wrapped her arms around him.

"Not yet," she whispered against his chest.

Reno shifted them so his weight would not crush her but he stayed inside of her. Then minutes later, he gently pulled away. Claire snuggled close to him.

"Damn, baby. What the hell was that?" Reno said to her once his heart stopped racing.

Claire just smiled.

CHAPTER 31

When I heard Reno on the phone with his mother, I blushed guiltily. He was going to be late and it was all my fault. After that marathon lovemaking session, Reno and I decided we both needed to shower.

So we took one together.

We took turns gliding the hot, soapy water over each other, and when I felt Reno slip that warm, wet washcloth between the folds of the most intimate part of me, that crazy need for him began to build again.

He took me once more under the hot pulsing spray of the shower.

It was going to be a great day. The best day. It was going to be an absolutely fantastic, totally awesome, wonderful day.

Almost as soon as that thought crossed my mind, I felt a cold breeze blow in through the open window. I leaned out to breathe in the cool fresh air. The sky was storybook blue and filled with white fluffy clouds. Suddenly the wind picked up and I watched as a lone, dark storm cloud appeared. For a fleeting moment the room was cast in shadow and the sudden change of temperature sent a shiver down my spine.

Then, just as quickly as it came on, the cloud disappeared, and the blazing sun broke through with its thick, warm rays. The breath I did not know that I was holding escaped from me in a long sigh.

I moved to the window again, and was relieved to see that the sky was back to the same storybook blue color. The white fluffy clouds winked at me from high in the heavens.

The air was light and breezy again.

But still, I couldn't shake that lingering feeling of darkness. The unexpected gloom that the storm cloud had brought threatened to rob the day of some of its promise. I told myself I was being silly and determinedly shook it off. I had a busy day full of classes ahead of me and I needed to keep my head in the game.

Today Reno had made plans to drop me off at school a little early because he was going to spend the day with his mother. We made arrangements for him to pick me up at the corner café later on. I thought I would treat myself to a sandwich while I waited, and I had plenty of schoolwork to keep myself busy.

Today was a special day for the McCabe family. Today was Reno's father's birthday.

At Dolly's insistence, once a year, Reno put aside that day to spend with his mother. It was the only real demand that Dolly had ever placed on her son.

In what may seem like a macabre tradition to some, but made perfect sense to me, Dolly and Reno spent the day graveside.

Along with the pots of lush green shamrocks and containers full of bright red geraniums that she would bring along to plant, Dolly also included a lunch of Petey's favorite foods. Reno told me that Dolly traditionally packed a picnic basket full of thick corned beef sandwiches, bowls of tangy beet salad, slices of salted, crisp pickles, and squares of rich chocolate brownies. Today, dark brown bottles of Guinness Stout would be raised in Petey McCabe's honor. Dolly and her son would spend a couple of hours together in the shadow of a large Celtic cross headstone. They would eat, plant, reminisce, raise a glass, and pay homage to the man that they both had loved.

Reno told me that his mother always did her best to make it a special day for the two of them. Because of that and a lot of other reasons, it was a day that, despite the circumstances, the two of them enjoyed. I knew that Dolly had had a lifetime of turning the bad into something good, and this day was no exception.

Good for her.

I had some small memories of Dolly from the time that Raine and I had spent that summer at the lake house in our childhood. Petey had still been alive then, but I don't recall ever meeting him, I had been so very young. Mostly my recollections from those days consisted of vague impressions of comfort, like warm soapy bubble baths, big soft beds, delicious homemade cookies, and a general feeling of well-being.

Along with those vague memories came a feeling of immense gratitude. I knew that even when she didn't have to be, Dolly had always been kind to Raine and me.

As I finished getting ready for the day ahead, I thought some more about Dolly.

She was a complicated woman. Although she spent most of her time surrounded by rough outlaw men, she had a natural refinement that always seemed to shine right through. She was tall and trim and moved with the poise of a ballet dancer.

Mrs. McCabe had the natural elegance of Grace Kelly.

But she had the soul of Grace Slick.

It was a well-known fact that Dolly could party with the best of them. She could drink most of the boys under the table, cook up a mean barbecue, hustle a pool game, and no one could beat her at cards. The small Rolling Stones tattoo that could sometimes be seen sitting jauntily on her left breast, and the small diamond stud on the side of her perfectly formed nose made her, in my eyes, the epitome of biker chic.

The years had faded Dolly's fiery, auburn hair to a softer shade. And although her thick curls mostly hid the smattering of gray, she had confided in me that she'd begun to put a colored rinse in her hair to cover those "pesky things." She needed reading glasses now to see the fine print. I knew from the sheen of sweat that sometimes came on her unexpectedly that she had some trouble with hot flashes, or "power surges" as she liked to call them.

And then there were those wrinkles.

From the corner of each of Dolly's eyes lay a fine network of tiny deep creases. They radiated out like sunbeams, an array of fine lines and crinkles that she made absolutely no effort to hide. Once, on one of our many shopping trips together, we had stopped at the cosmetic counter to try some fragrances. A well-meaning cosmetic clinician had approached Dolly and suggested a foundation to get rid of those fine lines of age. Dolly politely told the clerk that she was all set. That those wrinkles had nothing to do with age, and that she was happy to keep them just where they were, thank you very much.

On the way home she told me the heartbreaking and beautiful story of those tiny lines.

Dolly told me that the first one appeared almost like voodoo magic the morning after Petey had been killed. She said that after that, one by one, they slowly appeared like fault lines in her skin. In no time at all, a small network of wrinkles had fanned out like shattered glass from the corner of each of her eyes. For a while, it had seemed like every day there would be a tiny new line or crinkle. Finally about a year after Petey died, Dolly noticed that one day they had stopped just as suddenly as they had begun. Over the years, the lines had stayed exactly as they had appeared in that time of extreme grief. None of them went away and no new ones emerged.

Dolly told me that a few years back she had read a magazine article that referred to those fine lines as "laugh lines." She said that those words had horrified her so much that she hadn't been able to sleep for days after that.

Because Dolly knew that those lines had nothing to do with happiness. They were trails of grief.

Dolly knew that the pain of losing her young husband had been so complete and so deep that her poor heart had been unable to contain all that sadness. The hurt had risen upward, leaving in its wake fine scars of unimaginable sorrow.

Dolly told me that eventually she had learned to laugh again. But not to love again.

With time, Dolly told me, she had gotten used to living without him.

With enough time, she said, she supposed you could get used to just about anything.

CHAPTER 32

"Are you ready, Babe?" Reno's voice took me out of my musings. I took a quick look at the clock and hurriedly grabbed my school bag. Today was my psych seminar. The class I hated more than death itself, it was so boring. But I was already on the teacher's bad side, and arriving late with the rumble of pipes thundering through the ivy-covered brick passageways of the campus would not help matters.

As always, Reno got me to class on time. But I was almost late anyway, because today I just had not wanted to let him go. Usually I was okay with being in class while he roared off, but today the only place I wanted to be was where he was.

Well, that might not be quite true. The truth was that the only place I wanted to be was some place other than my psych seminar. Especially on a sunny Monday. The dentist's chair, cleaning out the bathroom at Reds, the gynecologist's office . . . anything would be preferable. Reno knew exactly how I felt about this course, so he had not been flattered or fooled by my transparent attempt to delay his leaving. After giving me a quick kiss and a shove in the right direction, he roared off without looking back.

I sighed and headed toward the lecture hall.

About fifteen minutes into class, I had to fight to stay awake. The stage lights were dimmed and a PowerPoint presentation flashed endlessly across the screen. Dr. Charto droned on and on.

And on.

As I looked around at the sea of students, I noted the bleary-eyed faces of my classmates. Their expressions of apathy and boredom validated my own. In the darkened auditorium, a vast array of laptops, tablets, and phones were secretly opened. Their screens provided a needed respite from the endless tedium of the class.

Basic public speaking rule number one. Never read a Power-Point presentation word for word.

Evidently, Dr. Sylvia Charto had not gotten that memo.

How this woman had ever become an educator was beyond me.

The woman bored me to tears, and judging from the activities of the students around me, I knew that I was not the only one who felt that way. More than anything, I was disappointed. When I had first enrolled in college, I had been really excited about all my classes, but the psych courses were something that I had particularly looked forward to.

Except for this one.

This one I hated.

More to the point, I hated the professor.

Psych 101/02 was a general education requirement and came with a three-hour weekly seminar. It was a prerequisite for lots of other higher level courses. There was no escaping it. Just about every student at the college had to pass through the doors to that lecture hall sooner or later. This thorn in my side ran for two semesters. Unfortunately the same professor taught both classes. Even after Julian's help with that first research paper and the study groups I attended on a regular basis, my grades never reflected the hard work I put in. At first, I had tried to force interest by being an enthusiastic contributor to the class. But my comments and overall participation had been met with such complete disdain that I had begun to take it personally. Honestly, the hostility that emanated from this woman seemed to come at me in waves. And it was not just that way in the lecture hall. Every paper that I handed in to her was marked up through and through. Red pen lines slashed through my hard work like bleeding sword wounds. If I hadn't been doing so well in my other classes, it wouldn't have been so glaringly apparent.

I resolved to get to the bottom of things.

When she did not respond to the third email I sent requesting a scheduled meeting, I had waited with a few other students outside her door during office hours. I watched while people who came after me went in and came out, and still she kept me waiting. Then, when she finally opened that door and called me in, she gave me ten minutes to everyone else's twenty. During that time she didn't answer any of my questions. However, she did suggest that I might be more comfortable at a two-year community college where "the expectations weren't so high."

I left that meeting with my head up, but I cried buckets onto Reno's back all the way home. Finally he had to pull over. When he asked me what was wrong, I was too ashamed to tell him what the professor had said to me. I just told him that I felt overwhelmed. Reno didn't buy it. He had seen all the hard work I had put into the class, and he had seen the caustic remarks Professor Wonderful had written on my papers.

He hadn't liked it. Or her. And it was with great reluctance that my man stepped back to let me handle the situation in my own way and in my own time.

"Just remember, Babe," Reno said to me. "Trash is trash. And this bitch is small-minded gutter trash. A few letters after this teacher's name don't change that. You ever get tired of working around that on your own, you let me know." Then my man added this, "But if you ever come out again with tears on that pretty face of yours after meeting with that piece of shit, I'm going in."

Reno stayed up half that night with me and quizzed me on the flashcards that I had so painstakingly prepared. The multiple choice tests were scored by a Scantron so there was no bias involved, and so far I was kicking ass on those exams. I thought that maybe if I did well enough, she would see me as something other than the "less than" that she evidently thought I was. I tried my hardest, but that just seemed to piss her off more. I found the whole thing shocking, because I thought that a professor who had over one hundred students per class should be a little too busy to hate on hardworking me. But then again, maybe I wasn't the only one who was getting this kind of treatment.

Evidently, the good professor did not approve of the company I kept. I had run into this kind of narrow-mindedness before when I was out with Reno. I knew that Raine and Glory had had it happen to them as well. It came with the territory. But I had never expected to find that kind of prejudice here, in a place of knowledge and learning. And I certainly never expected it to come from a professor. Someone who, in my mind, should be far too wise and enlightened to harbor an apparent hatred based on a stereotype.

But Dr. Charto made no secret of her disdain. When she first saw me with Reno, she gave us a look of such contempt that I felt it like a slap across my face. Reno saw it too, and had raised an eyebrow at her. To his credit though, he did not say a thing. I knew that he had kept quiet for my sake and I was grateful for it.

As it so happened, her office sat adjacent to the campus parking lot. More often than not, Sylvia Charto would be exiting her building just as Reno and I rode into the campus. The psych seminar was the first class of my day. This meant that oftentimes the three of us would be making our way across campus at the same time. Reno always walked with me to my first class before he headed off for the day.

The whole thing was very strange. At first Dr. Charto seemed content to walk behind us, but then she would increase her steps at intermittent times. This caused the three of us to arrive at the door to the building at the same time. When I entered first, I always politely held the door a fraction longer than I needed to, just to make sure it did not slam in front of her.

When she arrived at the door first, she would let that door slam right behind her.

Oh, yes she did.

And not just with a casual "oh, sorry" whoosh. Professor Charto would swing the door open wide enough to make sure that it shut right in my face. The first time it happened, I was so shocked that I just stood there for a second. Then I decided to give old Sylvie the benefit of the doubt, so I opened the door and went on toward class.

The next time she did it, I had figured it was no accident. While I was figuring, I had felt Reno's arm slide past me and slam the door open so wide that it caught the heel of the professor's sensible shoes and sent her stumbling toward the floor. She'd regained her balance, just short of sprawling onto the tiles. She righted herself and shot a scathing look at Reno.

"Well, I should not be surprised. You are evidently just as rude and ill-bred as you appear to be," Dr. Charto spat at us.

I gasped.

Reno had taken a step and stood between the professor and me. Then he said, "Really, bitch? You need a PhD to come up with bullshit as meaningless as that? I don't give two fucks what you think of me, but that's the last time you are going to disrespect my woman."

Professor Charto blustered and hissed like a fat little alley cat.

"Don't you dare speak to me in that manner. Do you know who I am?"

Really? She went with that?

Reno had leaned in so close to her that his nose almost touched hers. Her breath steamed his dark aviators.

"Yeah, I do. I know exactly who you are, Sylvie. Last name, Charto. Husband, Albert. 546 Commonwealth, Apartment C. Hundred-year-old Volvo in your driveway, tags 678VYC. I get that right?"

Sylvie had taken a step back, way, way back

Reno moved in again.

"Yeah, I got that right. Bitch, I know exactly who you are. And if you ever, *ever* slam a door into Claire's face again or take this conversation into that classroom of yours, you are going to get to know who *I* fucking am."

The professor had stumbled off, pale and shaken. I'd turned to Reno, my mouth opening and closing like a fish gulping for air.

Reno had kept his eyes on the professor until he saw her turn the corner into the hallway. Then he kissed me on the top of my head, spun me around, and said, "Get to class, Babe. You're going to be late."

Yeah, it was pretty safe to say that good old Sylvie and I had pretty much stayed out of each other's way since the door incident. I looked at my watch for what was probably the fifth time in half an hour. Reno should have picked up Dolly by now. I hoped that he was in for a more interesting day than I was.

I dug into my bag, pulled out an apple, took a bite, then flipped open my laptop and tried to follow along with the lecture.

It was going to be a long morning.

CHAPTER 33

It took about a half hour for Reno and his mom to drive to the cemetery. Reno routinely scanned the perimeter of his father's final resting place before he allowed his mother out of the Escalade. His father had been buried in a family plot that lay just outside Saints territory. Because Petey had not been a club member, and at the time Reno had still been a young boy, the territory boundaries had not been an issue. Eventually the area had been absorbed by Los Diablos Rojos. The president of the MC was Lucius Rieldo. Because the territories bordered each other, Prosper and Lucius had had a choice to make.

They chose peace.

Eventually that peace moved the two clubs to an uneasy alliance. Except for a few setbacks, the alliance had remained strong.

The first setback had come when Manny Rieldo, Lucius's nephew, kidnapped Claire and Raine.

The second setback came when Manny was made to pay for that stupid move.

The abduction of Prosper's daughters and the subsequent death of Lucius's nephew had been the cause of a major meet with the heads of the East Coast gangs. After much debate, his killing had been seen as a necessary and justified act.

Everyone had decided to play nice, and because of that, some pretty profitable deals had been made between the various criminal entities.

Everyone liked that payout.

Everyone had been on their best behavior.

All of them.

All of the *boys* had been quiet.

But all the local chapters had remained on alert, waiting to see what the fallout was going to be from Manny's mother. Since Manny's death, there had been rumblings about family disagreements. Manny had been Luisa Sievas's son.

Reno knew all about Luisa Sievas.

When that whole thing went down with Manny, the brothers did their homework. They wanted to be absolutely sure that if any blowback hit, they would know who they were dealing with.

Prosper had his associates do some checking into the whole Sievas family. It was important to know just how deep those family ties went with Lucius. Turns out those family roots had rotted years ago, and Lucius was fine with however Prosper had wanted to handle things.

That was a start.

But Reno had also done some digging on his own.

And it was a good thing he had. Because if the shit ever did hit the fan, Reno knew that Manny's mother could be a serious problem.

A very serious problem.

~

Yeah, Reno had a big ol' file on Manny's mama.

Like so many others, Lucius and his sister, Luisa, had emigrated from Mexico to the United States as children. Apparently, they had spent their childhood in the Liberty City section of northwest Miami. That information was telling in itself. Reno and the brothers had made a run through Miami a couple of years ago, and they had learned all about Liberty City. The hard way.

Reno could not even imagine growing up on those mean streets. It was not exactly what you would call a kid-friendly environment.

To make matters worse, Lucius and Luisa had grown up on 15th Avenue, also known as the Street of Death. Luisa had been the oldest of five children. When she was fifteen, her mother had died of hepatitis C, the kind brought on by shared dirty needle usage. Luisa and her brothers moved in with an aunt who had three kids of her own. Apparently, Tia Rosalie had a serious blow problem and a predisposition to being in the wrong place at the wrong time. Almost a year to the day after Luisa and her brothers moved in with her, the aunt died in a drive-by shooting.

By then, Luisa had become involved with a member of the John Doe gang. Prince Charming moved his woman and her four brothers into a five-room apartment, and in the next eight years gave her four sons.

In a clean sweep that ended the reign of the notorious gang, Luisa's baby-daddy was sent away. A couple of weeks after that, she threw her brothers out on the street saying she couldn't feed them anymore. Over the next couple of years, she spent a whole lot of time in and out of psychiatric units. Luisa's sons spent most of their childhood in foster care and, later on, in juvenile detention centers. Luisa survived by dealing, whoring, and working the system. It was rumored that for a while, she had been a mule for a small cartel. Eventually, she had proven herself to be too crazy even for the Colombians and was cut loose.

Over the years, she had somehow managed to form her own business partnerships and now ran a small, but serious, drug business.

In short, Luisa Sievas was one dangerous, psychotic lunatic. The file that Reno had on her was as thick as a shithouse brick. No doubt about it, she was the force behind some pretty heinous crimes. Over the years, her name had been linked with every offense imaginable. One of the worst was the shooting of a child.

Reportedly, Sievas had gone after a former associate because he had made some unflattering remarks about her family values. She sent her crew out to hit him while he drove home from his son's Little League game. The two idiots missed the father, but shot the son. They put two bullets in the side of the seven-year-old boy's skull right through his Little League cap. Word had it that when her goons reported back, she was furious that they had missed the target. But when she found out that they had hit the son instead, she was glad. She said that maybe burying his son would show the guy a thing or two about family values.

Whatever the hell that meant.

Yep, that bitch was just about as black hearted and soulless as you get. She was not someone that Reno had any intention of messing with. But if Prosper hadn't stepped up and taken the blame for Luisa Sievas's son's death, Reno would have. He didn't want that psycho killer blowing back her crazy ideas of revenge at Claire.

It would take a band of brothers to handle that kind of insanity. But so far it had been quiet.

CHAPTER 34

R eno?" Dolly stood in back of the SUV.

"Yeah, Ma?" Reno pulled back from his thoughts, but out of habit he scanned the city cemetery. The place was pretty quiet. A couple of cars sat a few roads over and there was a brown utility van parked on the road closest to them. About a half dozen or so people filled the area. Some were tending to the graves, while others paid respect to their loved ones. It was exactly what you would expect at a cemetery. Reno didn't see anything out of the ordinary.

"Will you open this for me, honey?"

Reno moved to his mother's side and unlocked the back for her. Then he leaned in and grabbed the picnic basket.

"Jesus, Ma, what do you have in here?" Reno groaned as his bicep leaped out from under his T-shirt.

Dolly looked perplexed for a moment. Then she laughed. " I brought some of the prettier rocks in from the garden. I thought that they would look nice against the shamrocks."

"And you packed them in with the food?" Reno looked at her like she had lost her mind.

"No, honey. Rocks are in the picnic basket. Food is in the duffle bag in the back." Dolly reached behind him.

Reno raised an eyebrow at her.

Dolly laughed at the expression on his face.

"Ma, picnic baskets are for food, duffle bags are for shit like sweaty gym clothes. I ain't eating corned beef that smells like dirty socks." Reno grimaced.

"Oh, relax. The food's wrapped up tighter than Fort Knox. Besides my socks don't smell and I don't sweat at the gym. I do a leisurely pace on the treadmill while reading my magazines. You know that."

Yeah, Reno had to give it to her. His mom, with her perfectly polished nails and her carefully arranged hair, had never been the *sweat at the gym* type.

"I packed the rocks in the picnic basket because it has a sturdier bottom. Now stop complaining and do what your mother tells you to do." Dolly grabbed a few of the lighter things, but left everything else for her son to carry.

Reno settled the picnic basket down near the vehicle and carried the chairs and the rest of the stuff over the perfectly trimmed lawn for his mother.

"When are we moving in?" Reno started to set up the chairs. New this year was a little portable camping table.

"Oh, hush, Reno." But she couldn't help but grin. Reno was right. Every year she added something new to their time with Petey.

"Hey, Ma? What do you say that next year we just dig Dad up and bring him on home?" Reno teased. "It would be a helluva lot less work, and you always pack up half of the house to bring over here anyway."

Dolly took a swat at her son.

Then, ignoring him, she reached out and lovingly dusted a fine layer of dirt from her husband's headstone. Reno watched as his mother muttered softly to herself, or maybe she was spouting off some bullshit to his father. It had been years, but Reno never could get used to Dolly's little graveside chats.

Reno looked around the cemetery again. He squinted his eyes and frown lines formed between his brows. He reached a hand up to rub the tight cords on the back of his neck. When he did, he felt the fine hairs on his skin rise up. Maybe all that thinking about the Sievas bitch had spooked him.

He just could not shake the feeling that something was headed his way.

And it wasn't something good.

Still seeing nothing out of the ordinary, Reno reached into his pocket, grabbed himself a smoke, lit up, drew deep, and relaxed. He thought about Claire and smiled. She would be in class by now. He was so damn proud of her. She was really kicking it with this whole college thing. Then Reno thought about the million other things that he had to do today before he went to pick up Claire, and he heaved a sigh. He didn't want to rush his mother, but he didn't have the whole day to spend either.

He finished the smoke, grabbed the watering can and went to go fill it.

As he did, some nagging instinct caused him to look around again at the quiet graveyard. The cars had left and with them had gone the graveyard visitors. The birds had even stopped singing.

What was it that he had heard Raine say when she was spooked? *Something wicked this way comes.*

When Reno's mother called out to him, he almost jumped out of his goddamn skin.

Jesus. What the fuck was wrong with him? It was midmorning on a warm Monday. In Reno's experience nothing bad ever happened on Mondays.

He tried to pay attention as his mother chatted on happily, but the uneasiness that Reno felt did not leave him. On the contrary, it actually started to grow. He looked around the cemetery again. And again Reno carefully scrutinized the landscape.

His eyes settled on the brown utility van to his immediate left. It was empty and had been there since they had arrived. Except for him and his mother, the cemetery was now deserted. The thought nagged at him.

Dolly and Reno chatted loudly and appeared to make themselves busy planting shamrocks and flowers, but actually Reno's mind was going a mile a minute. In his mind's eye, he saw each gardening tool as a potential weapon and gauged their effectiveness at close range.

Just in case.

He fought the urge to reach back into his waistband for his piece. Then he remembered that it wasn't there anyway. The brothers rarely felt the need to sport a weapon these days. No one wanted to risk a criminal charge of carrying concealed if they didn't have to. But Reno sure as hell wished he had his piece with him now. Because even though there was still no sign of a threat, the air was charged with a tension that he could not explain. He just could not shake it. He looked from the Escalade to his mother. Maybe they should just get the fuck in the car and take off. But the Escalade was several yards away and parked in a place that was totally unsheltered. If his instincts were right, that move would make the two of them open targets.

Reno needed a minute to think.

Maybe he was just being a paranoid asshole. Claire had accused him of that more than once. Not the asshole part, but the paranoid part for sure. He had to admit that he did get a little crazy when it came to her safety. But Claire was not here today and if he followed her rationale, he should be paranoia-free. Maybe the van had broken down or maybe it belonged to some homeless family who camped out in it all night. Who the fuck knew?

Reno only knew that it didn't feel right.

When Dolly murmured something to her son, Reno turned to look at her.

"Van? On the left? Is that what's got you so spooked, Reno?"

So his mother had felt it too.

Reno nodded his head once.

Then Dolly said loudly "Son, can you hand me that picnic basket? I'm just about parched."

Dolly was a quick thinker. Especially where the safety of her son was concerned. If Reno was spooked, then Dolly was spooked. Besides, she had clearly felt it too, the shift in the wind, the quieting of the bird songs, and that uneasy feeling that signaled that something was not quite right.

～

Although Dolly didn't want her son to leave the shelter of the headstone, her sixth sense told her that they might need that basket. The tightly woven container filled with rocks might be something that could be used as shield if they needed it. If it came down to it, they didn't really have anything else to defend themselves with. From behind the safety of the headstone, Dolly also took out two of the thick Guinness bottles. They could always be smashed and the jagged edge of the bottles could be used as weapons.

Damn it.

It was the one and only time Dolly wished her son was carrying. She never liked it when Reno came to visit her with that weapon stuck in his back. They had had more than a few arguments over it.

In Dolly's mind, carrying a gun was just asking for trouble. And not only from law enforcement. Live by the gun, die by the gun. As much as Dolly hated that old adage, she had lived to see it proven true time and time again.

Like many soldiers, Petey had somehow managed to bring back his service revolver from his days in Nam. He had loved that gun. He felt that it had saved his life more than a few times. Dolly's Catholic heart knew that was blasphemy. In her mind, Mother Mary had saved his ass, not a government issue. That damn gun had caused more fights in her house than anything else. But when Reno was born, that had all changed. There was absolutely no way Dolly was going to consent to having a gun in the house. Petey agreed and Dolly never saw the weapon again.

Then, one day after Petey's death, Dolly and Pinky were cleaning out his garage and found it. There it was, stored carefully away along with Petey's meager, but personally prized, possessions from his time in the military. At first, seeing the weapon had made Dolly furious, then the irony of it all had just made her sad. The gun had been locked away, but death had come for her husband anyway. Maybe the gun had saved his life in the war after all. She didn't know. Dolly only knew that it was still here and he was gone and nothing made sense to her anymore.

Dolly could not bear to get rid of the stupid thing.

But she had also determined that Reno would not have it, so after careful thought and planning she had decided what to do with the gun.

Holy Mother of God.

She had decided what to do with the gun.

Dolly pulled on her gardening gloves, grabbed the spade, and began to dig.

CHAPTER 35

Reno returned with the picnic basket to find his mother stabbing furiously at the soil. She talked nonsense about this thing or that and prompted answers from her son while she dug. Reno had no idea what she was doing. The way Reno figured it and if his instincts were right, they were probably running out of time. He had checked his cell a couple of times and found that he had no service. He couldn't reach the brothers. He was on his own.

Reno tallied up the weapons he had if it came down it. He had a couple of bottles, some rocks in a basket, and a two-dollar spade.

Great.

Reno knew that he could handle himself. He was a big guy. Tall, muscled, with lots of power behind his fists. He was smart, fast, and strong. It took a lot to take him down.

But Reno wasn't alone. He had his mom with him. And that changed everything.

Everything.

Next to him, Dolly was still on her knees digging with the intensity of a new puppy looking for his first T-bone.

What the hell was she doing?

Then he saw it.

His mother had begun to unearth what looked like a green torpedo-shaped object.

Dolly looked at Reno pointedly and said, "Reno, pick up that next geranium pot, would you? Now just take it out by the roots. Slowly. We are going to plant the pink one here and the red one over there. That variegated one should be right in the middle."

Dolly chattered away with the clatter of garden tools. Reno glanced at his mother, but she was intent on extracting the plastic cylinder from the ground. As more of the object became exposed, Reno knew what he was looking at. For some reason his mother had buried a piece of green PVC pipe.

What was she doing?

He whispered to her. "Really, Ma? A time capsule? You seriously want to take that trip down memory lane now?"

"Hush up, Reno, and let me think," Dolly whispered back.

Reno looked on in amazement as his mother's neon-pink garden gloves whisked over the object. She worked with deft hands, as she commenced to quickly rid the pipe of the dirt and night crawlers that clung to it. Then, in one quick efficient move, the gloves were off.

Reno looked on in fascinated silence while his mother tore off a piece of paper towel, placed it like a bed on the ground, and used it as a makeshift drop cloth. Carefully and methodically, she commenced to unscrew the wing nut on the end of the pipe that was fitted with an expansion plug. Reno watched on as his mother carefully removed the rubber bellows and exposed a heavily greased gasket.

"Well, will ya look at that? It worked!" Dolly whispered urgently to her son. "It's as dry as a bone. All these years and it's still as dry as the day I buried it."

Dolly blushed with pride.

And Reno still had no idea what was going on.

She carefully placed the greasy plug on the paper towel. Then she ripped off another piece of toweling and began to wipe clean the interior of the pipe. After she had cleaned off the grease at the end of the plastic tube, she tilted it up in order to release the contents onto her hand. Reno looked on as a shiny, padded, sealed envelope fell heavily into his mother's steady palm. Dolly quickly deposited it to the ground and ripped it open. Finally, she pushed the open bag over to her son.

Reno could not believe what he saw.

Could not believe it.

His mother had somehow managed to hermetically seal a firearm under a foot of dirt at his father's gravestone.

Reno let out a low chuckle.

His mother never failed to surprise him. Who else could come up with the exact thing that he needed at the exact time he needed it? Reno suddenly felt very sorry for any poor bastard that had to grow up without a mother.

But then he felt a rush of disappointment.

He whispered to her, "Ma, what about the . . . ?"

"Magazine?" she whispered back as a second smaller bag fell out and on to his hand.

Reno made a promise to himself at that very moment. He would never, ever make fun of his mother's fastidious attention to detail again.

"Ma, should I even ask?" Reno couldn't help himself.

"It's your father's," Dolly answered.

"This is Dad's gun? You buried it with him?" Reno was incredulous. And a little outraged. When his father had died, he had torn his father's shop inside out looking for that service revolver. His mother had insisted that she had no idea where it was.

He looked at the gun again and Reno immediately recognized the army issue colt 1911 .45. This was his old man's gun for sure.

"Ma, you lied to me about the gun?" he whispered. "You buried it?"

"And I'm not one bit sorry. Never wanted you to have it," she retorted.

"Humph," Reno snorted. "Well, I'm sure as glad as hell that we have it now."

Then he kissed his mother on top of her head.

"What else have you been lying to me about?" he asked, despite the seriousness of the circumstances.

"Hush, Reno. We don't have time for your sass. Will it shoot?"

"Yeah, Ma. Damn right, it'll shoot. It'll shoot just fine."

Reno examined the magazine and found that it was completely loaded. The gun held seven rounds of ammo. Seven chances to get it right. He instinctively articulated the weapon. Then he saw them. The notches for the four kill shots that his father had carved into the stock. If Reno's instincts were right, he would be adding more notches in the next few minutes.

A rush of startled birds flew from a nearby tree as a group of shadows moved against the sun-soaked lawn.

"Now, Ma." Reno held the gun loosely in his hand. "Hold the basket in front of you and move with me toward the car."

Dolly's hand shook as she lifted the heavy basket with two hands and carried it in front of her chest. Then she said loudly, "Damn, I'm getting old, honey. Looks like that's going to have to be it for today. You want to help me carry this stuff back to the car?"

Reno stood next to his mother. He also stood in front of her and behind her. When she moved, he moved. As they headed toward the relative safety of the car, Reno tried to shield her body with as much of his as he could.

They got within about five feet of the door before Dolly turned to glance toward the brown van. Reno followed her gaze to see three men start their approach.

And so it begins.

Behind the men stood a tall Hispanic woman. Reno knew instantly who it was.

Psycho Snatch had finally made her play. Madness and rage radiated from every pore in the woman's homely pitted face.

And she was smiling. Bitch must have done her homework.

Dolly went to Petey's gravesite every week like clockwork. Reno made the pilgrimage once a fucking year, and today was it. Yeah, it made sense. To Sievas's way of thinking, Prosper had taken out her son, so she was here to take out the closest thing that he had to one.

Reno heard his mother's sharp intake of breath.

Drawn purely by mother's instinct, Dolly readied a bottle to be used as a weapon and leaped to Reno with lightning speed. That protective move captured the assailant's attention just long enough for Reno to raise his weapon. Reno pushed his mother hard toward the Escalade and yelled for her to get in.

The report of gunshots echoed through the quiet graveyard. For what seemed like an eternity, Reno aimed, fired, and dodged, aimed, fired, and dodged until he had cleared his way to the car. As he fumbled to push the keys into the ignition, he gave a quick glance over to his mother, who now leaned heavily against the door.

"Ma . . . ?"

"I'm okay. I'm all right. Go, son. Go! Go! Go!" Dolly yelled.

The engine rumbled and turned over. Reno glanced quickly in the rearview before he shifted into gear and saw the two desperados lying dead on the ground. Their eyes were open unblinkingly. Their dark blood stained the asphalt.

Where was that last asswipe?

"Reno, straight ahead," Dolly yelled to him.

When he looked through the windshield, Reno saw that the third guy stood in front of the vehicle with a .22 leveled right at him.

His mother screamed.

Without a moment's hesitation, Reno stomped his foot fully down on the gas pedal and floored it. Reno saw a look of surprised terror on that ugly face before the body flew high and bounced over the hood of the Escalade. He hit the windshield with such force that it cracked his skull and the glass at the same instant. Reno grunted with satisfaction as the body rolled off the car and joined the other dead men on the ground.

Road kill.

Before he could breathe the slightest sigh of relief, a sound on the passenger side caught his attention. Dolly's screams had turned to deep guttural wheezes.

Reno turned toward his mother and what he saw made his blood run cold.

Luisa Sievas was hanging on to the door. She had pushed her skeletal body through the open window and her hand was placed hard up against his mother's throat. With the kind of strength reserved only for the damned, the bitch was strangling his mother. Dolly thrashed while she scratched and clawed at her assailant. Before Reno could act, Dolly reached down and groped for the broken bottle that sat on her lap.

Luisa's dilated pupils bore a crazy drug-induced look. The foaming spittle of a rabid dog trickled from the side of her thin mouth. Her fingernails were dirty and broken where they held on to Dolly's throat.

"I'm going to strangle the life out of your whore of a mother. Mommy here is going to die knowing that her precious baby boy is next. That cocksucker president of yours destroyed my family. Now I am going to take his." The sound of Luisa Sievas's voice came straight from hell.

Still struggling against the death grip that Luisa had on her, Dolly's fingers finally found the makeshift weapon. With all the force of an enraged lioness, she pushed the heavy, jagged-edged glass deep into Sievas's neck. Luisa released her grip on Dolly just long enough for the air to pass into her lungs and for his mother to let out a deep snarl.

Reno swerved the car sharply to the left and then to the right in an effort to dislodge the homicidal maniac. Incredibly, the bitch still held on. Even with her throat bleeding out, she was still screaming threats at Reno.

Dolly finished the job. She shoved the razor-sharp end of the bottle as hard as she could into Luisa's neck.

Bull's-eye.

Reno turned to see Luisa's blood splatter out from her jugular vein in long, pumping streams. Her hand immediately left Dolly's throat and frantically clutched at her own bleeding neck.

Unbelievably, the crazy bitch was still hanging on to the moving vehicle.

Reno reached across his mother then, placed his hand over the face of the dying woman and pushed hard. Blood pulsed out from her neck and across the Escalade before Luisa Sievas fell away from the door and back onto the hard ground. Reno pulled up beside the thrashing body. Then he leaned out his window and pumped his last bullet right between her eyes before he sped out of the cemetery.

CHAPTER 36

Reno put the pedal to the metal and expertly navigated through the narrow streets of the city before he finally reached the relative safety of the highway. All the while, Dolly bravely fought down the nausea that threatened to overcome her. Her breath came out in shallow gasps while she struggled to keep the terror at bay. She stuck her head out the open window and breathed in the fresh cool air.

"Ma?" Reno's voice sounded far away. Dolly willed herself back from the edge of that extreme fear.

"I'm good, son. I'm okay. Let's get home." Dolly reached over and patted Reno reassuringly. Then she put her head to the backrest and closed her eyes. She took in a few deep breaths and felt the adrenaline slowly begin to move out of her system. For Reno's sake, she needed to push that panic aside. After all, they had just left four dead at the cemetery and were driving in a bloodstained motor vehicle with the windshield cracked. The very last thing Reno needed was a frantic woman beside him. Getting stopped by the highway patrol was not an option.

They needed to get back to the compound. They needed to get home safe and sound.

There would be time later to fall apart.

Dolly willed her heart to stop beating out of her chest. She clasped her hands together to stop them from shaking. Her mind raced and her throat hurt.

She had just killed a woman. A woman who, together with three men, had tried to murder her and her son.

But why?

Although Dolly had a lot of questions, she knew that they would have to wait.

Thank God there would be time enough for that.

Light and shadow flashed against her closed eyelids, and she felt the unmistakable blinding nausea and pain of a severe migraine coming on.

As Dolly fought to regain a semblance of control, the SUV begin to slow down to a less frenetic speed and the tension in her body released a little bit. Every mile brought them closer to safety. The rhythm of the engine lulled her shocked mind into a blessed stupor.

A blare of horns suddenly startled her into a foggy awareness. The SUV's speed had reduced dramatically and it was now careening between the lanes of the highway. Dolly's eyes flew open and she took a hard look at her son.

Reno's face had turned an ashen gray, and his eyes struggled to stay open. Her son's foot had fallen off the gas pedal and his grip was slipping off the steering wheel. He was slumped over, trying his best to hold on. To her horror, a crimson spot of dark, wet blood had begun to seep through the left side of his shirt.

Her son was bleeding.

"Reno. Reno? Reno!" Dolly repeated her son's name over and over again.

"I'm okay, Mom," he managed to groan out. "But you're going to have to grab the wheel. Motherfucking sons of bitches shot me."

"It's okay, honey. I got it. Lean to the side. Can you lean to the side, Reno?" Dolly fought to keep her voice steady.

She reached over, grabbed the wheel, and somehow managed to maneuver the car over to the breakdown lane.

"Honey, I'm going to pull you over toward me. Can you help me slide you over?" Dolly tugged and pulled at her son.

Reno did his best to move, but it took every bit of strength he had left.

"Oh, my God. Oh, my God. " Dolly whispered.

"Ma," Reno ground out. "In about a minute, I'm going to pass out. You've got to make some sort of a compress and put pressure on the wounds. Can you do that, Ma?" Reno's eyes were glazed over and his words were barely above a whisper.

Dolly thought quickly. "I got some blankets and clean rags in the trunk."

Reno nodded and leaned heavily against her.

She opened the door to the stopped vehicle and tugged her son over to the passenger side. Then Dolly quickly ran around to the back of the Escalade. She unlocked the trunk and grabbed the blankets and clean rags that she always kept handy. When she climbed back into the car on the driver's side, she saw that her son had lost consciousness. She worked quickly in the confines of the vehicle. Dolly tore open Reno's thin T-shirt. There was so much blood. She had no idea where it came from. She moved Reno carefully and found a bleeding wound on his side. Dolly's eyes swam and her mouth filled with the bitter bile of pure fear, but somehow, she found the strength to control that terror as she folded the towels up into a pad and applied pressure to the wound. Then Dolly tore off a strip of blanket and wrapped the makeshift bandage tight against him.

Blood continued to flow over her hand. Where was it coming from?

When Dolly lifted her eyes to her son's shoulder, she found her answer.

Reno had been shot twice.

Dolly repeated the steps and once again attempted to staunch the flow of blood.

Reno's eyes flickered as he fought his way back. She knew that the pressure must be agony for him. Reno winced and let out a low groan. His hand flexed with what strength remained and knotted into a loose fist. The scent of fresh blood filled the air.

Reno's eyes met hers.

"No hospital, Ma . . . promise me . . . Jules will know what to do . . . He'll know . . ."

"I know, baby. Don't worry, son, I'll get you to him." Dolly tried her best to reassure him.

She had to get him help. He was losing a lot of blood.

Live or die. His life was in her hands.

She would not let her baby boy succumb.

Dolly straightened her spine, and fought back the tears and the terror. With fear in her heart and a prayer on her lips, Dolly covered her son with a thick blanket.

Then she threw the car into gear and moved it back into traffic.

Despite what she had promised, Dolly's first reaction was to bring her son directly to the closest emergency room, and then deal with the consequences later. Whatever they were, they would be better than a dead Reno.

She would gladly do prison time for the four deaths at the cemetery, if it meant that her son would be free to live out the rest of his life.

But when she thought about it again, she knew that bringing Reno to a hospital would mean police officers, and detectives, and probably even the FBI. From experience, she knew that once it was revealed that Reno was one of Prosper's boys, they would arrest first and ask later. She couldn't even be sure, given the standards of small-town justice, that Reno would get the medical care that he needed. And even if he did, there was a better than good chance that her son would wake up from surgery only to find himself handcuffed to a bed and facing serious time. She knew that Reno would rather be dead than spend the next twenty-five caged in a prison cell.

Damn it.

Dolly glanced over at her son and saw he had his eyes open again.

When her eyes touched his, she knew he could see the pain, the love, and the indecision written on his mother's face.

"Ma, I'd rather be dead . . ."

Tears filled Dolly's eyes.

"I know that, son. I know."

"Then no fucking hospitals. You promised me, Ma. You promised . . . Call it in . . . Call my brothers . . . Jules'll know . . ." Then her boy mercifully closed his eyes again and passed out.

Holy Mother of God.

Dolly couldn't lose her boy. She could not lose her baby. She knew that it was true; she knew that Jules had patched up at least half of the brothers before. But Reno had lost a lot of blood.

Think, Dolly. Think.

She willed herself to keep calm and follow the speed limit. She reminded herself for the millionth time that she could not risk getting pulled over or even worse, get into some sort of accident. She prayed in earnest to Mother Mary and then to the archangel Michael.

The off-ramp to the clubhouse came into view just as the bars returned to the cell phone. Dolly had the presence of mind to use the untraceable prepay that Reno carried with him. She made a desperate call to the clubhouse. Thank God Prosper answered. In a stream of somewhat incoherent babblings, she let him know what had happened.

His voice calmed her. He spoke quietly and deliberately. He somehow got her to tell him what her exact location was so that he could send an escort detail out to meet them. Prosper asked Dolly a few more questions about the extent of Reno's injuries. Then he reassured her that Jules was at the clubhouse and on standby. Prosper handed off the phone to Jules and he asked her a few more questions. Prosper made Dolly stay on the line with him until she heard the distant rumble of pipes and caught sight of the boys cresting the horizon a few miles off.

Dolly hung up the phone then. Her boy was going to live through this. No question. Whatever it took. Whatever he needed.

Reno was not going to die.

Not today. Not on her watch. And if that meant that she had to raise an army to keep him alive, then that is exactly what she would do.

She hesitated for a fraction of a second, then Dolly picked up the cell and dialed one more number. She gave her name to the woman who answered the phone. There was a moment of hesitation then a series of clicks. Then the receptionist was back on the line.

"I've been instructed to put you right through, Mrs. McCabe. Please hold while I connect."

After a few moments of questions and answers, Dolly ended the call. While she was not certain that she had done the right thing, she knew for sure that now she had covered all the bases. Whatever happened next, life or death, she could be reassured in her own heart and mind that she had done all she could to get her only child, her baby boy, the kind of help that she knew he needed.

And that was all that mattered.

Would there be repercussions for her actions today?

Absolutely.

There was no doubt about it.

But she would have to deal with them later. And that was just fine with her.

CHAPTER 37

The guy next to me looked up from his small electronic game. For the last twenty minutes, he had been playing an online video game. The entire storyline seemed to center around a herd of zombies and a group of cowboys who took turns hiding behind things and then randomly popped up to shoot at each other.

The game was inane—childish and crudely conceived. It was not even close to the most mediocre game on the market. And still, it was infinitely more interesting than Dr. Charto's stupid presentation.

"My turn," I whispered to him. "Hand it over."

My classmate and would-be zombie assassin held my eyes in commiseration. "You have got to be shitting me. Still? She is still reading that?"

I nodded, shrugged, and held my hand out to receive the game.

He shook his head and handed it over. Then he reached for his phone and started to text his girl exactly what he would like to be doing if he wasn't stuck in Psych Seminar 102.

Who could blame him? I had some of those same thoughts myself.

I spent the next ten minutes killing the thirteen zombies hiding in the train station, thus securing my lead and winning the game.

I looked up at the wall clock. Ten minutes to go. Almost over. I snuck a peek at my classmate's phone and smirked. Although I was tempted to do some sexting of my own, I forced myself to refocus.

Despite the slight video game lapse, I was determined to do well in the class. I worked and reworked every assignment that was given, I was never late for a lecture and I never missed a class. I was so determined to do well that up until recently I actually sat right in the first row of the lecture hall and had listened intently to everything that the professor had to say.

Then I snapped.

The final straw came for me when I gave what I thought was an intelligent response to one of the professor's bullshit questions. And she rolled her eyes at me.

She rolled her eyes.

I could take a lot; I *had* taken a lot. But the sting of that public humiliation hurt like a thousand angry yellow jackets. After that I just gave up. So now I sat in the back row, shadowed in the cool dark of the lecture hall. And while I still paid attention, from the safety of those distant seats, I did a few eye rolls myself.

My stomach rumbled as I sighed deeply. Eight more minutes to go.

While the guy to the left of me spelled out the words *blow job* in all capital letters on his phone, the girl to the right of me checked out the price of tickets to Cancun. She turned to me with a smile and said, "Just a few more weeks until margaritas on the beach."

I smiled back.

Then I watched as she widened her eyes and licked her lips. "Now, this just got real interesting."

I followed her line of vision.

Someone had opened the door to the lecture hall, and whoever it was cast a large shadow against Sylvia Charto's extremely boring but painstakingly prepared presentation. And that someone was the last someone that I would ever expect to see in Psych 102.

I watched in fascinated silence with the other ninety-nine students in the darkened auditorium as the instructor took in his worn leather chaps, outlaw cut, long dark hair, and bulging biceps. She stared at Crow as if he were a rotting piece of meat.

Every other woman in that room stared at Crow as if he were dessert.

The professor took one long last look at the Hells Saints soldier. Then she spoke in a voice that dripped with outward disdain.

"Just how many of you *are* there?"

"You want to rein that shit in now, Sylvie, and shut right the fuck up," Crow growled loudly at her.

Apparently, Reno had shared.

I could feel the shock and the silent cheer that filled the room.

Professor Charto paled and grabbed the corner of her desk for support.

Then she shut right the fuck up.

I watched on in stunned disbelief as Crow's eyes quickly skimmed the lecture hall. Then he turned and nodded to the prospect who stood with his arms crossed and his feet firmly planted in front of the entrance. At his boss's signal, he reached over, flipped on the switch and released a flood of bright fluorescent light. Crow stood front and center of one hundred suddenly silent psychology students and ran his eyes up and down the rows of stadium seating.

I tried to make my way to the main aisle as quickly as possible.

"Excuse me . . . Sorry . . . Pardon me," I murmured as I stumbled over feet and backpacks.

The industrial lighting did not quite hit that back row and as I continued forging forward, I saw the look of frustration cross Crow's face. Suddenly, he cupped his hands to the sides of his mouth and shouted for me.

"*Claire!*" he yelled out.

Oh, my God. Did I hear that right?

When he bellowed out my name for the second time, I was sure that I had.

Panic.

There was a distinct and underlying tenor of panic in Crow's voice when he called out to me.

Jesus.

Panic?

There had been only one other time that I'd heard anything even close to it from one of the Hells Saints brothers. And that had been the time that Raine was in the hospital about to deliver Willow much too early. That strangled sound had come from Diego when he had thought that he might lose my sister and the baby. That had been the time that Ellie had kidnapped and tried to kill us both.

Oh no. Oh no. Oh no.

I finally reached the center aisle and took the steps two at a time. My classmates sat in their seats mesmerized by the somewhat bizarre scene that had unexpectedly unfolded before them.

The bad had found me.

CHAPTER 38

I'm here! I'm coming." I ran toward the podium. Without sparing a glance at the instructor, I threw myself at Crow. I didn't ask any questions, I didn't pause or hesitate. I followed silently along as he grabbed my hand and led me out of the door to where Pipe, Riker, and two prospects waited for us. They started their engines the minute they saw us. The sound of pipes rumbled loudly through the air, blowing hot exhaust onto the expensive turf of the Hill Crown College campus. Evidently, the brothers had not seen the "No Vehicle Beyond This Point" posters that were plastered all over the area.

Across the green, three campus security men headed our way.

It was pretty safe to say that the Hells Saints presence had created quite a stir at the quiet college.

But I didn't care.

Because I was scared.

I didn't know why Crow was here, but Reno wasn't.

Reno had not come for me.

Why isn't he here?

A big black train of terror thundered toward me. It blocked out the sun and blew fire clouds of steam down my throat. It was heading right for me. And terror had me tied to its tracks.

I couldn't breathe.

"Claire?"

"Claire!"

"Honey, we've got no time for you to freak. I need you here. With me. Now."

Crow's voice broke through to me.

As I turned woodenly to him, I felt him lift my arms and strap me into something heavy. Then he covered me with a black hoodie that was at least two sizes too big for me. Something in the back of my mind told me that I had just been outfitted with a bulletproof vest.

"Crow?" I whispered.

I looked around to see that the boys were all carrying concealed.

Apparently, I was getting an armed escort home. "Please tell me what's happening," I pleaded.

"I can't go into it now, Claire. Just know that me being here means that we're containing some shit. I'm taking you to the compound and I'm driving right through anything that tries to stop us. The boys are going to be on the side of us and behind us. I want you to tuck your head as close to me as you can get and hold on tight. Make sure you lean in hard. Okay, Claire?"

I nodded to him. Crow zipped me up and pulled the black hood over my helmet.

"Time to ride, babe." Crow started the engine and I got on behind him.

I knew that bulletproof armor was not for containing a small amount of shit. Bulletproof meant containing serious shit. It meant that shots had been fired. I was getting an armed escort home because that shit had evidently not been contained soon enough.

I held on tight and started to pray.

Reno. Raine. Willow. Prosper.

Prosper. Willow. Reno. Raine.

Willow. Prosper. Raine. Reno.

I had heard once that by speaking someone's name, you held power over their destiny. Maybe if I said their names over and over again, I could protect them from whatever this newest threat was. Maybe if I said their names over and over again I could keep them alive.

Please. Please. Let them be safe.

Crow flew furiously past posted speed signs. He deftly wove in and out of traffic as the brothers rode protection around us.

I sent up one final prayer as we reached the locked and guarded gates of the compound.

Please, sweet Jesus. If you take my man, then take me with him.

If you take Reno, then take me too.

Take me too.

CHAPTER 39

Three armed men that stood at the gate buzzed us in. As we drove up the long driveway of the compound, Crow nodded to several more who I did not recognize. All of them were heavily armed and wore Nomad cuts. As we rode past the last one, Crow lifted a hand in greeting. In answer, the brother raised a large automatic weapon over his head and yelled out what sounded like a battle cry.

Oh, my God.

I felt that panic rise and take flight, lifting me off the seat. Crow leaned back into me and with his free hand he squeezed my thigh in reassurance.

But I did not feel reassured.

Because whatever had happened, whatever this was, it had turned the Hells Saints Compound into a battle zone. Someone moved in front of the bike with a raised hand to stop Crow. My mind went into high alert. I leaned into the Apache warrior. My ears strained for any scrap of information that would help me. Feeling the tension increase in Crow's already rigid body, I scanned the perimeter and inhaled the charged air. I looked at the compound through new eyes and I took everything in at once. The sights, the smells, the sounds.

A group of cars littered the parking spaces. New ones seemed to be arriving by the minute. They were filled with the wives and children of the brotherhood. All of the MC families were here. An order must have come down to get the families safe under lock and key.

The Saints were in lockdown.

Still scanning, I landed on Diego's SUV, and Glory's car.

That had to be a good sign.

Feeling hopeful, I scanned for signs of Reno.

Where was Reno's bike?

From across the yard, a movement caught my eye. The clinic. Someone was coming out from the clinic.

It was Pinky and she was holding Willow.

She was holding Willow. And she was crying.

Pinky was holding Willow and she was crying.

Where was Raine?

Oh. My. God.

I tore off my helmet, jumped off the back of the bike and ran toward the clinic. Through the muddy field, over the rocks and tree stumps, I flew. I fell once and barely landed before I got up again. I did not falter one step as I shed the vest that weighed me down. Somewhere, someone was calling my name. I kept on running and I just kept getting faster. My legs and arms were pumping as boatloads of adrenaline streamed through me and propelled me forward. I kept my eyes on the prize. Straight ahead. All the while willing the ones I loved to walk out of that door.

Diego came out of the clinic.

Not Diego.

Prosper followed him, his hand on D's shoulder.

Not Prosper.

I held my breath. The door slammed shut behind them.

No one else exiting.

Where was Raine? *Where is Raine?*

Oh, God.

Reno.

Where are you, Reno?

Almost there now, I was still getting faster. I couldn't stop. I was

220

going to bust right through. My body braced and tensed in anticipation of hitting the heavy wooden doors.

Instead it hit a mountain of flesh.

That mountain pulled me hard toward him. One arm snaked tight around my waist; the other held the back of my head.

Trapping me.

Stopping me.

He held me close, immobilizing me. Steel and granite imprisoned me in a python's death grip.

The force that I hit him with knocked the air out of me. It didn't move him back. Not an inch.

Then Prosper's arms closed around me with a quick forced pressure. I was lost in a web of panic. Blinded with fear. Terror tunneled inside of me and pulled me inside out.

Then there was only the harsh reality of Prosper pulling me back.

"Breathe, Claire. Honey, stay here with me. Don't go, baby. Stay here. Stay here." He was holding me tight.

Then tighter.

His gravelly voice reached down into that long dark tunnel and brought me back from the edge.

"Reno," I heaved. "Raine."

"Raine's okay, honey. She's okay. She's here. Helping Jules." Prosper still held the back of my head; his mouth was tight against my ear.

Raine's okay. Raine's here. Relief made me weak.

Then. *It's Reno.*

"How bad?" I whispered.

"He's been hit. Twice. One grazed his left side and took a chunk outta him. No exit wound on the other one. They're in there now getting it out. He's alive. And that's good. That's real fucking good, Claire."

I beat against Prosper's chest and felt my legs go out from under me.

The wounded animal that had long ago taken refuge deep within my soul rose again and began to wail. I could no longer contain that long, mournful sound. My sobs echoed throughout the compound. Hearing it, the brothers rose to their feet. Every one of them felt my pain.

My father held me with everything he had. I felt his heart beat against my own. The raw power that emanated from his body was doing its best to move that strength through from him to me.

"I swear to you. I promise you. *I goddamn promise you,* he is gonna come out of this."

"Hospital. Please, Prosper, we need to get him to a hospital." I did not even try to keep that panic from spreading out into my voice.

Prosper shook his head against me. "Jules has got this. He does, Claire. It's not his first time at the rodeo. Hospitals report that shit, honey. Not good for our boy."

Prosper held me against him for another minute as my body quaked with uncontrollable fear.

"Dolly's inside waiting for you. She's a damn mess. She's going to need you. Diego has to come with me, so Willow's going to need her aunt while her mother's in there helping to patch our boy up. Everybody needs you here, Claire. Including me. I cannot think clear, I cannot do what I know that I have to do. If I don't know that you are going to be all right."

Prosper pushed me gently away from him. Then he used his free hand to wipe the tears from my eyes and to push the hair off my face.

"Listen to me, Claire. I know this does not give you a whole lot of turnaround time, but it is what it is. You being anywhere but here in this moment ain't gonna do anyone any good. The falling-apart shit is going to have to wait. Do you understand me, sweetheart?"

I nodded my understanding.

Reno is alive.

I pushed away from Prosper, reached in, grabbed the flask from his cut and took a deep swallow of the vile stuff that sat in the bottom of the silver savior. Then I coughed, sputtered, and took another hit as I felt the burn hit my belly and throw flames of heat throughout my body.

I stood on tiptoe, pressed my face against him, and took comfort in feeling Prosper's warm stubbled cheek. I inhaled the tobacco and musky scent that was so him. I held my father close for a moment, drawing from his strength. I steadied my breath. I felt the flow of blood pulse through my brain and the oxygen feed my lungs.

He's alive.

I looked toward the door that led to the small waiting room of the Hells Saints Compound Clinic. Prosper was right. My family, *my man* needed me. This falling-apart shit was just going to have to wait.

CHAPTER 40

While I took another minute to compose myself, Prosper snarled questions and barked orders into a walkie-talkie. Apparently, something was going on at the front gate.

"Yeah? Now? You have got to be shitting me. Who? Who did? Jesus. Why the hell . . . when? Yeah. Yeah. No, goddammit." He was running his hand through his hair in exasperation.

He asked a few more questions, and then with a final note of resignation, Prosper added, "Just send 'em up."

I looked questioningly at Prosper, but his eyes had narrowed on the dirt road ahead.

We didn't have long to wait.

Kicking up road dust as it rolled toward us came a shiny black Cadillac. Its dark, heavily tinted windows gave no clue to the occupants inside. The car slowed its pace as it drew near. With its sleek approach and sudden dramatic stop, it reminded me of a crouching panther.

We watched in silence as the driver door swung open wide to reveal a hand heavily adorned in eighteen-karat gold, followed by the arms and then body of a Calani suit, Bruno Magli shoes, and Bulgari sunglasses. Even from where I stood, I could detect the clean, crisp scent of his Tom Ford cologne. I didn't know his name; I had never heard him speak. Day or night, his eyes were always hidden behind dark glasses, but if you looked up *mob boss driver* in the dictionary, I felt certain that there would be a picture of this guy.

Someone had called the Italians.

The driver moved formally to the back passenger door of the Cadillac and opened it to reveal Gianni Di Biacco, front boss to the Bonzini family.

Now this was a face I knew.

Gianni was not a big man. He stood about five feet ten in shoes. He had a full head of salt-and-pepper hair, gleaming white teeth, and eyes the color of richly roasted espresso beans. His toned, fit body was covered in golden brown skin and gave testament to his Mediterranean heritage. A long thin Sicilian nose sat elegantly on his face and against his arched eyebrows. Despite his nefarious affiliations, or maybe because of them, Gianni exuded wealth, good taste, and excellent breeding.

Gianni had what you would call magnetism.

As we silently looked on, someone else emerged from the Corinthian leather-upholstered interior. He had the same golden skin and elegant demeanor as Gianni, but this man was older, smaller, and balding. In his hands he carried a large worn medical bag and some sort of soft-sided, hard-lined cooler.

Before Gianni had a chance to approach us, the door to the clinic opened and Dolly came rushing out. I barely recognized her.

Dolly's complexion had paled to a sickly, chalk-white. Her hair hung in startling and wild disarray. Smeared mascara had created deep, black hollows under her eyes, and her bottom lip was split and bloody where she had bitten it through. Her throat showed the beginnings of bruising, and her eyes were swollen to red puffy slits.

As she moved past me, I could detect that telltale smell of earth and metal. As I looked closer, I could see that Dolly's hands were covered with rust-colored smears and her shirt was stained in large splashes of deep crimson. Fine, thin, red lines spidered out on her neck, chest, and arms.

Dolly was covered in blood.

I felt myself get dizzy again. Prosper instinctively reached out for me, but he kept his eyes on the scene unfolding before us.

When Dolly reached Gianni, to my surprise, he moved in and brought her close and tight to him. Despite the two-thousand-dollar suit and the impeccably clean, white, cuffed shirt that he wore, he pulled the bloodstained frantic woman hard against him. I could see the back of Dolly's shoulders begin to heave and I heard her soft hiccupping. The compound turned thick with quiet, except for the gasps of Dolly's sobs, and the sound of Gianni's voice comforting her as he brushed the tears from her eyes.

I felt Prosper stiffen beside me.

"Goddamn wops," he murmured under his breath. But then his gaze fell on the worn leather medical bag, and I detected the smallest sigh of relief coming from him.

Gianni stepped aside. He seemed to be introducing Dolly to the man with the satchel, then the three of them headed toward us.

Gianni extended his hand first.

Prosper returned the handshake. Gianni proceeded with introductions.

"This is a friend of ours, Dr. Vincent Abrino. He is here to offer his services."

"What makes you think we need *services*?" Prosper kept his eyes on Gianni.

"Me. I brought him here," Dolly moved to Gianni's side. She wrung her hands again and her eyes leaked. A high-pitched frantic tone of pleading desperation took over her voice. "Reno needs him, Prosper. He might need something . . . he might need blood . . . he lost a lot of blood . . . I didn't know . . . I don't know . . . I don't know if Jules . . . I don't know how to help him . . ."

I knew exactly how she felt.

Because I felt it too.

I felt sick with that same desperation.

I went to stand beside her. Pinky and Glory, who were heading toward us from the kitchen house, had heard Dolly's plea. Now they stood beside us as well. Flanking the doctor now on all sides, we stood and waited.

Prosper looked at the women. His women. Then his eyes met Gianni's. Gianni brought his shoulders up to his ears and stretched out his arms with the palms up in mock surrender.

The gesture was so classically clichéd that it was almost comical. But the situation was too dire, too critical, and too desperate to be humorous.

We all looked back at Prosper, waiting and wondering what he was gonna do.

Prosper narrowed his eyes, rubbed his hand over his chin, and sighed.

Then he looked at the doctor.

"What's in the cooler?"

"Type A negative plasma," the doctor answered as if he were used to being questioned.

Prosper nodded. "Open it and the bag."

The doctor turned to Gianni. Prosper saw that hesitation and didn't like it. He addressed Gianni, with a hard challenge written all over his face.

"You got a problem with that?" Prosper punched out the words.

Gianni stood for a minute and looked Prosper in the eye. I felt a deep fear flood me. I was afraid that Prosper was not gonna play nice, and that Gianni was going to take his ball and go home.

"I got no problem, but be careful, my friend. I understand this is your family that we are talking about, and I understand family. But I am here on request, to offer my services. I didn't come knocking on anyone's closed door. If these services are no longer required, we can just as easily leave," Gianni spoke with deadly calm.

Dolly made a strangled cry next to me. Prosper's gaze fell on her. Then he looked straight at me.

"Please, Prosper," I whispered.

Prosper hesitated a moment longer, then he turned to Gianni.

"I understand why you're here, and who brought you here. And I'll be dealing with that shit later on." He paused then and looked straight at Dolly. "Right now, though, I'm man enough to admit that we can probably use the help that your doctor, here, can provide. But, one of my own just got jumped in the goddamn cemetery with his mother at his side, and until he can tell me exactly what the hell happened, I am going to do what I need to do to keep this club and the rest of my family safe. So invited or not, doctor or not, *friend* or not, I'm still going to look in those fucking bags before I let you anywhere near Reno."

Gianni gave a barely perceptible nod. "I understand." Then he turned to his doctor. "Open them."

Prosper quickly inspected the bags, then nodded to the clinic.

"Come with me. I got my boy, Jules, working on Reno now. Not sure how he's going to handle interference."

Gianni nodded and the three of them headed toward the door of the clinic while Dolly led the way.

I turned to Pinky and Glory and noticed for the first time that they had a fresh pot of coffee and a tray of sandwiches in their hands. The thought of eating made me sick, but I knew I was going to need the coffee.

"He's alive," I said. My throat felt jagged and raw from the pressure of holding in screams of despair and fear.

"And he's gonna stay that way, honey." My friend wrapped her arms around me.

Then the three of us followed the men into the building.

CHAPTER 41

We had been waiting in the front room of the clinic for what seemed liked days, but really it was just a few hours.

And a few hours was long enough.

Dolly and I sat together on the hard metal chairs. Throughout the afternoon, the brothers drifted in and out in a show of support. Someone was making sure that the coffee was kept fresh, and at one point a pack of cigarettes and a bottle of whiskey had been added to the tray. A constant stream of tobacco smoke and muffled voices drifted in through the open windows.

The Hells Saints and their families were holding a vigil for one of their own.

Pinky fussed around Dolly and me like a mother hen. She brought Dolly some clean clothes, but Dolly refused to change.

"I'll change when my boy is out of danger," Dolly had whispered without looking at her.

I understood her unwillingness to leave for even a moment, but I wished she would go and clean up.

I really did.

The sight and smell of Reno's blood and God-knew-whatever-else all over Dolly like that made me feel ill. I leaned my head against the wall, sighed deeply, and almost gagged on the thick smell of dried gore.

Gianni had left us intermittently to go do whatever a mob boss did in situations like this, but for the most part, he had endured the hard metal chairs and the loud incessant ticking of the clock, right alongside Dolly and me. His suit jacket was off and the stark white cuffs of his sleeves were rolled up to reveal strong dark forearms. His tie hung from his back pocket and the first two buttons of his shirt were opened.

I felt Gianni's eyes on me and turned to look at him. His expression of deep sympathy and understanding touched me. I got up and began to pace the room, back and forth, back and forth. While I kept my eyes fixed mostly on the loudly ticking clock, I also watched the exchanges between Gianni and Dolly.

Dolly seemed to be barely aware of his presence, but Gianni watched her closely and anticipated her every need. He knew how she took her coffee and made her nibble from the food tray. Once, when Dolly shivered, Gianni got up to close the window. Then when he saw her fan herself, he opened it again. He remained solicitous and kind. There were several times over the course of those hours when Prosper arrived at the clinic door. He had checked in on us, then he had nodded to Gianni, and they left together. Each time the two men came back, there was a new hardness in their eyes and a grim set to their mouths.

Now the front boss got up and stood in front of Dolly while Prosper waited at the door.

"Come, Dolly. Your boy is going to be all right. Between that hulking Viking in there and my doctor, nothing is going to happen to him. Let's go and get you cleaned up."

Silence.

"Dolly? *Andiamo, cara mia.* Let's go."

Dolly looked confusedly at Gianni, as if she could not believe that he would dare suggest that she should leave her son.

Even to wipe the grim evidence of arterial blood off her skin.

Please. Please, listen to him. The thought pounded through my brain.

Then Gianni nodded his head gently toward me. Dolly, more than a little annoyed with him, followed his gaze. When I felt her look at me, I turned to her and tried to smile in reassurance. But I just couldn't manage to pull it off. Instead, I just stared dumbly at Dolly, my eyes taking in the horror of her blood-soaked countenance.

Dolly's eyes trailed the length of me, assessing. Then she looked down at herself, perhaps seeing for the first time what the rest of us had been looking at for hours.

Her blood-spotted hands fluttered in her lap like birds. Then they reached for me.

"Claire, forgive me."

I felt immediately contrite.

In her place, I would have done the same thing. I knew that Dolly was afraid that cleaning off Reno's blood would be like washing away the man himself. Like tempting fate. She wanted to do nothing to turn the tide against him. I knew she was afraid that the dried crimson stain might be the last thing she would ever have of her only child.

It was crazy thinking.

Her thoughts were morbid and gruesome, and filled with faulty reasoning.

And they made perfect sense to me.

"I am going to change, honey. I'll be right back." When Dolly moved to get up, Gianni was immediately at her side. Prosper had returned once again and stood at the doorway.

When Reno's mother walked past me, I reached for her hand. Dolly took both of my hands and covered them tightly with her own. The two of us, the two women who loved Reno with all of their hearts, held on to each other for dear life. We drew what strength and hope we had left, pooled it together and sent that energy out to whatever God was listening. When Dolly bent her head to say the Our Father, I was shocked to hear the strong voices of Gianni and Prosper join ours.

A strong and sudden sense of doom and panicked guilt struck me.

"Stay, Dolly. You don't have to wash up for me," I whispered to her.

"No, honey. Gianni's right. I want to be fresh and clean when I go in to see my boy. I'm just going to go freshen up a bit. Don't let him die while I'm gone, honey. Promise me."

I squeezed her hands tight.

"I promise." My eyes shone bright with tears.

Then I watched Dolly and Gianni close the door behind them.

"Willow?" I turned to Prosper.

"She's fine. Glory has her. She gave her a bath and put her to bed," Prosper said softly. "You okay, honey?"

Three little words.

I fell apart, just for a moment. I sputtered and heaved and clutched at his shirt. I laid my head on his chest, drinking in the comforting familiar scent of him. While I felt his hands rub my back in small circular motions, I cried a minute's worth of tears.

Then I righted myself and looked into his eyes.

"Is he going to make it, Prosper?" I sniffled.

"Hell, yeah, he is. No doubt in my mind, honey. No doubt. What's that saying? Only the good die young? Sons of bitches like Reno, they are too damn mean to die."

Prosper tried to smile at me.

But I didn't even try to smile back.

Prosper cleared the deep rasp from his voice before he continued.

"That boy in there is tough, honey. He's a fighter. You know that Jules knows his shit. All that time he spent in the field as a medic and all the brothers he's patched up around here. Reno's in good hands, honey. And that doc that Gianni brought in, he works on his crew all the time. Best there is. Between the two of them, they've got every damn thing they need and more. Besides, Raine is in there helping too. You think for a minute that your sister is going let anything happen to your man? Reno's going to pull through this."

"It's been a long time; he's been in there a long time." I could feel the adrenaline of anxiety shoot through my system and I began to shake.

Prosper pushed me away from him, but still held me tight and looked into my eyes. Then he said, "That's a good thing, Claire. In this case, time is on our side."

"I don't understand." My chest felt like it was going to burst from the fear that I had been keeping at bay.

"Means he's fighting. Means he ain't dead yet."

Means he's fighting. Means he ain't dead yet.

I looked at the clock.

It had been four hours.

Four hours.

Four hours and four million years.

I didn't know how to feel about time any more.

CHAPTER 42

Leaning against the inside of the car door, Reno had watched through dull eyes as his mother fought back the panic. He wanted to call out to her and reassure her that things would be okay. But he didn't have the strength for it. And really, Reno didn't know if he was going to make it, he only knew that he wasn't dead.

Yet.

But he also knew that he had lost a lot of blood and that he had been slipping in and out of consciousness. Pain and nausea radiated like hot jagged streaks of white lightning through his body. He fought to stay awake, but as soon as his eyes began to focus, they would close again. Thank God, his mother had somehow managed to take over the steering wheel. As he leaned against the passenger door, Reno had strained to listen for the sound of sirens, or the report of gunshots, or metal meeting metal, or anything at all that would signal danger, but all seemed clear.

He heaved a sigh of relief before he passed out again.

Now Reno's eyes began to focus slowly. His consciousness was a slippery thing that he still could not get a firm hold on. The pain and loss of blood made it impossible for him to tell the difference between reality and fantasy. Reno teetered on the edge of darkness. When he momentarily broke through, he saw two faces hovering over him. Their distorted and disembodied features made him feel like he was looking through a fun house mirror. He tried to lift a hand to reach up to them, but when he did, he felt a sharp burst of pain radiate from his shoulder.

Then the darkness came again.

Eventually, sounds began to break through the haze. The distant rumble of pipes, the hum of machinery, the soft cadence of voices weaving in and out of his dulled senses. The colorless ceiling above him faded to black and then came back again. The rectangular lighting directly overhead gave off an eerie yellow glow. He moved his head slightly and experienced an explosion of pain that snaked down his left side. When he inhaled, a fresh burst of something fresh and cool seemed to sharpen his dull senses.

Shit.

He was hooked up to an oxygen tank.

He hoped that he was not in a goddamn hospital.

A moment of panic surged through his body and he lifted both his wrists. Once he found them free of handcuffs, he relaxed.

His mother must have listened to him and driven him back to the compound.

Yeah, he must be in the clinic.

Thank God, he thought, before he passed out again.

It was a fight to stay awake, but Reno had been shot before and he knew the drill.

He won the battle for consciousness for a few minutes, then for longer minutes. Finally, he was able to stay alert long enough to gather his wits about him.

Slowly he felt his body begin to report in. One limb at a time. He felt the sting of the needle that was buried in the vein in his arm, and the pull of the tape that held it in place.

So he had an intravenous drip stuck in him.

Okay. What else?

He could move his toes and his fingers, but the rest of his body felt sluggish and heavy. He continued to fight though the haze to take further inventory. His shoulder was numb, and his left side throbbed dully.

Breathing deeply, it took a while for him to verify where he was and to try to remember the details of what had happened. Reno closed his eyes and tried his best to clear his fuzzy mind. Then he opened them again.

Jesus. The cemetery.

Motherfuckers.

They had been at the cemetery.

That bitch and her boys had tried to take him out at his father's grave site.

A horrible thought came to him then, and Reno was filled with a fear so thick he almost gagged on it. That fear threatened to kill him in a way that a dozen bullets could not do.

Claire.

Had they gone after Claire too?

Reno moved to rip the IV out of his arm.

Just then, the door creaked loudly on its hinges and the thud of leather boots hit the floor. Reno turned his head to see Jules at his bedside.

"Welcome back, Brother," Jules said.

"Claire?" Reno choked out the word.

"She's fine, man. Your woman is just on the other side of that door. Prosper sent Crow out to get her as soon as we heard."

Reno slumped in relief. Then he almost leaped out of the bed.

"Ma?"

"Right out there with your woman. Tough one, she is. Drove you here."

Yeah, that's right. He remembered now. All those goddamn blankets, he had almost died from the heat alone.

Reno attempted a wry grin, but it turned quickly into a pained grimace.

"Me?"

"It might be a while before you can get it up again, Brother." Jules smirked.

"Fuck you," Reno smirked weakly. "Send Claire in here, I'll get it up right now."

"No doubt, you horny bastard. Tubes coming out of you left and right might be a problem, though," Jules shot back.

"Seriously, man. I've been taking inventory. Fingers, toes, everything seems to move. That mean I'm going to be okay?"

All of the brothers feared that one shot that would leave them in a chair.

"Yeah, clean shots, bro. No fragments. You are going to be one sore motherfucker for a while, but you're going to be okay." Jules looked pleased with himself.

"Smug bastard," Reno said. But relief riddled his voice.

Jules just smiled.

"Prosper's been pacing around the compound madder than a goddamn wet hen. You up for some questions?"

"Yeah, I'm up to it." Reno's head was back on his pillow.

Jules radioed over to the clubhouse.

"He'll be here in a minute. What happened?" Jules asked him. "Do you remember anything?"

Reno searched the recesses of his mind. Bits and pieces flashed before his eyes.

"The fuckers shot me."

"Yeah, the fuckers did. Looks like they used .22s. Stupid motherfuckers should know that it takes more than a .22 to kill a brother."

"Three men and a woman. All dead. I shot two of them, then another asshole tried to blow a hole in the windshield, so I ran right through him."

Jules nodded. They both turned to see Prosper and Gianni Di Biacco walk through the door.

"You okay?" Prosper took in all of Reno at once. His hard eyes missed nothing

"Better than okay, Boss."

Then Reno nodded toward Gianni.

"What's he doing here?"

"It was his doctor who patched you up, right alongside Jules here," Prosper answered.

"No shit?" Reno looked at Jules.

Jules nodded once, but didn't say anything.

"How did he know?" Reno spoke to Prosper, but he eyed Gianni suspiciously.

"You don't want to know," Jules muttered under his breath.

"Oh, yeah I do." Reno was beginning to feel that dull ache throb through his left side again and the pain was pissing him off.

"Let me guess, you and the doctor here just happened to be in the goddamn neighborhood?" Reno looked at Gianni now.

The doctor had entered behind them and said something to Gianni in harsh Italian.

Gianni put his hand up.

"I dragged my personal physician away from a family obligation to assist your man in saving your life. Your tone has offended him. And me," Gianni said calmly, but his eyes glittered.

Reno didn't give two shits who he had offended, or who Gianni had dragged from where.

"Yeah, well I'll get to the apology part later. But for right now, I want to know what brought you to the compound with a doctor in tow, right in time to save my sorry ass, because I know sure as shit a brother did not call you."

There was a pause that went on a little too long.

"What the fuck, Prosper?" Reno asked again.

"You're not gonna believe it," Jules muttered.

"Try me."

"It was your mother," Jules said.

"My mother?" Reno lifted his head off the pillow and looked at the three men.

"What do you mean, my mother?"

"Dolly called Gianni," Prosper confirmed.

"My mother called this in to the mob?" Reno croaked out. His pain had begun to spark and he felt that burn.

"Yeah, she did. She called him on the way in. Dolly called Gianni and told him that she needed his help. And he came with that help," Prosper said as casually as the situation would allow.

Reno let those words settle for a minute. He was having trouble digesting them.

His mother had called Gianni for help.

And he came with that help.

Even if it meant dragging his guy away from some family celebration.

Gianni had dropped everything and came when Dolly had called him.

Jesus.

Because getting ambushed and almost shot to death wasn't enough, let's add this to the damn mix.

"That debt? Mine to repay. Not hers." Reno looked Gianni in the eye.

Gianni looked like he was about to say something, then simply nodded.

Reno let his head fall back on the pillows. His woman, and his mom, both safe.

"Three men and a woman?" Prosper asked Reno.

"It was that whore Sievas," Reno answered. The pain had settled and begun to blaze.

"You sure?" Gianni asked.

"Tall, bony, long straggly hair, pockmarks all over her face. Ugly as sin. That her?" Reno growled out.

"Yeah. That's her," Prosper said grimly. "You shoot her?"

"Yeah. I shot her. Right after Ma rammed a broken bottle in her neck."

There was a moment of stunned silence, then the three men looked toward the doorway that led to the room where Dolly sat and waited.

"Dolly?" Prosper and Gianni both said at the same time.

"Yeah, she had no choice. Bitch came at her through the window. She almost strangled her to death." Reno sank back deeper into the pillows and a slick sheen of sweat covered his forehead. He let out a soft moan. Jules moved everyone aside, gave another quick check to the IV in Reno's arm, and then he took his pulse.

"Enough for now. Everyone get the fuck out." Jules crossed his big arms and stood in front of his patient.

Reno called out a begrudging thanks, before he closed his eyes against the pain.

CHAPTER 43

Raine had finally come out to give us an update. Reno was conscious and talking. Dolly rushed to the door, but apparently Jules had radioed the clubhouse for Prosper and Gianni. In order to get the answers to some pretty important questions, they would be first to see Reno. Dolly paced like a mother lion outside the clinic door waiting for them to make their way across the compound. She and Prosper exchanged a few heated sentences about priorities, but I stayed out of that particular showdown. I was just glad that Reno was alive, talking, and ready to receive visitors.

I could wait.

Pinky persuaded Dolly to go for a cool-down walk while Prosper and Gianni were in with Reno. I was invited to go with them, but I didn't need to cool down. I needed to talk to my sister.

Raine gave Dolly a long hug and whispered soothing words in her ear. Dolly nodded tearfully and let herself be led out the door with Pinky. Raine stood with her hands supporting the small of her back as she swept the hair out of her eyes. Then she bent a little backward in an attempt to alleviate the strain of the recent hours. Her tired eyes went to me and she smiled.

My hands shook and Raine took them into her warm, steady ones.

"How is he really?" I asked. The snake of fear uncoiled deep within me and made it hard to breathe.

My sister smiled gently. "What do you want first, honey? The good news or the bad news?"

I shook my head, unable to speak.

"The good news," Raine said, "is that we got the bullet out." Then she grinned with weariness as she quickly added, "And the bad news is that you are going to have to put up with that crazy Irish brawler for the rest of your life."

"Yeah?" I squeaked out as a flood of relief surged through me.

"Yeah, honey. He's going to be just fine. Jules and the doctor fixed him up just fine. I'm not going to lie to you, Claire. He was in pretty bad shape when Dolly brought him in. He was really, really lucky. He lost a boatload of blood by the time he got here, but we were able to stabilize him before we went after that bullet. Did anyone tell you anything? Prosper? Dolly?" my sister asked me.

I shook my head.

"Prosper told me a little, Dolly added a little more, but I don't know much," I said.

"Okay. Honey, let's sit for a minute. Reno was hit twice. Both on his left side. One of the bullets grazed him, but it took a big chunk out of him. The doctor and Jules were able to clean that up and stitch it without too much difficulty."

Then she paused.

"The second wound was a little more complicated. He got hit in the shoulder, same side. It was a nice clean shot, which means it hit a lot of soft tissue and no bone. That's good—no bone fragments to worry about. Bone fragments can be dangerous. They can travel or settle in places that can cause problems. Reno being so damn muscular didn't hurt either. But he had already lost a lot of blood when he came in." Then she sighed and said again, "He was damn lucky, honey."

My blue eyes fixed on hers.

"Thank you, Raine. Thank you. I love you." I placed my head against hers. The complete feeling of relief made me weak.

"I love you too, little sister. I didn't do much, but I'm glad that my nursing degree finally paid off for more than treating Willow's gas or Diego's exhaust burns."

We stayed like that for a minute. Raine kissed the top of my head before she moved away and asked, "Does Glory still have Willow?"

"Yeah. She has her in Prosper's rooms at the clubhouse. I think he said something about a bath, but I don't remember . . ."

"It's okay, honey. I'll find her."

After what seemed like forever, Prosper and Gianni finally emerged. Without waiting one second longer, Dolly streamed past them toward the door that would lead her to her son.

Prosper raised an eyebrow. "Me and that woman are going to have a long talk."

"Good luck with that," I heard Gianni mutter under his breath.

"Yeah, I hear ya." Prosper nodded in agreement. Then he turned and looked at me.

"You okay, honey?"

"I'm okay." I nodded.

"You going to go on in and see your man?"

I shook my head. "I want to give Dolly some time with him first. She needs to see for herself that Reno will be all right. Then she can go home and get some rest," I said.

I would have my time with Reno. Once in that room, I did not intend to leave him again until he was well.

When Dolly walked out the door a few minutes later, her eyes brimmed with happy tears.

She came over and hugged me close. "He's asking for you, honey."

"Thank you for coming today." I surprised Gianni by giving him a small hug.

Prosper scowled and grunted beside me.

"And don't yell at Dolly, Prosper. If it were me in there, or Raine, you would have done the same. You would have stacked every deck you had to make it come out okay. And you know it," I said.

Dolly looked suddenly uneasy, but there was a light in her eyes that even Prosper's scowl could not erase.

I left the three of them to work it out and went in to see my man.

CHAPTER 44

I pushed the door open, but stopped just on the other side of it. I knew that the brothers had added on to the clinic, but I had not realized that the building extended this far back. There was a single corridor with one door on the left and one door at the end.

I opened the door to the left first.

Holy shit.

If I had known a room so fully equipped existed here on the compound, I could have spared myself some of the fear that I had just gone through. Because, as far as I could tell, this room could rival any hospital surgical unit.

Everywhere were monitors and stainless-steel everything. A heavy smell of antiseptic wash permeated the air. Off in a corner sat boxes and boxes of gloves, a covered tray of surgical instruments, a small autoclave, and a deep sink. A good-sized closet area held several large tanks of compressed gas. Two halogen lights waited off to the side next to a glass-fronted refrigerator.

I saw a few balled up pieces of bloody gauze through a hazardous waste container and wondered who had been on cleanup detail. The place was scrubbed and ready for the next illegal medical emergency.

Wow.

I left the room and headed down the hallway toward the last door.

I stood in front of it and willed my heart to stop pounding.

I took a deep breath.

Then I walked in. Reno sat propped up in a hospital bed, naked from the waist up. A yellow iodine-type solution coated the ridges in his hard stomach. Large padded bandages covered his torso and his shoulder. He had an IV stuck into his arm. He looked too big for the bed, too powerful to be lying on the stark white sheets. His eyes seemed too bright in his pale face, and there was a hard line to his mouth.

But he was alive. And he looked beautiful.

"Claire." His eyes met mine.

My whole body melted with relief at the sound of his voice. I stood frozen with gratitude and offered up a silent thank you. I was too afraid to move. I was paralyzed with fear that this was an illusion, a dream that I would wake up from to find a very different outcome.

"Babe," Reno called softly to me again, "come here."

I walked unsteadily toward the bed. I wanted to reach out and touch him, but my hands were like lead weights at my sides.

I knew, I just knew, that if I reached for him, he would be gone. I knew that he would disappear and be forever trapped in some dark magician's magic spell. Or he would be snuffed out like a candle flame that was caught in a too-strong wind.

And I knew that if Reno disappeared, I would die. Right there on the spot.

"Closer." Reno's gaze touched me everywhere. I moved until my knees almost touched the side of his bed.

"Closer," he said again.

"Reno . . ." I looked at the IV in his arm and the big pieces of gauze that covered most of his chest.

"I don't want to hurt you," I said softly.

"You won't." His eyes held mine.

Still I hesitated.

"Claire, come here," he whispered to me.

I leaned in and over him then. My hair fell loose and brushed against his bare skin. My tear-stained cheek pressed against the rough stubble of his jaw. I felt the heat from Reno's body rise through the thin fabric of my blouse as my breast softened into his hard chest. The musky familiar scent of him was edged with the metallic smell of blood and the unmistakable odor of antiseptic.

I inhaled deeply.

He smelled wonderful.

As if on its own, my hand reached out to him and laid itself over the small patch of skin that was not covered by the protective bandages. I could feel the rise and fall of his warm chest. I pressed with the slightest measure of force against the place that covered his heart.

I wanted to feel it beat. I needed to feel it beat.

"I can't feel it." I looked at him helplessly.

"Can't feel what, Claire?" Reno had closed his eyes again and had leaned against the pillows. His big hand covered my own.

"I can't feel your heart, Reno. I can't feel it beating." My voice cracked with the sound of desperation. A part of me had gone a little crazy.

"It's all right, Claire. I'm okay, baby." Reno's amber eyes flew open and were on me now. His hand squeezed mine.

"We're going to be okay. I'm not going to let anything take this away from us, honey."

I heaved against him now. Safe in the power of his love, but not even close to recovering from the shock of almost losing him.

"It's been hours since they came for me. They came to school, Reno. And Crow didn't tell me . . . I didn't know why . . . I didn't know . . . they came to get me . . . you weren't there and I didn't know why. Prosper told me that you'd been shot . . . And there was

blood . . . Dolly was covered in blood . . . The doctor came and then
. . . nothing . . . for hours and hours . . . no one came out to tell us
. . . to tell me . . ." My whole body shook with released adrenaline.

"Shh," Reno smoothed my hair and murmured to me. "It's
okay, baby. Everything is okay. I'm going to be fine. Just fine."

I nodded "I know that. I do. I know that," I heaved.

It was true. I knew that it was true. Reno was going to be fine.
Just fine. He was going to be sore and uncomfortable and laid up
for a while. Reno was all right, but I was falling apart.

"I don't want to ever lose you," I managed to choke out.

"You won't," Reno sighed into my hair.

Then he grabbed my hand and gently pressed my fingers to his
neck.

He pushed them against his pulse point.

"There, baby. Feel that? I'm here. Trust that. Keep your fingers
there all damn night if you need to. I'm not going anywhere."

I looked at our entwined fingers. His big, callused hand held
my smaller one prisoner. I knew it was a matter of only milliseconds,
but it seemed like forever. Then I felt that strong steady rhythm of
his pulse. Like tiny drums. The beats pounded against my fingers
like a thousand tiny drums of celebration. They pumped and circu-
lated the life-giving blood to and from his heart.

His heart.

"Baby, don't cry anymore. It's going to be okay." Reno pushed
the hair out of my face, wrapped his hand around the back of my
neck, and he pulled me closer.

He knew.

He was the one who was hurt. He was the one who was lying in
a sick bed. His body was the one that had survived the deep wounds
left from a spray of bullets.

Reno was the one that was wounded.

But he knew that I was the one who had almost died.

He saw the unmistakable signs of the deep terror that had burned a hole deep within me. He could see the razor-edged fear and the panic. He recognized the shock that coursed through my veins, and the desperation that made me want to curl up inside of him.

He knew.

So he reached to me, pulled me close, and he kissed me. At first gently and tenderly, and then with all the strength he had left.

I felt his body rise against me and his hand wrap itself in my hair. His tongue moved ever so slowly against my mouth leaving in its wake tiny trails of light and love. He traced my lips with his finger, slowly letting me taste him. When he felt me sigh against him, with small, slow movements, he parted my lips. Taking his time, he explored every moist, secret place of my mouth. His tongue found mine and plundered it like it was a long lost treasure. I groaned when I felt him withdraw slightly from me, but then he was back again. Reno pressed warm soft kisses on the corners of my mouth, up to my temple and in my hair. Then he moved downward and rained soft kisses down my neck, all the while soothing me with words. His big hand cupped the back of my head, then he pulled slightly back on my hair until our eyes met.

"You are never going to lose me, baby, and I am never going to lose you. I'm sorry, Claire. I'm sorry that shit touched you today. I never wanted any of this life I chose to blow back on you. I'm sorry that I let you down, honey."

Oh, my God.

"Stop it, Reno. Everything good that ever happened to me was because of you. The bad came but it didn't take you away. It did its worst and it still didn't kill you. You were stronger than it was. You didn't let me down," I said hoarsely.

And suddenly I realized that was true. Were there still things we had to work out? Still things we had to talk through? Sure there were. None of this erased the fact that there were still parts of Reno and me that didn't make sense. But I also knew that without him, nothing at all made sense. Without him, none of the rest of it mattered.

Reno sighed softly against my hair, then he leaned deeper into the pillows, taking me with him. Drawing me close to his right side, he finally succumbed to the events of the day. I lay nestled close to him for a long time, then I fell into a deep dreamless sleep.

CHAPTER 45

This convalescence shit sucked.

Absolutely, totally sucked. Reno hated being laid up like this. Fucking hated it.

He had too much damn time to think. He could not stand the thought of lying in a goddamn bed when he should be out handling business with his brothers.

It wasn't his first time mending from a bullet. But he had never been shot up this bad before.

And it didn't help that he replayed the shooting over and over again in his mind.

When had he become such an unobservant idiot? Brothers who lived their lives unaware did not live long.

This was all his goddamn fault.

On a quiet Monday morning, in the shadow of the Celtic cross that marked his father's grave.

The bad had come.

If he had not been busy giddy-upping all morning long, acting like a teenage boy who had just gotten his first blow job, Reno would have been ready.

He should have sniffed the danger in the air the minute that he had stepped out of the car.

But he had been too busy thinking about being dick-deep inside of his woman.

That was the thought that plagued him. Self-recrimination rolled over him in boiling waves of rage.

And that was just one thing, on a shit pile of other things, that gnawed at Reno's gut.

First on the list was that psycho killer Luisa Sievas.

The thought of her filled him with a primal and deadly fury.

He wanted that pock-faced insane bitch dead.

Again.

The cut glass to her throat and the bullet in her evil, black, fucking soul was not enough.

He wanted to kill her again, slowly.

While he lay in bed gagging on pain pills and feeling the sting of needles stuck in his arm, he thought of all the things that he would have liked to do to that she-bitch. The dark thoughts were always a little different but all along the same lines. In those first hazy days of recovery, it was that anger that kept him sane.

The bitch had gone after an unarmed man and his mother paying respects to his dead father.

Reno wanted to kill her again.

He wanted to use a chainsaw on each one of her limbs. Then he wanted to filet her with a dull, serrated knife. He wanted to spend days peeling that pockmarked skin away from her bones. Reno wanted to hear the pop and crackle of each of the bitch's vertebrae as they snapped like twigs under the weight of his fingers. He wanted to look her in the eyes and see the heartless whore's pupils dilate in pain and horror, as she watched her intestines splash and splatter on the ground in front of her. He wanted to cut out her tongue and shove it up her ass. Then he wanted to feel the pull of the knife as he carved the eyes out of her sockets. First the left, then the right.

Yeah. Reno wanted to kill Luisa Sievas again. And again. And again.

The fact that he was lying on clean white sheets with fluffed pillows under his head while the rest of that bitch's crazy-ass crew was out loose somewhere, possibly planning their next fucked-up play against his brothers, or even worse, against their families, was enough to make him writhe in fury.

He knew that Prosper and the other bosses were all over it. Bloodletting would not be enough. Ten pints would not even come close to covering it. Every crew within five states who had any kind of affiliation at all with the Saints was in lockdown. There would be a major meet soon, just like there always was when shit like this went down. Every fucking country heard from. Each with their own stake in the outcome, each looking out for their own interests, each with their own opinion.

But this time it would be different.

Because even in the underworld of motorcycle gangs, Italian mobsters, Russian mafia, black gangstas and all the rest, there existed a code. And that code was pretty clear. No one screwed with the hereafter. Even in the ruthless world they lived in, or maybe because of it, this kind of jump hit just did not happen. Whites, Blacks, Italians, Mexicans, and Asians each had their own ideas of what they held sacred. But the one single truth, the one universal agreement that crossed all colors and clubs, was that the dead were left in peace. There was enough hell in this world for each and every one of them. There was no need to have that violence follow this life into the next one.

That Colombian bitch was straight up crazy pulling that shit. Bands of brothers all over the East Coast had been standing in line to take that gash down for years. Many of them had been looking for an excuse for a very long time to put a bullet between her eyes. The only problem that they would have with him taking her down is that they did not get a chance to do it themselves. Now the alliance just had to figure out how far this assassination plot extended. They had to determine if it was merely personal, as Luisa had screamed out that it was, or if it was something more far-reaching. Prosper and his brothers kept Reno informed. He knew that things had been set in motion to right this wrong. Like artfully carved chess pieces, the outlaw nations had made some strategic and carefully planned moves. Reno had listened closely, gave his input, and felt some of the impotent rage leave him.

Luisa Sievas's crew, what was left of them anyway, were dead men. Outlaw justice would be served.

CHAPTER 46

The light breeze blew in through the window and danced through the long strands of Claire's soft, dark hair. She looked hot, sweaty, wet, and annoyed. And unbelievably beautiful.

It was a week before Jules gave Reno the go-ahead to take a full shower and shave. The hot stinging sprays of the water coupled with the cool mentholated foam made him feel healthy and whole again. And it had covered his woman with provocative wet splashes all over the front of her T-shirt. Yep, so far, for him at least, the day had been a win-win. Jesus. She looked good enough to eat.

She started to leave.

"Claire," he called to her.

He could see the back of her shoulders lift and rise with barely controlled restraint. A whoosh of air shot out of her in a deep sigh.

She was getting riled. Reno suppressed his smile before she turned around. "This bandage is seriously messed up," he said.

"No, it's not, Reno. It's perfect. I just wrapped you myself. You are fine." Claire stared at him with more than a glint of anger in her eyes.

"It's really uncomfortable. You didn't do it right this time. I can feel this big knot in the back of my spine," he fired back at her. "Baby, why would I make this shit up?"

"Can't you wait until I come back?" Claire was pulling at the thin fabric. She might as well be wearing nothing. He knew she was embarrassed by the way she kept blushing and putting her hands in front of her. She looked so damn sexy he wanted to jump up, pull her under him, and bury himself deep inside of her. For days.

"No, I can't, Claire," Reno said evenly.

Pulling again at her shirt and sighing deeply, she went to his bedside. She reached behind him to feel for the knot.

He smelled her hair and felt the cool damp part of her shirt flatten slightly against his heated chest. Her wet puckered nipples pressed into his warm skin. She reached far behind him with both hands, and searched for the source of his discomfort. He put both his arms around her.

"There's nothing back there." She started to pull away from him. "There's no knot. Just like I said."

He pulled her back hard against him. "No? Put your arms around me again like that, baby. I'm sure I felt something."

Then he pulled her off her feet and fully onto his chest. With amazing alacrity for a wounded man, Reno shifted Claire to his good side and moved his knee over her small body, successfully trapping her next to him on the bed.

"I'm wet," she said exasperated as she struggled against him.

"Already, babe? I barely touched you." Reno grinned at her.

Claire shook her head at him. "The way your moods have been swinging lately, I figure I have about a three-second turnaround time before you shove me off you and order me to go get you some Chinese food."

Reno pressed her closer and began nuzzling the sensitive place on her neck.

"Have I been that bad?" he said softly against her.

"No," she sighed into him. "You've been worse than that."

His fingers on her back pressed and kneaded the tension out of her tight muscles.

He felt her go soft and still against him. "That feels so good, Reno. I guess I didn't realize how tired I am."

"I know I've been a pain in the ass, Claire. What you've done for me, the way you've been here, honey, it hasn't gone unnoticed."

Reno massaged her neck and shoulders for a while, then his hands drifted along to the sides of her breasts. The soft therapeutic massage had begun to turn into something else entirely. Reno felt himself go hard against his woman. It seemed like forever since he had been inside of her.

"Reno, your bandages," Claire breathed when he pulled her body closer against his.

"Forget the bandages, baby." Reno's hand was inside her wet shirt moving up toward her swollen nipple.

"Your stitches are going to open," she whispered.

"Forget about the stitches too. If they split, I'll just have Jules sew me up again. It would make his day. You know how he loves to inflict pain." Reno pressed warm soft kisses insistently on her neck, while he caught a nipple in between his thumb and forefinger. He tugged it gently just the way that he knew she liked it.

Claire stilled for a minute, and Reno took that advantage. He pulled the shirt over her head and reached back to release the clasp on her bra. Her breasts bounced free of the restraints, and he dipped his tongue over the large dusky tip of her nipple. When he felt her arch into his mouth, he moved his hand to grasp her heavy breast fully. Then he began to suckle her greedily, first one, then the other, then both. Reno's hands left Claire's breast to move firmly up her thighs and to skim over her denim shorts. With a practiced flick of his fingers, he had them unbuttoned and unzipped in no time at all. Then his touch moved lightly over the smooth branches of the willow tree inked into her flat stomach. Lovingly, he traced every branch and each finely drawn leaf. His callused fingers dipped down past the trunk, and still lower to the intricately drawn, wide-spread roots. She felt so incredibly good, he could not get close enough to her.

He couldn't hold back a small grunt of pain as he shifted onto her.

"Honey, let me," Claire murmured.

She put her small hands on his shoulders and surprised him by pushing him down back onto the pillows.

She moved away from him quickly, arched her hips, and dragged her shorts and panties down. Then Claire bent over him, beautiful and naked.

She smiled shyly at him, but her eyes filled with a hunger that matched his own. She moved gently over him and pressed her small hands against his strong hip bones. In a careful move, Claire straddled Reno; when her breasts swung heavily over him, Reno almost shot his load like a horny teenager.

Claire took command and touched her soft mouth to Reno's hard body. She trailed small tender kisses along the firm lines of his chest and down to his abdomen. She navigated easily past the carefully wrapped bandages. Then her mouth moved lower.

"Claire, you don't have to . . ." A shot of pure pleasure ran through Reno and almost brought him off the bed.

Claire raised her beautiful blue eyes. "I want to, Reno," she whispered in a voice that was husky with need.

The sound of that warm rasp was enough to make Reno's head swim. Sensual waves of pleasure built and crashed over him again and again as Claire teased him with her tongue. She moved the wet, pink tip until it slid over the long, hard length of him. Swirling and darting, sucking and nibbling, she fed on the musky, salty, rich velvet of his skin.

And Claire took her time.

She moved her mouth over and over again, experimentally, each time taking more and more of him, taking him deeper and deeper. Reno willed himself to stay absolutely still, but he clutched at the bedsheet as if it were a lifeline and he was a dying man.

And a part of him was dying. The part that fed on vengeance. The part of him that yearned for bloodletting and violence, for pain and revenge. All of the nightmares and self-recriminations of the past few days were replaced with the purity of the now. Strains of pleasure shot through his veins in long molten threads and chased away the deadly iciness that Luisa's attack had left him with.

Claire had pushed them all away, and had left him with this moment.

There was only her. There was only him. There was only love.

When he cried out to her in a rich deep moan, she edged back up his body like a sleek lioness. She looked deep into his eyes then put her mouth to his, catching his lower lip in small playful tugs. Then Claire pulled back quickly, arched her back and tossed her long beautiful hair.

Kaleidoscope.

Cracker Jack Surprise.

Brass Ring.

Reno lifted her in his arms and seated her fully on top of him. She felt so hot, so tight, so wet that it almost took his breath away. He slid his hands down to the soft skin at her hips and settled her deeper, rocking her, shifting her, loving her. He murmured his encouragement, and he felt her heat and flood with the friction the new position created. He watched her face as her eyes closed and a flush of pink crept over her. He felt her begin to tighten and build and suddenly her beautiful eyes were focused on his in an expression of lust and wonder.

"Reno," she cried out to him.

"That's it, baby. Let it go, let it go, Claire." Reno ground deeper into her with a need as deep as her own.

When he felt her shudder and begin to pulse with release, he held her hips tight to him, and gave himself up to the wonder of her. The entire world stopped. The rumble of the pipes, the distant shouts of his brothers, the roar of engines, even the call of birds and hum of insects ceased to exist.

It was only Reno and Claire, and a kaleidoscope of light, hope, and love.

And life.

There was life.

With Claire by his side, there would always be life.

CHAPTER 47

Time moved on in an uneasy rhythm for a while after the shooting. Reno's road to recovery continued to be rocky, but steady. Rocky because Reno continued to drive everyone around him absolutely crazy, and steady because each day he pushed himself to be the best that he could be.

In a gesture that was as shocking as it was unexpected, Dr. Charto gave me more than ample time to complete any classwork that I had missed. The rest of my professors followed suit, and I worked night and day to catch up.

I think everyone was grateful that things had turned out the way they had. But the day of the shooting had set off a chain of events that no one could have foreseen. While the local authorities of the towns involved hadn't really cared too much about a few drug dealers being gunned down, it turned out that the feds had a real interest in who had taken out Luisa Sievas and why. There were no surveillance cameras anywhere on the city cemetery property, thank God, nor were there any witnesses to the shooting. However, it did not escape the authority's notice that the four bodies and spent shells were all in close proximity to the headstone of Petey McCabe, the father of a foot soldier in the Hells Saints Brotherhood.

For a few weeks, the feds had been all over the club. The Escalade, with its smashed windshield, dented hood, and streams of blood splattered throughout, had been chopped as soon as it hit the compound. Any attempt at questioning Dolly or Reno as to their whereabouts or involvement in the shooting had resulted in the club lawyering them both up and was quickly squashed. An early-morning search of the compound conducted by federal, state, and local authorities had revealed nothing. However, a few eyebrows were raised at the content of the clinic and a charge was levied against Jules for practicing medicine without a license. Within hours, Gianni came through with documentation that the clinic and all of its contents belonged to "his guy," so those charges were dropped.

Under tremendous pressure from just about every organized club in the northeast, the Los Diablos was absorbed by the Almas Oscuras. The A.O. had just started their charter on the East Coast so the crew could patch over and become an integral part of the club's organization. This allowed them to satisfy the edict passed down by the outlaw alliance and still maintain their dignity. Prosper and the other heads of the various crews were meeting behind locked doors more often than ever before, and most importantly, the uneasy peace had been maintained. Matters, at least for now, seemed to have worked out as best as they could have.

Everyone I loved was safe, alive, and reasonably happy.

Yeah, everyone I loved was reasonably happy.

Except for me.

In the aftermath of Reno's recovery I found myself once again in the grip of nightmares and crippling fear. Because the closer that Reno and I got, the more I realized how very much I had to lose. There were still things that needed to be settled between us. There were things that needed to be said that could change everything.

And those things needed to be said by me.

I just couldn't seem to find the courage to say them.

CHAPTER 48

It was a beautiful day. Warm and sultry with just a hint of a breeze. I had taken my last finals the day before and I was looking forward to the first free day I had had in a while. Glory had taken off early in the morning to attend a huge farmers market a few towns over so I had the house to myself. I had just finished putting in a load of laundry and was heading upstairs to put my bathing suit on and head out to the dock.

I heard the screen door slam shut and turned the corner to see Reno standing in the living room.

"Babe, we have to talk."

I looked past him toward the driveway and saw the club van parked outside. I knew he wasn't well enough to ride his Harley yet. I didn't know what could be so important that it brought him over to the lake house in the utility van. But the thought of what it could be frightened me, and not just a little.

"Is everything okay?" My eyes swept his body. He looked just fine. Great, in fact. Reno still had some time to go before a full recovery, but there was a notable air of renewed health and strength about him recently that I was glad to see.

"That's what I'm here to find out." He nodded to the couch. "Have a seat, Claire."

Reno waited until I sat down. He remained standing and looked at me from across the room. Then he scrubbed his hand once over his face and sighed deeply.

"There's something I have been meaning to say and I've been putting it off. But I don't want to do that anymore. Not after the shit we've just been through. So I'm here today to say it." Reno was not smiling.

I nodded and felt my mouth go dry.

"Baby, I know we've been through it. From the very beginning you and I have been riding a shit storm of bad luck, but the hell of it is, we always manage to get to a place where we find ourselves together again. And that's the good part, that's the fucking great part, yeah?"

"Yeah," I said softly. "That's the great part."

"But the rest of it, I can't do anymore."

"Can't do what anymore?" I felt sick.

"I can't have you in my bed, on my bike, and in my goddamn head twenty-four hours a day and not have all of you. It's just not enough for me. And it's never gonna be enough."

"I understand." I nodded miserably. "And I'm sorry. I tried, Reno, but I'm just no good at this." The words flew out of my mouth. I hadn't known they were there until I said them.

"No good at what, Claire?" he asked.

"This." And I waved my hand between us.

"*This*? I don't understand what you are talking about."

"Going the distance," I answered him.

The room was closing in on me. I felt it coming on. Like a freight train. The awful truth. The truth that I had hidden from everyone, even from Raine.

"Tell me why, baby. You've got to tell me why that scares you, Claire," Reno said quietly. "You hiding from me after everything that you've been through, that *we've* been through, I get it. But that shit is done. It's over and we have got to find a way to move past it.

Because when we are together, it's fucking perfect. You in my bed is *perfect*. Nothing has ever come close to that. Not for me and not for you. You know it and I know it. But for some reason that scares you, for some reason you get to a place where you start to forget all that, and if we don't do something about it goddamn soon, then I'm going to start to forget that too. And that would be a real shame. That would be a real fucking shame. I have tried, baby, I really have tried, but for the life of me, Claire, I can't figure out why you do it. I don't know why you keep running from me. So me and you, we aren't leaving this room until we figure that out. Then we decide to either move forward or let this thing between us go once and for all. But either way, babe, I have to know and you are going to tell me."

Reno paused then and gave time for his words to reach me.

Then he said this: "I love you."

I felt the flutter of my heart beat against my chest.

"I fucking love you, Claire. Loved you for a long time. Loved you from that first time I saw you. Loved you from the first time you came dancing down those damn steps and stood behind your sister trying to hide from me. And I want you. All of you. I want to go to bed holding you, and I want to wake up next to you. I want my ring on your finger and I want my babies in your belly."

"There are things that you don't know, Reno. Things that if you knew, they might change the way you feel about me. Things that might change what you think you want with me." Somehow I managed to get the words past the lump of fear that sat heavy in my heart.

"Is this about Manny, Claire? Is that what we are talking about? Because I was with Prosper when we found him. I know what happened, and I am glad you had the balls to do it."

I shook my head.

"That's not it. That haunted me for months, but I worked that through," I whispered.

Then I added, "Prosper helped me to work that through."

Reno growled. "It should have been me helping you. I fucked up. I'm sorry I left you alone in that. Is that it, Claire? Are you still pissed that I wasn't there for you? Because you have got to know that I will never leave you alone again. Not ever."

"I don't blame you, Reno. I never really did. I missed you and I was hurt and angry, but I didn't blame you. I know how tired you must have been of me always pushing you away," I answered in a low voice.

We each let that truth settle for a minute.

"Then what is it, honey? Talk to me," Reno said.

"Your babies," I choked out.

"What?" Reno pulled his hand through his hair.

"I can't give you that." My heart broke open, and the pieces scattered on the floor.

I looked at Reno, then. Shame and guilt surrounded me like a deep, dark, hooded cloak. Because I hadn't been able to stop Jamie. Not from hurting me or the life inside of me that had barely begun.

Reno stared at me. He kept his expression blank. I didn't know what he saw when he looked at me.

"Tell me what happened, Claire," Reno said.

"It was my fault. All my fault. I knew what he was capable of and I stayed anyway. I stayed too long." My face felt like it was on fire, and the tears that had begun to form in the corners of my eyes spilled down my cheeks. The shame and the disappointment that I had kept locked inside myself was almost more than I could bear.

"Jamie . . . he knocked me around while I was pregnant. And I . . . I . . . lost the baby. There was a lot of blood and they tried but they couldn't stop it. There were complications and now . . . I can't . . ."

I angrily wiped the tears from my face.

I hated remembering. Hated it. Hated myself for letting that happen.

My hand went to my stomach, to the tattoo that hid the small scar that had been a constant reminder of the "complications."

The silence seemed to stretch on forever. Reno's eyes were on me. Finally I was done hiding. Finally he knew everything. Everything.

"Is there anything else you want to tell me, Claire? Anything else that I don't know?"

I didn't hesitate.

"No, there's no more. Reno. That's all of it."

Isn't that enough? I thought.

He didn't move toward me, but his eyes were soft when he spoke. "It's done, Claire. It's over. He's gone, baby."

"He will never be gone, Reno. It will never be over."

"No, that's where you're wrong. It's over. Today. Right now. It's gone. That sick motherfucker is dead and buried and he's gonna stay that way. You have to help me, though. You have to let me in, Claire. Let me in, so I can keep him and all the bad shit that he brought with him out. He's gone, and I'm standing right here and I am not going to let anything ever hurt you again."

In Reno's voice I heard a thread of gentle fury that I had never heard before.

And I wanted to believe him.

I wanted to believe him. More than anything I had ever wanted in my life, I wanted to believe that Reno could keep the bad out. I wanted to believe that I had finally found someone who was strong enough to stop the misery that always seemed to find me.

"I'm scared, Reno," I whispered.

I felt the tears wet my cheeks.

"Don't cry, Claire." Reno still had not moved. "Baby, please don't cry."

CHAPTER 49

Reno could not take his eyes off the woman that he loved. The tears spilled down her face, and her small shoulders shook with the effort of holding all that in.

He felt a fury build inside of him and rage so hot that it burned itself out soon after it started. Reno wished that Jamie wasn't dead. He would have given his left nut to have the chance to kill that sonofabitch over and over and over again. Some men were just motherfucking monsters.

Reno knew that everything depended on what he said next. He searched for the words, and came up with the most honest ones he could find.

"I'm scared too, baby. I'm afraid of that place that you go to. I'm afraid that the next time you hide, you'll run so far from me that I won't be able to find you."

Reno stayed where he was. He stood absolutely still, but he kept his eyes glued on her. His voice was soft and gentle. Reno spoke slowly and waited for each word to reach Claire's scarred and broken heart.

When he spoke, it was with all the love and conviction that he absolutely felt.

"You won't have to survive losing me, Babe. I'm here. Right here. I'm still standing and I'm gonna stay standing. I'm not going to let anything hurt me. I'm not going to let anything hurt us. Nothing will get to me and nothing will get past me to find you. I swear my life on it. And if there ever comes a time when I think that I can't stop that bad by myself, then I am going to raise an army to do it with me. You will always, always be safe with me, Claire. And baby, with you is the only place that I want to be."

Then he put his hands out toward his woman, palms up and in surrender.

"But, you have to help me. You have to give me the chance to prove it to you. You just have to be brave one more time, honey. You just have to stop being afraid long enough to let me love you."

Reno took a deep breath.

"And I don't give a shit about kids, Claire. If you decide you want them, then we'll find a way."

Reno smirked and rubbed his jaw.

"But I'm guessing that taking care of you is going to be a full-time job."

He could see that Claire had started to breathe again. That haunted look had finally begun to leave her eyes and was slowly being replaced with something else. Something that looked like hope. She took one long last ragged breath.

"I've made some mistakes, Reno. I've done some things that can never be undone. Things that I will regret to my dying day, things that have changed who I am."

"Aw, baby, who the fuck hasn't?" He looked at her.

And there it was, the beginnings of a small smile. That one slight curve of Claire's mouth set Reno's heart to soaring.

"I know who you are, Claire. I see how hard you try. I see how brave you are. I know that underneath all that fucking beauty is a kindness and a strength that I want to be around. I know the worst and the best of you, baby. I understand exactly who you are and you are everything I ever wanted."

He let those words drift and settle like a soft blanket around her. Then he continued.

"But this isn't about me, honey. I knew what I wanted the minute I laid eyes on you. This is about you. This is about what you want. I ain't a bad man, Claire, but I have done some pretty fucking bad things. And safe to say, with the life I lead, I'm going to do more bad things. But none of that will ever touch you. I swear it. I won't lie to you, cheat on you, or ever lay a hand on you. And I'll try my goddamn best to stay out of jail."

Claire smiled fully at the last part.

"So this is it. Me and you. The good and the bad. But there is just one more thing. If you want me, if you're in this with me, then you're in it all the way. You and me. I'm asking you for forever, baby, and I ain't settling for anything less. Nothing less, Claire. Do you understand what I am asking you, honey?"

Claire nodded her head and said softly, "I understand."

Reno looked at her.

"If you want that too, if you want *me* too, then you need to come to me. You need to come and take what you want."

Reno stood with his arms by his sides and his heart on his sleeve. The hardest thing he ever had to do was stand still and wait for Claire to cross that room.

Thank God that he didn't have long to wait.

It took less than three beats of his heart for her to decide.

She closed the gap between them in just a few steps.

And she took it. All of it.

This man was hers.

And she was his.

Forever.

CHAPTER 50

I awoke to find myself tucked safely under Reno's arm. The rising sun had just begun to stream in through the blinds, casting the room in shimmering beams. I turned and found his eyes on me, warm and smiling. He kissed the top of my head and slipped his hand through mine. Thin rays of light skipped and danced over our entwined fingers. Reno stretched out our clasped hands and held them to capture the light.

"A perfect fit, baby."

I moved my fingers around his, sighed deeply, and let myself feel the joy of the moment

"So what's it going to be? Round? Square? Teardrop? Or that one that points on both ends?" His words were laced with tenderness.

"Not the one called a teardrop, Reno. I don't want that one." I felt the panic edge my voice.

Reno pulled me closer. "No, babe, not that one."

"There's a girl in one of my classes. I like her ring," I offered, suddenly shy.

"Yeah?" Reno grinned. "What's it look like?"

"It's in the shape of a heart."

"Done, baby," Reno said and kissed my hair.

I shifted closer to him and felt the last, final bits of tension release. Relief, happiness, and something undefined coursed through my body and warmed me.

"Are we really going to do this, Reno?" I whispered to him.

He pulled my hair back and looked into my eyes.

"Yeah, babe, we are really going to do this."

I sighed happily against him. Reno's hand moved to my stomach, his thumb made small circles against my skin. I peeked at him from under my lashes and saw a smirk begin to form on the side of his mouth.

I took the shit-eating grin on Reno's face to be a good sign.

Phew.

Because I had something to say.

I inhaled deeply and positioned myself up on one arm. I wanted to get a good look at Reno when I laid it out for him. I grabbed the bedsheet and brought it tight against me. Wanting no distractions, I looked down at the sheet, saw some cleavage, and raised it even higher. I needed his full attention.

The movement of self-protection did not escape those beautiful amber eyes.

Reno arched his eyebrow. "Babe?"

I inhaled. "Reno, I love you, I do . . ."

"*Do not, do not* fucking tell me that I am about to hear a *but* in there, Claire."

"No, Reno. No buts. Absolutely no buts," I spoke quickly to reassure him.

"I love you, so this doesn't really matter," I muttered.

As Reno watched me, his eyes grew wary. "What doesn't matter, Claire?"

"Nothing. I mean everything. I mean it all matters, *we matter*. Of course, we matter. Except that . . . if we are going to do this anyway . . . maybe we could . . . I mean, everybody likes cake, right?"

Holy shit.

I sighed.

My heart began to race and my thoughts were stuck somewhere in a swirl above my head.

Reno pulled his hand through his hair, looked at me and said, "Babe, you're doing that thing you do again. Just focus and tell me what the fuck you are trying to say."

I held my breath for a second.

Then I went for it.

"A wedding, Reno. If we are going to do this, then I would like to have a real wedding."

I waited, and Reno waited too.

So I inhaled deeply and let all my little girl dreams come out in one big rush.

"My mom and Raine didn't get to have that. And I want that. I have always wanted that. And when I say *that*, I mean all of it.

"I want a big white cake with loads of flowers made from icing, and one of those long white runners that will lead me to you. And I want bridesmaids—Raine and Glory walking in front of me holding flowers and wearing dresses that match. I want Willow to be a flower girl. I want her to wear a little white dress with a ribbon sash that matches the bridesmaids' dresses."

When I heard Reno clear his throat, I continued on before he had a chance to break in.

"And when it is announced that *the groom may now kiss the bride* I want you to kiss me long and deep. I know that some people don't think a full-on kiss is appropriate, but I don't care. I want to remember that kiss for the rest of my life. Oh, and talking about that, I want pictures. Lots and lots of them. I want to drink pink champagne from crystal glasses. I want our guests to throw rice at us and blow bubbles from those little plastic bottles. I want flowers on the tables. I want to hear the words *'til death us do part*. I want to say *I do*. Reno, ever since I was a little girl I have dreamed of saying *I do*."

Reno had not moved a muscle. And when that sheet slipped a little, in my exuberance to explain my whole wedding scenario, his eyes did not drop from mine.

"Anything else?" Reno asked, not giving me one hint as to what he felt about my whole grand scheme. Usually I would let that stop me, but I figured this was probably going to be my one shot.

And I was going to take it.

So I continued, letting the words flow out in a rush of enthusiasm.

"I know it's a lot. I know maybe you don't want those things, or don't feel the need for those things. But I have always dreamed of those things, Reno. I was that little girl. The one who wrapped a towel on her head and pretended it was a veil. The one who made wedding bouquets out of dandelion weeds and broken ribbons."

I sighed wistfully at the memory and added, "I cannot even begin to tell you how many times Pink Bunny and I promised to love, honor, and cherish each other."

Reno smiled at that.

Then because I knew my chances of Reno being a white-wedding kind of guy were slim, I added, "But all of that really doesn't matter. Because I love you. I really, really do. All those walking-down-the-aisle dreams, they were really about finding a man like you. *I wished for you, Reno*. And in a world where wishes hardly ever come true, I know how lucky I am to have found that. I know how lucky I am to be loved by you. So if you are dead set against the whole big wedding thing . . . make no mistake here, that is what I am talking about, then I can live without it."

Phew. I sat back. Exhausted.

Reno took a minute to consider.

"I am not going to be handing my brothers some plastic shit filled with bubbles, Claire."

I could live without the bubbles. Bubbles were definitely negotiable.

"Okay, forget the bubbles," I said.

"Not letting anyone throw food at me either." Reno's eyes narrowed.

Food? Oh, geez . . .

"I'm okay with no rice," I said. I actually kind of loved the rice thing, but if the rice had to take one for the team, so be it.

"Anything else?"

"I kiss you when I want. I don't need anybody telling me that *now I may or may not* kiss my woman on our wedding day." Reno arched an eyebrow.

Really? Did he not get the symbolism there? But, okay.

I nodded in agreement. "You can kiss me constantly. From start to finish if you want, Reno."

I held my breath.

Reno nodded.

"What does that mean, that nod, Reno?"

"It means okay, Claire," Reno answered.

"Okay? Like okay everything, okay? Or okay just part of it, okay?" I asked him. Then I held my breath in hopeful anticipation.

"Means okay everything, Claire. Plan the wedding of your dreams, baby. Whatever you want. We're good on the green, I got this." Reno smiled at me then.

So this is what it feels like when dreams come true.

The little girl in me jumped up and down and threw bright yellow dandelion bouquets in the air. My inner child watched happily as ribbons danced gaily around us, and their streamers wrote *thank you* in the wind.

The woman in me expressed that gratitude in a very different, but no less enthusiastic, sort of way.

Much, much later, as I was falling asleep in his arms, Reno pulled me close to him and whispered against my ear.

"I wished for you too, Claire."

CHAPTER 51

Two days after Reno proposed to Claire, he went to see his uncle.

When they heard the chiming signal of the security monitor, Dolly and Pinky had just gotten up from the table and had begun to clear the dishes. Prosper sat deep in his favorite chair and lit up his weekly Cuban cigar. It was late Sunday afternoon, and the tradition that had begun when Petey was alive had continued on long after his death. Reno had been just a kid when his dad had passed on, but Dolly knew that he remembered those Sunday dinners well. She noticed and appreciated that her son tried to make an appearance whenever he had the time.

"Sorry I missed dinner, Ma." Reno bent down and kissed his mother's cheek.

"Happy to see you up and around. How you feeling, honey?" Dolly hugged her boy close in answer.

"I'm good thanks to my kick-ass gun-toting ninja mother," he teased her. Then his eyes warmed. "You okay?"

"Yeah, honey. I'm doing just fine."

Reno kissed his aunt in greeting. "Hey, Pinky. Mind if I steal the boss man for a couple of minutes?"

"You got about a half an hour before the game starts," Prosper growled, but Dolly didn't miss the light in his eyes at seeing his nephew.

Dolly watched Reno walk toward the office with his uncle. The wild child that she and Petey had conjured up together. God, she missed her big, rough husband. Reno was so much like him. Loyal, smart, handsome, and too damn stubborn for his own good. Reno was the best thing that Dolly had ever done, the best gift that she had ever been given. Dolly loved her boy with all of her heart.

But she was not blind to his faults.

She knew that Claire and Reno had been spending a lot of time together since the shooting. She had seen the panic and heartache in Claire's eyes during those long hours that they had sat together at the clinic. A person had to be just about blind not to see the love they had for each other. But Dolly had watched this thing with Claire and Reno unfold, then snap back and close tight before her eyes too many times to be overly optimistic. Dolly had bit her tongue at every twist and turn. Her boy was a damn fool if he let that sweet thing slip away. But that was exactly what he had been before, a damn fool. Drinking, whoring, and fighting. *Damn, damn fool.*

Dolly knew that whatever it was that had made Reno act like a goddamn ass would work itself out. She also knew that the times it did, her son would always find his way here. Not to her, but to Prosper. Eventually, Reno talked just about everything out with his uncle. Dolly knew that Prosper had been waiting for that too.

But Dolly also knew that time wasn't going to be on Reno's side forever. Dolly realized that for Prosper, this situation was different, because it involved one of his girls. She understood that it was a true testament to Prosper's love for Reno that he had kept silent this long. Today, she hoped that Reno had come here to honor that and explain himself if he could, or to seek Prosper's counsel if he couldn't.

Dolly held her son close in greeting and hoped for the best. She stood by her sister-in-law and the two of them watched Reno and Prosper head toward the back of the house to the office.

"He looks good. Don't you think? Apart from being a little pale and a little skinny, I think he looks good." Dolly tried to keep the anxiety from her voice and failed.

"He looks great, honey. Your boy is going to be just fine," Pinky reassured her.

"I'm glad he's here. Wish the hell I knew what brought him here, though." Dolly was looking at the closed door.

"I hate it when they go into that room. I can't hear a thing," Pinky commented to her.

Dolly watched as Pinky put on a fresh pot of coffee, "I had hoped that you'd found a way to get around that by now. Are you sure there is absolutely no way that we can hear what's going on in there?"

"You know, as well as I do, that I have tried about a million times over the years to listen in on what's being said behind those closed doors. Sweet Jesus, Dolly, you've been right alongside of me with your ear to that door for most of those times. That goddamn room is locked up tighter than a farmer's daughter on a Saturday night." Pinky sighed.

The two of them stood together and looked toward the tightly closed doors.

"I'm worried." Dolly turned to her friend.

"About Reno?" Pinky made herself busy setting up the coffee tray. Then she searched under the cabinet and came up with the good stuff. Pinky brought out the bottle that was reserved for special holidays, the very good news, and the very bad news.

"Yeah, it's Reno. I don't know, Pinky. God knows I love that boy, and I'm the first to admit he hasn't always been an easy child to raise. But he always kept that sweet side to him. Always kept his head," Dolly sighed, looking for the words. "Things seem to have calmed down now, but you know as well as I do that there have been times in the past year or so when my boy's been lost. That trip out West—all that drinking and fighting and . . ."

"Whoring," Pinky finished for her.

Dolly nodded. "Whoring."

"Honey, Reno was a good boy, and he's grown to be a good man." Pinky looked at her friend.

"I don't know." Dolly shook her head. Doubt created worry lines between her brows. "It's this thing with Claire."

Dolly poured a generous shot from the best bottle in the house into her black coffee.

"You don't like Claire?" Pinky asked. She was confused.

"Honey, of course I like her. I love her. Absolutely love her. Raine and Claire both. Remember that summer? That little tiny thing with those big, blue eyes following her big sister everywhere? It took her a week before she would let us put a comb to her hair."

Pinky smiled at the memory. "Jesus, it took me two weeks before she would let me get her into the bathtub, then she liked those bubbles so much, I couldn't get her out. The child bathed four times a day after that first time. Her little fingers used to get so wrinkled, I was worried that one day, all the skin was going to fall right off."

"And that dirty little pink bunny that we could not pry out of her hands." Dolly smiled too. "I thought for sure something was going to crawl right out of that thing."

"Oh God, remember that? She finally let me wash it, but only if she could watch. That baby girl got out that little green plastic stool and sat right in front of the washer, and then the dryer, until that old, fat, stuffed bunny came out."

They both laughed at the memory.

"She's grown to be a beautiful woman, honey, and I thank the Lord that he brought them both back to us safe and sound." Pinky was Dolly's best friend in the world, but Dolly couldn't forget that, for a while, in her mind at least, Pinky had been Raine and Claire's mother. And for a woman who had known early on that she would never be able to have children of her own, that had meant a lot.

With all that history between them, it was safe to say that even though Pinky loved Dolly like a sister, Pinky also loved Claire like a daughter.

Dolly knew they were about to walk a very thin line.

"So what is it about Claire that's not sitting right with you now, Dolly?" Pinky asked. Then she took a sip of her very hot coffee.

"Oh, honey. It's not that. I'm just worried that if Reno ever gets it into his head to go back to those wild ways, he's gonna permanently ruin his chances with that sweet girl." Dolly sighed.

Pinky visibly relaxed. They were in perfect agreement on this one.

"That would be a damn shame," Pinky said. Then she added with force, "Prosper will straighten him out."

"I hope the hell so," Dolly answered.

Then they both looked toward the closed door of Prosper's office.

The two women sat and talked together as the sun started to fade in the sky. The loud ticking of the clock did nothing to help with the building anxiety they shared. At one point, Dolly got up and paced in front of the heavily carved wooden doors that led to the office. Pinky watched her for about five minutes before she couldn't stand it any longer and then she put her ear to the door. After a minute or so, she reported that she thought she might have heard something being kicked or thrown against the wall, but she couldn't be sure.

CHAPTER 52

Reno watched as his uncle splashed Johnnie Walker Blue into the two shot glasses that he had set out on the table. Prosper's windowless office sat in the back of the house. Behind the rich oak panels, its partitions were lined in lead. Two large safes were hidden in the walls as well. One safe had a small arsenal of weapons, and the other contained a bundle of cash and some documents that Prosper found useful to have around.

To the bare eye, the office looked like any other room in the house. The room was Prosper's nod to Pinky's determination to give them "normal" in the times when they found themselves at home together. The house had the means of security it needed to provide a safe environment for the founder and president of the Hells Saints MC. But as Pinky had put it, "that doesn't mean we have to be reminded of it every damn day."

Prosper had insisted that he had agreed to the changes in the house in order to make his wife happy. But Reno suspected that despite all his bluster, Prosper actually liked the sense of normalcy that the home provided. Although his uncle was still a tough bastard, Reno could see that time had mellowed him. Raine and Claire and the birth of his first grandbaby had mellowed him. He was past sixty now, and while Reno doubted that Prosper would ever completely be done with his outlaw ways, his whoring, fighting, and heavy drinking days were a thing of the past.

Reno and Prosper both downed the first shot, and Prosper leaned over to fill the glasses again.

Reno reached into his pocket and pushed a small blue box toward his uncle.

"Too damn early for my birthday, son." Prosper looked at Reno.

"Open it, man." Reno nodded to the box.

Leaning back and taking his time, Prosper snapped the velvet ring box open, took a look, and snapped it back closed again.

"You proposing to me, Reno? 'Cause let me tell you, if I see you going down on one knee, I'm going to put a bullet in your goddamn skull."

"Yeah, really funny, Boss." Reno was not amused.

Prosper did not smile either.

"So what the fuck is this about, Reno?"

"I love her, Prosper." Reno said it straight.

"Is that what love looks like to you, asshole?" Prosper's eyes glittered.

"What the fuck are you talking about?" Reno fired back. But his uncle's reaction was just what he had expected.

"You were there, man, you know exactly what I'm talking about. Oh, no. That's right. No, you weren't. You getting shot up does not fucking excuse what was happening before that. Does not excuse any goddamn part of it. You were out there doing the dirty on the West Coast while your girl was not eating, not sleeping, and generally just making herself sick with the thought of offing that cocksucker. Not to mention that she was still dealing with the rest of the shit storm that she's been through. You left her alone in that," Prosper snarled.

"Yeah, well, we worked it through," Reno snarled back.

"Really? You worked that through? Was that before or after your cock slammed every whore from coast to coast, and you took to the ring with your bare fucking fists?"

Reno looked Prosper in the eye.

"After."

Prosper sighed heavily.

"Goddammit, Reno, I don't know who is stupider. You for thinking you can make this thing work, or her for giving you a chance to try."

"You got no right to call her stupid, Prosper." Reno's body was tense and primed. The muscle in his jaw jumped.

"No? Well, she's been mine a hell of a lot longer than she's been yours. That right there gives me the right, Reno. Gives me a lot of other fucking rights too. I've lived a hard life, made some hard choices, and there have only been two things that I have ever regretted. One was leaving those two little girls with their good-for-nothing father, and the other was leaving their mother, knowing that she was making the biggest mistake of her life by pushing me aside. Claire's a lot like her mother. She's a runner, Reno. Just like Maggie."

"I know that." Reno agreed. "Been talking all that out with her—Manny, and that fuckhead, Jamie—the whole deal. I am hoping now that's it out, she won't feel that need to run."

"What's that dead junkie got to do with our girl? Fucker's been gone for a while now." Prosper's eyes narrowed.

Reno didn't hesitate to lay it out for his uncle.

"Cocksucker beat her when she was carrying his own. He hurt Claire so bad that she lost the baby. Just about tears her apart to even talk about it. She can't have any kids, Prosper. And no one knows that shit. Not even her sister. It messed her all up."

Prosper's mouth closed into a hard line and his eyes slit to daggers. He bunched up his already taut muscles and clenched his fists. With barely controlled rage, he stood and paced the floor like a captured beast. All of a sudden, the room seemed too small to cage the big man in. He growled and heaved and sputtered. Furiously, Prosper picked up the shot glass and threw it against the wall with such force that bits of it came back and landed on the table. The bottle quickly followed.

"Motherfucking, cocksucking, sonofabitch." Prosper stood clenching and unclenching his fists. He felt the shots of anger-driven adrenaline course through his body in long rapid streaks. It took a while before all that rage landed. When it did, Prosper punched his fists bloody into the oak wall.

"That shit's on me. On my goddamn watch. You're telling me that Claire's got to live with the reminder of that good-for-nothing junkie every time she sees a kid, or a pregnant woman? Bastard will never be gone for her." Prosper didn't seem to know what to do with himself. Pacing like a tiger, kicking and throwing anything that got in his way.

Reno waited him out.

"Goddammit, Reno. No wonder she runs. How the hell is she ever supposed to want to stick around long enough to feel something that always brings her pain? How's she supposed to want something that she's never had? Except for the little I gave her, and I was gone too soon. Fuck Jack, for being a weak sonofabitch. And fuck Maggie too, for never seeing him for what he was. This is on me."

Prosper laid his arms down hard on the table. The tiny razor sharp shards of glass embedded themselves into his skin. Points of crimson glistened and pooled.

Reno saw the sorrow in his uncle's eyes. And the guilt.

"I got this, Prosper. I've got her. I'm there. I just have to keep it that way. I've got to admit it, me acting like a dick for all those months didn't help matters. But like I said, we are getting past that. And that other shit, Prosper, that ain't on you. Raine and Claire are two of the kindest, strongest, smartest women that I've ever known. Part of that is because of the shit they've been through. That shit taught them to be tough. They are beautiful inside and out. They are survivors."

Prosper shot back, "Bullshit, Reno. They were babies, *babies* when Maggie died. No kid should ever have to be strong to survive. Not separating those kids from their weak, pathetic father was flawed, fucking thinking on their mother's part. I never should have gone along with it. And that is something that I will regret until my dying day."

Prosper looked hard at his nephew then.

"Knowing the kid part, and all the rest, you willing to take that on, Reno?"

"Yeah, I'm willing. More than willing. So much more than that. I love her. I can't breathe without her. Shit, Boss, I wouldn't want to. I don't want to be in a world without her in it. Honest to Christ, when I was lying in that car bleeding my guts out, my only fucking regret was that I would never be able to make right all that had gone wrong between us." Reno leaned forward. He had his hands on his knees, and he looked his uncle straight in the eye. "But now I have that chance and I am not gonna fuck that up. She loves me too, Prosper. Feeling that, knowing it to be true, I can take anything on."

Then Reno ripped his heart from his chest, held it in his hand, and placed it out on the table in front of the man that he loved.

"Like you said, she's your own. Question is if you want me there. I have to tell you, I'm going to marry her. With or without your blessing, Prosper. But for her sake, and for mine, sure would be nice to know you're good with this. So when it comes down to it, do you think I'm good enough for your daughter, man?" Reno's hand shook as he put it on the table. His whole body tensed.

Prosper leaned in too. He dropped his hand hard on his nephew's shoulder.

"You're my own too, son. You have been a part of me ever since the day you came out red and screaming. I was there that day, and I've been there ever since. I stepped up when your pop died, not because I had to, but because I wanted to. Hell, yeah, I think you're good enough. But, I'm telling you right now, that whoring shit is done. I got a good idea what brought you to that, but now that's over. And not just for now, you marry my girl, you keep that for her, forever. I know what goes on in the club, and I don't give two flying fucks what the other brothers do. I had this same talk with D. Yeah, I did. I told Diego the same thing about marrying Raine that I am going to tell you about marrying Claire. I don't give two shits where you get hungry, son, but you eat at home."

Reno nodded. "Would never do that to her."

Prosper took a good long look at his nephew, then nodded.

"Claire's good with this? You sure she wants to marry your sorry ass?" Prosper reached for the box again, opened it and took another look.

"Yep." Reno's clenched fists started to open and relax. "She does. Can hardly believe it myself."

Then he joked, "Tying her to the chair 'til she said yes probably had something to do with it. A little trick in persuasion that I learned from my uncle."

Prosper snorted and then gave out a low chuckle. "You didn't learn that from me. I ever try that with Pinky, she would untie herself and use the rope to hang me."

He let out another slow chuckle, reached into the box on the table and offered Reno one of his Sunday cigars. The two men sat in comfortable silence for a few minutes.

Reno watched as the tension slowly began to leave Prosper's face.

"I didn't know that they made that shit in the shape of a heart. Nice fucking ring." Prosper reached for the ring box again.

"Yeah, as soon as she said yes, I drove to every damn jeweler in the county. I finally settled on this one." Reno leaned in and looked at it too. "Hope she likes it."

"Are you kidding? Claire is going to goddamn love it," Prosper reassured him.

Reno smirked at his uncle.

"She wants this big-deal wedding. Cake, white dress, champagne, and all the rest of it."

"Yeah?" Prosper grinned.

"Yeah." Reno grinned back.

"Jesus, the women are going to be all over that," Prosper said. "They've got a baby girl running around to spoil the shit out of, and now there's going to be a big fucking wedding to plan. Dolly and Pinky are going to think they died and went to heaven."

Then he added thoughtfully, "I guess we fucking deserve some happiness around here."

Prosper and Reno sat together for a while then, each in his own happy thoughts.

Then Reno watched as Prosper got up and moved to the wall safe. After a few spins and clicks, the heavy door swung open.

Prosper reached in and found what he was looking for. Then he took a cloth from the wet bar and made an effort to clean the booze, the glass, and the blood off the table. When it was cleaned well enough, he threw down a blue-backed document.

He nodded to Reno. "That is yours."

Reno was confused. "What are you talking about?'

"Read it." Prosper leaned back in the chair with his muscled arms crossed in front of him. He watched on as his nephew tried to make sense of the document.

"This is a land deed," Reno said, still perplexed. "This ain't mine. I don't own any land."

"Yours now, son," Prosper said.

"What the hell are you talking about?" Reno asked again.

"It's a couple of acres. Extends off the property line of this house here. There's nothing on it. It needs clearing. But it's on road front, has sewer lines and all that shit. If you are up for putting the work into it and having a mean sonofoabitch like your uncle here for a neighbor, it's yours."

"Mine?" Reno carefully skimmed through the pages of the document.

"Yep. Consider it a wedding present. For you and Claire."

Reno fell speechless. He looked at his uncle. Then he looked down at the land deed in his hand. Then back to his uncle.

"Shit. I don't know how to thank you," Reno said gruffly.

"Don't need to thank me. You're my goddamn nephew and I fucking love you." Prosper put his hand hard on Reno's shoulder. "But if you mess this up with Claire, I'm going to put a bullet right through your heart."

Reno scrubbed his hand over his face and grinned. "Don't start loading that six shooter anytime soon, because you're going to be disappointed. There won't be no need to shoot me, Boss. There won't be any need at all."

"I know that, son." Prosper grinned back. "Now let's go tell your mother and your aunt the good goddamn news. You know those two hens have been sitting with their eyes glued to that door ever since we walked in. Drives my woman crazy, absolutely insane, that she can't hear through these walls."

～

Dolly and Pinky, who had given up on the coffee and a little somethin' somethin' an hour ago, were now just filling their cups with a little somethin' somethin'. The two worried women looked up as the heavy doors to the office slammed wide open.

The first thing they saw when those heavy doors opened was Prosper holding heavily on to Reno, as the two of them powered out together through the wide archway. Prosper had Reno's neck in a stranglehold tight against him and his big forearm ran wet with streaks of blood. Long, thin shards of embedded glass caught the light and glistened against his heavily tattooed forearm. Dolly and Pinky looked past the two men, and what they saw through the open office door made their blood run cold. The wall was splattered and stained, chairs lay broken on the floor, and smashed glass littered the smooth blue carpet.

The two women reached under the counter for each other's hand at the same exact time. This could not be good.

Unexpectedly, Prosper's face broke out in a big grin. He pulled Reno in tight to him one last time, then he placed a big resounding man kiss on his nephew's head.

"Women, looks like you got a damn wedding to plan." Prosper looked very pleased with himself.

Dolly looked at her son and her son looked right back at her. Then Reno smiled a smile that his mother had not seen on his face since the Christmas he got his first dirt bike.

"Yeah, mom. I'm going to marry Claire. You good with that?" Reno moved to put his arms around his mother.

"Yeah, baby boy. I'm good with that," she answered. Dolly hugged her son close. A satisfied sigh of relief broke through from her anxious heart. Then they both turned to Prosper who had gathered his woman into his arms and kissed her hard. Pinky blushed and seemed to be fully enjoying every bit of her husband's attentions. But then she pushed away from him, took a good long look at his arm, and handed him a shot from the good bottle.

Prosper, Reno, and Dolly watched Pinky walk down the hallway toward the bathroom to retrieve the first aid kit. When they heard her long-suffering sigh, they grinned at each other.

And for that one moment, all was right in their world.

CHAPTER 53

Today had been a good day. An early morning rain had washed away the sticky humidity of the last few hours and had left in its place a light clean breeze. The heavy veil of mist had moved on at midmorning and the sun in all its glory had finally broken through. Its warm rays came streaming down in thin beams, and turned each remaining droplet into small prisms of light.

Reno and Prosper had taken a step back from clearing the land that would be our home, and I had taken a step back from finding the perfect wedding dress which, according to Raine, I had already found several times over. When I refused to shout out "Yes to the dress" at the most recent perfect-fitting, just-right-priced wedding gown, my sister accused me of enjoying the whole shopping experience so much that I refused to choose one.

She was not wrong.

But today was the day to put all personal endeavors aside and give back.

The Hells Saints had just completed a weekend of their annual charity event and everyone was feeling the satisfaction that came from a good deed done. I had counted seventeen patches in the past two days. All charters and allied clubs had come together with their friends and families for a charitable run. The event had ended in a weekend of horseshoe, pool, and dart tournaments, raffles, live music, and a grand finale clambake. Even Glory had put aside her aversion for being anywhere that Jules might be and had come out to help. And even though it hadn't been expected of us, Glory, Raine, and I showed up the next day to help Dolly, Pinky, and the boys clean up.

"Well, that's about it," I said to Pinky.

"Thank heavens, that's over until next year," she sighed. "I don't want to see another plate of potato salad for the rest of my life. Or at least for the next twelve months."

I smiled at her. I finished putting the tin foil, plastic wrap, silverware, and various pots and pans back into the cabinets.

"Let's go grab a beer and join the boys, what do you say?" Pinky suggested.

"Great idea! I could use a couple of cold ones right about now," I responded. "I'll go and grab the cash crew and be right there.

"I'm going to just run the dishwasher and organize a few things in the fridge," Glory said to me.

I turned and put my arms gently around her shoulders. "You can't avoid him forever, honey."

Glory looked at me, a small measure of sadness darkening her light blue eyes. "Sure, I can."

But then she grinned. "It was a great couple of days, Claire. It felt good being a part of it."

I squeezed her tight and said, "Have a beer before you go?"

Glory nodded. Then she turned and began piling things into the refrigerator.

I knocked softly at the club office door, and Diego answered it.

I could see Jules and Raine seated behind him. Prosper leaned against the corner wall. A pile of checks sat on one side of the desk, and several stacks of cash were on the other side. A couple of ledger books and a calculator were placed in front of them.

"How'd we do?" I asked.

My sister smiled. "Great. Better than last year. After we pay for the food and some of the other expenses, we have raised about ten thousand dollars in donation money. I just wrote out the check to the East Coast Wounded Men and Women in Military Project."

I nodded and smiled. "That's great. I called them yesterday and told them that we would have a check ready for them. They said they would send someone to come get the money. Prosper, please remember to make sure you are around for the photo. I want to take a picture of you donating the money and send it in to the local papers."

"And I already told you, Claire, that I don't want my damn picture taken." Prosper's voice grumbled out into the room. "Last time we did something like this, the Associated Press picked that shit up."

"Worried about Interpol?" Diego grinned at him. Jules looked up from the pile of money and chuckled.

"No, smart ass. It's just that it ain't about that," he snarled.

I crossed my arms and looked at him.

"And I told you that a little bit of good press never hurt anybody. This club does a lot for the townships and nobody knows about it, and that's okay. A few thousand here or there for the schools or playgrounds, that's the kind of give back that's expected, I guess. But this is more than that. A lot of the guys in the charters are veterans, and they're proud to do their part. It's not like the Saints are exactly rolling in good press, lately."

Prosper snorted but everyone else nodded in agreement, a gesture of goodwill could not hurt.

Prosper went on to grumble and I countered each grumble with a well-pointed argument. It didn't matter, anyway. I had already called the Project about our donation and they were eager to receive it. I just hoped that once they were here, Prosper would consent to the photo op. If not, I would sic Pinky on him. Despite his grumbling and protests to the contrary, there really wasn't much the big man could deny her.

And more often than not, Pinky was on my side.

With the money counted and the compound cleaned, it was time to take a well-deserved break. I went back into the kitchen and put a few beers and the rest of the leftover sandwiches on a tray. Then I headed for the picnic tables. Everyone but Glory came out for lunch, and I noticed a measure of disappointment in Jules's eyes. We sat at the large tables drinking and eating and talking; we were just like any other family after a weekend of hard work.

The distant roar of an engine signaled that someone was coming up the road to the compound. We all turned to watch as the SUV made its way up through the open gates of the Hells Saints property. It stopped in the parking area right in front of the three large flagpoles. The tallest pole sported the American flag, the other one flew the club flag, and the third had four smaller flags displayed. Each one represented a branch of the military. The vehicle had an insignia on its door. I didn't recognize the vehicle, but I felt the boys quiet and tense beside me.

About half an hour earlier the two men in the SUV had stopped right outside of the town line. They had pulled into a convenience store, parked, and grabbed the two large garment bags that were draped carefully over the back seat. They walked into the small establishment dressed as civilians, but walked out spit-and-polished. Two hundred and thirty-seven years of tradition now covered their lean, strong bodies. Their black shoes shone up at them and reflected the burnished brass buttons of their coats. The blood-red stripe hung straight against the deep blue of their pressed pants. Around their necks sat a tight, rigid red-trimmed collar. Their white gloves were folded perfectly, left over right, and tucked next to a shiny brass buckle.

The major shut off the engine and looked at the gunnery sergeant. He nodded and the two men climbed out of the SUV. Their shiny black shoes kicked up the dust and gravel from the driveway as they walked purposely toward the group of men and women that were congregated at a large picnic table.

As the deep hazy sunset lined the backdrop of the woodland, Major Elmswood focused on the forearm of the biggest man at the table. He kept his eyes glued to the tattoo that read in simple script, *Always Faithful. Always Loyal. Semper Fidelis.*

The men at the table all stood at the same time. With wary eyes, clenched jaws, and squared shoulders, they surveyed the two officers walking toward them. Sergeant Nickerson noted that three of them sported military tattoos. Then he glanced again at the group of flags flying high over the compound.

They know, the sergeant thought to himself.

A pretty girl with long dark hair and bright blue eyes leaned across the table and spoke first.

"Oh, look, Prosper. The men are here for the check. Wow, that was fast. And they are all dressed up too. That will make a nice picture." Then she smiled brightly at the two officers.

When she went to move from her seat, the large man she had addressed as Prosper put his hand on her arm.

He spoke to her with surprising gentleness. "Claire. These men are not here to pick up the check, honey."

And then he paused and added, "Where is Glory?"

CHAPTER 54

The refrigerator was full to the point of bursting. Glory stood in front of it with her hands on her hips, and tried to find room to put the various leftover casseroles, cold salads, and desserts. *What a mess,* she thought to herself, as she gave up looking for a place to put the large containers. She would have to remove most of the contents of the refrigerator and start over.

"Glory."

She turned at the sound of her name to see Prosper's eyes settle gently upon her. His big body partially blocked the two men behind him.

But only partially.

As the two uniformed officers stepped out from behind Prosper, Glory started in surprise. Then her eyes took in the crisp dress blues, the shining brass buttons, and the sheathed sabers at their hips. Both men had their hats in their hands.

Marine officers.

Glory's hand flew to her stomach, then it fluttered up to her heart where it stopped and lay shaking. She looked past the men to find that Jules had entered the kitchen. His gaze spoke to her with such tender sorrow that it made her knees weak. Jules shoved his way through to her. She reached out and twisted the fabric of his T-shirt into a tight knot in her fist.

"No." She looked at the officers. "*No.*"

"Ma'am . . ."

"No," she whispered.

"Ma'am . . . are you Glory Thomas, the sister of Captain Hallelujah Thomas?"

"No." Glory's voice bordered on hysteria.

"Please, ma'am," The officer spoke gently.

Jules murmured something soft and low, his hand placed firmly around her waist.

Glory nodded.

"I am sorry to be here today, ma'am. We have received word from his unit commander that Captain Hallejulah Thomas has been very seriously injured in . . ."

"He's wounded?" Prosper broke in. "Why the fuck didn't you call? Isn't the notification process for you to call unless he's . . . ?"

"Stop! Stop don't say it! Please don't say it, Prosper," Glory choked out.

Prosper didn't say it and Glory took a step away from Jules and stood on her own.

The two Marines kept their eyes on Glory.

"My phone." She looked helplessly at them. "I dropped it off the dock yesterday. It's sitting at the bottom of the lake somewhere."

"I understand, ma'am," the major continued, "your brother was very seriously injured in Kandahar, Afghanistan, earlier this morning when his convoy hit a roadside bomb. Gunnery Sergeant Harris is your casualty assistance officer and he will be here to help you with anything you need."

"How bad is he?" Glory whispered.

"We don't have all the details in yet, ma'am. We do know that Captain Thomas has been airlifted to Landstuhl Regional Medical Center, ma'am," the sergeant answered.

The silence was deafening as the officers gave her time to process. Prosper and Jules stood right where they were.

"Where is that? I don't know where that is," she said weakly.

"It is next to the US air base in Ramstein, Germany, ma'am."

"I need to go to him," Glory moaned. Her eyes were glued to the sergeant.

"Yes, ma'am. I can arrange that for you."

"When? How soon can I go?" Glory fought through the daze.

"I can get those orders in place as soon as you are ready, ma'am," the sergeant assured her.

"I'm ready now," Glory whispered. "I'm ready now. I just need to go home first. I need to do a few things . . . I need . . . I need . . . Oh, God. God. I'm not sure what I need . . ."

"Glory." Jules took a step toward her. His eyes filled with concern and longing.

Glory put her shaking hand up in a barely controlled stop motion. "Stop. Stop, Jules. Don't say a word. Don't come near me again. Don't touch me."

She stepped back and leaned against the counter to steady herself. Her voice was filled with steely determination and heartbreaking vulnerability.

Jules moved toward her anyway.

Glory shook her head and panic filled her eyes.

"If you ever loved me, if there is one shred left of what you felt for me, then please, *please* stay where you are. If you touch me, Jules, if anyone touches me, I am going to fall apart. And I can't do that. I can't do that. *Please stay where you are.*"

She looked at the officers then. Her face filled with fear, misery, and raw nerve.

"Ma'am." The sergeant stepped forward.

"I'm ready." Glory took a deep breath and straightened her spine.

"Tell them I'll call them when I can," she whispered to Prosper.

He nodded. His eyes filled with deep sympathy and grave concern.

Then Glory turned and silently walked out the door behind the two marines. She didn't look back, she didn't whisper a name or say good-bye. She just put one foot in front of the other, got into the SUV, and watched as the door closed on her shattered world.

CHAPTER 55

Glory let us know the minute that she had landed in Germany. But it was a while before we heard from her again, and then it was just intermittently. We knew that Hal had not been expected to survive even long enough for Glory to arrive at his bedside, but thank God he had. Glory seemed loath to discuss his injuries or prognosis in any great detail when she called, and sensing she needed a welcome relief from the pain and fear of worry, I tried to entertain her as much as I could with club gossip and wedding plans. I had no idea when or even if she would ever be back, and even though I missed her horribly, I knew that she was where she needed to be.

Despite or maybe because of the recent past events, Reno and I decided to push ahead with our wedding. I still had my heart set on a big white extravaganza, but what had happened first to Reno and now to Hal had changed my perspective on things. I didn't want to wait, and since Reno had felt things were taking way too long anyway, he was happy to tie that knot as soon as possible.

And once I seriously had begun to look at venues, I realized that it didn't make sense to delay any longer in order to book just the right place to hold the reception.

Because the right venue would not have us.

Neither would the in-between venue.

Nor would the *I am so not having my wedding here* venue.

It turned out that no business establishment in a hundred-mile radius was up to having the local chapter and extended membership of the Hells Saints brothers tearing up their function halls. Initially, every call I made gave me a choice of available dates. It was only after Reno and I had thundered to the proposed venue, seated on the Harley and dressed in Hells Saints leather, that each event planner suddenly developed a conflict with the booking.

I got it. I did. And part of me didn't blame them. The boys weren't actually quiet partiers. But I had not given up entirely. Not until the day that I called the last possible acceptable place, and a kindly woman with a smoker's voice took pity on me.

"Honey, the word's out. No one in the tri-state area is gonna book you," she said in between puffs.

"I don't know what I'm going to do," I whispered tearfully. "I had my heart set on a big white wedding."

"Aw, doll, take some advice. Your club's got some nice pieces of property and a few bars, so I've heard. If you don't want to have it at one of your own establishments, then do it yourself. Rent a few of those pretty white tents, the nice ones, the ones with the sides and the plastic windows that look like cathedrals. Then you get yourself some of those put-together wooden dance floors and some pretty tables and chairs. You can even get those portable potties. Not the nasty ones, I'm talking about the nice ones that come in a trailer with air conditioning and real flushable toilets. As far as the food goes, just get it catered in. You can have carving stations, a buffet, or a sit-down dinner, whatever your little heart desires. Don't fret, honey. You can have yourself a real nice wedding. Flowers on the table and all the rest. All the movie stars are doing it that way. Hell, you can even cross state lines and get a bunch of fireworks."

Then she lowered her voice. "My daughter has a side business— she's a wedding consultant-slash-event planner. I can give you her number, honey, would you like that?

I sighed into the phone, "I would like that very much."

"All righty, then. You got a church lined up?" She wheezed.

"Yes, we have a church," I answered. "Father Andrew at the non-denominational church in Pierpoint said that he would marry us."

"That church is a beauty. My girl will help you do it up right pretty, sugar. Flowers for the church, white Cinderella dress, fifty bridesmaids if you want them, then you can go on home and have yourself a party."

I took her suggestion and wrote down her daughter's number. I may have given up on the venues but not on the dream.

CHAPTER 56

"Oh no." I looked at the storm tracker on my laptop and felt my heart sink.

I stood and scanned the lake house property from the living room and sighed. The chairs, tables, and the portable dance floors had all been delivered earlier in the day. The large event tents were erected and staked in place, their white walls were pulled back and danced gently in the breeze. Several beautifully decorated cocktail bars were set on and around the dock area, just waiting to be stocked with top-shelf liquor. Thousands of intricately strung, tiny white lights hung daintily from carefully chosen tree branches.

The lake house was all dressed in white and ready for a wedding. I sighed heavily and turned away from the window.

"What's the matter, Babe?" Reno asked. His voice called out to me, but his eyes were glued to the television screen in front of him.

Exasperation leaked out of my voice.

"I am not going to let anything stop me from becoming Mrs. Reno McCabe tomorrow. I am going to walk down that aisle in my perfect white wedding dress and into your arms. Even if I have to wade across a stream of mud, run between streaks of lightning, and jump over fallen trees to do it."

Reno tore his eyes away from the game and looked at me. "You expecting a string of disasters, Claire?"

I pouted and pulled back the curtain to frown at the deceptively clear sky.

"I have been monitoring the weather forecast and it looks like a low pressure system is moving in tonight, just in time for tomorrow. There's a good chance that it is going to rain on our perfect day, Reno. After all the planning, and the expense, and the hoping, and the dreaming. There's going to be wind and rain and thunder. It's going to ruin everything," I fretted.

Tears gathered in my eyes and crept into my voice.

With a click, Reno turned off the television, came up behind me, and pressed his chest against my back. Then he wrapped his arms around me, and we both looked out into the large yard.

"It looks pretty, baby. You did a great job," he said against my hair. "Everything is going to be beautiful."

"I wish that Glory was going to be here," I sniffled.

"Is that what's bothering you, honey? The boys said they were all ready to go with the Internet streaming. She'll be able to see the whole thing."

I nodded and settled against him. "It won't be the same," I whispered.

"She's where she needs to be, honey," Reno said softly.

"I know. I know that," I sighed.

Then I turned to him. "What if it does rain, Reno? What if it pours and ruins everything?"

Reno held on to my waist. His fingers gripped me softly.

"What if it does?"

I frowned at him.

"Look, Babe, the ceremony is in the church, right? It's been a while since I've stepped into a house of God, but I think they have doors and walls like other buildings to keep out the rain, right?"

"You know they do, Reno. And I do not appreciate you taking this lightly," I scolded him.

"Me?" he asked with mock outrage. "I am not taking this lightly at all. Nope. Not at all. Actually, Claire, we might have a bigger problem than the weather," he said with a teasing tone.

"Stop it," I said. But I couldn't keep the smile out of my voice.

"No. I mean it, Claire," he insisted. "I haven't talked to you about it yet, but now that we are doing the whole *I'm worried* thing, I actually have some fears of my own."

I narrowed my eyes at him. "And what would those be?"

"It's the holy water at the church. I am worried that it is going to start boiling up when the brothers walk in. Just like in one of those horror movies." He smirked.

"Cut it out, Reno." I twisted in his arms, but I couldn't keep in the small laugh that escaped me.

"That's better, Babe." He grinned at me. Then he drew me in and pressed his mouth lightly to my own.

"Claire, you have been fretting over one thing or another for weeks now. It's all going to be okay, honey."

My lips returned the kiss, but my thoughts were still racing.

"But what if it rains all over our wedding?" I persisted.

Reno looked at me for a minute and sighed. His tone was gentle when he spoke.

"And what if it does, honey? By this time tomorrow, you're going to belong to me. You and me, baby, *husband and wife*. In the eyes of God and in the eyes of the law, you are going to be mine. *My wife*. By this time tomorrow you're going to have my name."

"Mrs. Claire McCabe," I whispered. "It sounds good."

"It sounds fucking great," he whispered back.

He paused then and looked hard at me.

"That's all that's important, Claire. The rest, shit, it's just a party. And we can party anytime, anywhere. God knows, over the years the brothers have proven that. So, let it rain. Let the heavens open and pour down with all they got. Because none of that matters. What matters is me and you. Tomorrow you are going to walk down that aisle in a white wedding dress, with flowers in your hair and a promise on those beautiful lips of yours. And I'm going to be waiting for you. We are going to vow to love each other 'til the day that we die. And even beyond that. Then I am going to kiss you. We are going to have our first goddamn kiss as man and wife. And that kiss is going to be so fucking sweet that we are going to think back and remember it for as long as we live. After that we are going to eat and drink and celebrate with the people that we love and who love us, yeah?"

"Yeah." I nodded.

"I know that you have this dream of a perfect wedding in your head. But the dream is me and you. And baby, we are already there."

At his words, I felt all the tension leave my body. I reached up and put my arms around his neck. Then I ran my fingers gently through his freshly cut hair, and I pressed my body against his.

"I love you, Reno," I said against his lips.

"I love you too, baby. Now what do you say you stop worrying for a few goddamn minutes and come upstairs and help me celebrate my last night as a single man?"

I smiled, nodded, and let him lead the way.

Much, much later as I lay next to Reno and listened to the steady rhythmic sound of his breathing, a deep well of happiness surged and swelled inside of me. I loved this man more than I had ever thought possible. I loved him more than I ever thought I was capable of loving.

And we had been through so much together.

The path that had led us to this place had proven to be littered with land mines filled with dangerous emotion. Its banks had been built on matters of life and death. On every step of this steep climb, our love had had to fight to survive.

And now, here we stood with our hands clasped and our hearts bound. Together and triumphant at the journey's end.

Reno and I had finally, *finally* gotten to this wondrous place full of promise. A place that was full of light and love and the happily ever after. And the best part of all was that tomorrow would not be the end of that journey. It would be another even better beginning, another chance to start again. I sighed deeply as that first big splatter of rain hit the bedroom window and the wind picked up and beat the shutter rhythmically against the clapboard.

I settled myself deep into the bed, and I thought about the flowers and the tents and the twinkling lights. I thought about the delicate lace of my gown and the soft butter of the dress leathers that hung waiting in the closet next to it.

But it was all good. Because I realized more than ever before that what Reno said was true. The important stuff wasn't out in that yard. It wasn't in the tent or in the flowers or in that perfect white dress. It was in the love that had brought us here.

I knew that at times, life could be just like the weather—unpredictable, unyielding, and almost impossible to control. I knew that one moment it could be filled with calm winds, and the next moment it could be filled with stormy seas.

But I also knew that with my man by my side, I could weather any storm.

So feeling that and knowing it to be true, I closed my eyes and snuggled in deep beside my man. My heart was filled with the promise and excitement of all the coming days.

And if I woke up in the morning and found a gale storm had hit the coast and shattered the wedding preparations to bits, it wouldn't matter.

Because I had found my safe harbor.

Reno was right.

Let the rain fall.

ACKNOWLEDGMENTS

I would like to thank Helen Cattaneo at Montlake Publishing, whose professionalism, warmth, encouragement, and sound advice have made becoming a member of the Amazon family such a pleasure. I got lucky when you found me, Helen.

A special shout-out goes to my developmental editor, Kristen Stroever. I have learned so much from you. Thanks for sharing your talent, vision, and enthusiasm with me and helping to make Claire and Reno's story all that it deserves to be.

I would like to thank all the readers of my debut novel, *Raine Falling*. Without your letters, encouragement, reviews, and fearlessness in taking a chance on a new author, I would not have had the courage to put Claire's story out there. Thank you!

Finally I would like to thank Amazon, which has changed the face of publishing as we know it. What a gift you have given novice writers who have the talent, determination, and dedication to succeed but found the waters of mainstream publishing too difficult to navigate. Both as a reader and a writer, I have benefited from your visionary endeavor. Hats off to you!

ABOUT THE AUTHOR

Photo © 2014 Dawn Brundige

Paula Marinaro was born and raised on the North Shore of Boston. She currently lives with her husband in a cozy little house on a lake in Western Massachusetts. She holds an Associate Degree in Criminal Justice, a Bachelor of Arts Degree in Sociology, and a Masters Degree in Education. She considers herself to be a lifelong learner and enjoys international travel. She is extremely proud to be the mother of two children, Jake and Leah. Her debut novel, *Raine Falling*, was published in 2014.